I0688754

BEASTS OF PREY

THE FERAL SENTENCE – BOOK 1
BEASTS OF PREY – BOOK 2
PRIMAL INSTINCTS – BOOK 3
REIGN OF BLOOD – BOOK 4
GAME OF DEATH – BOOK 5

Shade Owens
www.shadeowens.com

Edited by Nikki Busch
www.nikkibuschediting.com

RED RAVEN PUBLISHING

ISBN: 978-1-7775422-4-5

PART ONE

PROLOGUE

My name is Lydia Brone.

As of today, I'm nineteen years old—at least, I think I am. I've been keeping track of the date in my head, hoping not to mix up the months that have thirty-one days with the ones that only have thirty. I was never any good at remembering such a simple thing; my phone's calendar app used to do it for me.

That is, before I was sentenced to serve three years on a remote island known as Kormace Island—the Island of Killers—for having accidentally killed my mom's boyfriend while he was assaulting her.

If my calculations are accurate, I've been living here eleven months and four days. I know I'll eventually lose count, but I must keep trying. The irony in all of this is that I was sentenced literally twenty-six days after my eighteenth birthday.

I keep wondering: would I have escaped the fate of Kormace Island had I been convicted at the age of seventeen? According to a news article I read quoting Mr. Milas, Attorney General of the Department of Justice, "Minors will be exempt from this new cost-efficient approach to sentencing."

New approach, my ass.

I've met women on the island, including the chief of our previous clan—I'll elaborate on the *previous* bit later—who've been stuck here for over forty years.

And the whole spiel about minors being exempt is bullshit, too; several months ago, we found a nine-year-old girl (Elektra—a name she picked out for herself) who said she'd been dropped off by a black helicopter. But I still wonder if maybe, with enough eyes watching in court, I might have dodged this barbaric bullet had I been seventeen.

I know what you're wondering: how am I surviving Kormace Island?

Well, for starters, I was fortunate enough to wind up under Murk's reign—a fierce and more-than-capable leader who somehow managed to establish a small, yet well-structured society of female convicts. She did this by assigning each woman a job, allowing them to contribute learned skills. In exchange, these women were granted access to food, water, shelter, and clothing. They were also compensated with pearls, the society's currency, which could be exchanged for various goods, such as soaps, lotions, tools, and weapons.

By night, we resided in the Village—a charming enclosure with sleeping tents and cabins located west of the jungle—and by day, we made our way to the Working Grounds—an open space surrounding a majestic waterfall and a crystal-clear bay—to complete our tasks.

While under Murk's reign, I was assigned the task of Hunter, or more specifically, Archer, due to having twenty-twenty vision. I made friends, mostly fellow Hunters, and some enemies because of my position. I was ambushed and threatened at knifepoint one evening and forced to split a portion of my weekly earnings with my masked attacker.

Good news—I figured out who orchestrated the attack behind the mask and beat her senseless. I admit, this hadn't been my intention, but after barely surviving a horrific attack by our sworn enemies, and after running for hours to escape a rapidly spreading wildfire, I snapped.

Sorry... I'm jumping ahead.

When I first arrived at the Village, a clan known as the Northers attacked us. They're commanded by Rainer, a woman who, many years ago, decided she wanted no part in Murk's society and separated along with other similar-minded women.

After this attack, Murk took it upon herself to

begin training Battlewomen as a defense strategy in preparation for another attack. Unfortunately, we couldn't have anticipated the next attack...

One of the Northers infiltrated our society, managing to sneak poison into the women's breakfast and spreading illness across the Village. As luck would have it, I missed breakfast that morning, having fallen asleep in the jungle, and returned to the Village to find hundreds of bodies lying around the breakfast fire. As they began to wake from their poisoned states, the Northers attacked.

It's important to note that several months before the attack, Kormace Island experienced a terrible drought that caused the jungle's moist green vegetation to wither to a yellow crisp. Fire arrows came whistling from the sky and into the dry grass around us, causing a vicious blaze that spread across the land. Women were slaughtered as they woke and others chased with shivs and hunting spears amid the thick gray smoke.

Some survived, but most didn't.

The fire spread across the southern part of the island, leaving behind nothing but ash-coated decay, which is now known as the Dead Zone. Then, almost as if by miracle, a tropical storm came sweeping in, bringing with it torrential downpours and winds so powerful we were forced to return to the Working Grounds and seek shelter inside of the waterfall.

Although many women are still missing, including our chief (Murk), the few of us who crossed paths after the attack have managed to salvage what's left of our society by working together and building a new home for ourselves. Word has it that several of my friends are still out there, and I won't stop until I find them.

I know the road ahead isn't going to be easy, but as a good friend of mine recently told me— there's always hope.

CHAPTER 1

"There'd better not be any rain dripping on my face at night," Franklin said, crossing her pale tattooed arms over her flat chest. She shook a loose strand of her short chestnut brown hair out of her face and gave Coin the stink eye.

Who did she think she was, anyway? She stood there, arrogant, biting down on her thick bottom lip and tapping her fingers against her biceps.

I wasn't a fan of her know-it-all attitude and constant opinions, but from what a few others had told me, she was a good fighter, and that was something we needed. I'd simply have to get used to her.

Coin stood up straight, stretched her back, and impatiently ran her hand against the grain of her hawk-style shaved head. She was much shorter than Franklin, but also much thicker. Over the last few days, I'd come to realize that Coin was patient by nature but explosive when provoked. She placed both hands on her waist, her dark veins bulging through the black skin of her hands, then sucked on her gold tooth and said, "Girl, this is what I do. If you wanna build your own shelter, here you go." She held out a handful of rope and a giant banana leaf, but Franklin pointed her nose upward and rolled her eyes.

"Coin knows what she's doing," Fisher said, looking up at Franklin from behind her narrow black eyes. She rubbed a hand along the tight, dark-haired ponytail on her head that always looked greasy. "She's a Builder."

Hearing Fisher's voice, Franklin sighed and walked away. Although no official status had been granted, everyone knew Fisher was in charge. Having hunted by her side for nearly a year, I knew she was more than capable of leading our new group of women.

She was young, vibrant, and dominant by nature. There was a coldness to her that often came across as insensitivity, but I'd come to see Fisher's true self—she was loyal like no other; she defended her friends even if it meant putting herself in harm's way.

Fortunately for me, I'd somehow managed to fall inside of her friendship circle. The others, not so much, which was probably a good thing if Fisher was to have any authority over them.

She retightened her ponytail and wiped droplets of sweat off the tip of her pointed nose. She was beautiful, but the island had changed her.

She had bubbly scarred skin across her left shoulder and thin cuts—seemingly the result of a bird attack of some sort—across her high cheekbones. She smirked sideways at me, revealing crooked teeth. "Not too bad, is it?"

I looked around at our new home. It was incomparable to the Village—an enclosure with dozens of suede leather tents surrounding a fire pit—but it was special in its own way. After fleeing the Working Grounds, many of us headed northeast in search of habitable land, only to stumble upon a peculiar space amid dozens of humongous trees you'd only find in a fairy tale.

A few women stayed behind, including Coin's friends, who believed that their only chance for survival was to remain inside the waterfall located in our old Working Grounds.

I'd seen big tree trunks in the jungle before but nothing like these. They must have measured the size of a small house in diameter. Their bark had a red tint to it, and the one farthest at the back had an oversized cavity deep enough to provide shelter—something Fisher claimed as her own the moment she set eyes on it.

The ground was covered in leaves—a mixture of ugly browns and faded greens. The tree leaves overhead were vivid reds and oranges, with patches of yellow at their tips. It was evident that they too had been starved of water during the drought. There were bushes upon bushes of bright yellow flowers, vibrant purples dangling from the trees, and translucent mushrooms growing around tree roots.

The ground was damp due to the recent storm, and there was a cool moisture in the air that carried a salty, earthlike smell. Most rivers and streams we'd passed during our trek had flooded, bringing water to all plants across the island. Maybe this meant the drought was finally over.

I closed my eyes and breathed in the scent of moist earth—something I hadn't smelled in a long time. If there was one thing I would miss most about our previous home, it was the Working Grounds' waterfall. Although undrinkable because it was salt water—something I'd always found unusual—it was the perfect cleansing water. And, with the distillation contraptions built by the Farmers in our society, it became perfectly drinkable.

In our new home, there was a small stream of fresh water that ran through the enclosure of giant trees. Amid the colors of the jungle, the water looked brown, but it was cool to the touch and so smooth it made my fingers feel soft after splashing it on my face.

Everest, an older Ukrainian woman I'd met only recently, slowly dropped down onto her hands and knees, cupped a handful of water into her wrinkled hand, and raised it to her dry lips.

"Whoa!" Fisher said.

Everest rolled her tired gray eyes up at Fisher like she'd been asked to run a marathon.

"You can't drink water without knowing where it comes from."

I was shocked to hear this. We'd filled our water bladders with fresh water during our hunts many times over.

Everest separated her cupped hands and the water fell back into the stream. Her eyebrows, two straight lines that were barely visible, came so close to each other they almost touched. "Vy not?"

"You could get sick," Fisher said. "We don't know this place. That water could be crawling with parasites."

I leaned into Fisher. "Thought we used to drink fresh water during our hunts."

She smirked. "That little fall? It's clean. We know where that water comes from. We've been drinking there for years."

"So vat?" Everest went off. "Ve have all zis fresh vater, and ve can't even drink?"

Fisher only stared at her and walked away. I watched the back of her head as she disappeared behind an orange flower bush. Everest and I exchanged a confused look, but within seconds, Fisher was back with what appeared to be two pieces of massive vines dangling in both hands.

She threw one of them by Everest's knees, and the other, on the ground to be taken by someone else.

"Vat's this?"

"Grab that end of it and suck," Fisher said. "There should be rainwater in there. You can thank the storm."

Everyone lunged toward the second vine, but Fisher released a quick, "Hey!" and their eyes met hers. "Put your lazy asses to work and go get some more."

As everyone began scattering, Fisher rolled her eyes. "Bring a knife, too."

I glanced down at Everest, who was sucking on the tip of the vine. She was having a hard time of it, so she dangled it above her head in hopes that gravity would simplify the task. How long had she been on this island, anyway? Had she spent most of her life here, or had she committed a crime late in life? She was monotone and blunt when she spoke, but I knew there was goodness in there, somewhere.

She took one final lick of water and straightened her rounded back. Ellie quickly came to her aid, scooping her up by the arm and helping her to her feet.

I smiled. If there was one thing I was grateful for, it was having found Ellie after the attack. Ever since I'd first stepped foot into the Village, Ellie had been the only one to show me any affection, and not only because it was her job as the Village's peer worker to show me the ropes, but because there was something so pure and innocent about her. We'd spent countless hours every morning talking about everything from the island to completely irrelevant topics such as time, space, and the afterlife.

She pulled her long wavy brown hair over one shoulder and looked back at me through squinted chocolate-colored eyes. She knew I was watching her. I smirked, remembering her soft lips against mine and the way she'd pressed her body against me. Ever since she'd kissed me, I'd been unable to think of anything else. I didn't care where I slept, what I ate, or how badly my muscles ached after a day of hunting—all I wanted was for her to kiss me again.

"You guys going hunting soon? I'm hungry," Hammer said.

I instinctively glared at her, but quickly released my anger. If I was going to live with her, I'd have to get over the fact that she'd been the one to threaten me at knifepoint. Sure, I'd lost many pearls because of it, but the slowly reducing swelling on her fat face was payback enough. I couldn't remember how many times I'd hit her, but evidently, it was enough to earn back a measure of respect.

She quickly stepped back and raised two chubby hands. "Respectfully, I mean," she said. "And if there's anything I can do to help, I'm here."

I much preferred this new Hammer. I remembered first meeting her in the Tools tent: a small tent filled with tools, weapons, and satchels. She still looked exactly as she had then—a boyish haircut and a rounded body with pale blotchy skin and fat rolls under her triceps and above her pants. She had red pimples, or acne scars, across both cheeks. But what I remembered most about the old Hammer was her arrogant attitude and how she'd tried to rip me off.

I couldn't hold onto this. Hammer had incredible weapon-crafting skills, and the truth was, we needed her.

"There is something you can do to help," Fisher said, staring intently at her.

Hammer nodded like a child, her eyes round and her lips curved into a grin.

"Get outta my face," Fisher said.

Hammer's smile evaporated.

"Have a little respect," Fisher said. "I'm talking to Brone right now. We'll go hunting when we go hunting."

Hammer nodded quickly and turned away.

"Hey, Ham," Fisher said. "There actually is something you can do for us."

"What is it?" Hammer asked.

"We need more arrows."

Hammer nodded again and joined a few other women around a small fire that had taken nearly an hour to set up due to the forest's dampness.

"Can you believe that?" Fisher scoffed. "Who does she think she is?"

I glanced sideways at Fisher, wondering if maybe the power was already going to her head. But, at the same time, had Trim—the leader of the Hunters, who we had yet to find—been sitting here, Hammer wouldn't have asked her to go hunting. I supposed fear did earn respect, in a sense.

I didn't feed into it. Instead, I looked up at what appeared to be trees touching the sky and back at Fisher. "What should we call this place, anyways?"

She smirked at me and tilted her head back to take in the gigantic trees' magnificence. "I've seen trees like this before... When I was young, my abuela took me and my sister to some Redwood National Park out in California. She saved up for months to take us on that trip. She said it was something we had to see at least once in our lives."

There was a reminiscent smile on her face as she gazed toward the sky. I could tell the memory was still vivid in her mind. I didn't want to interrupt her experience, so I sat there, watching her relive her childhood.

"Redwood," she finally breathed.

CHAPTER 2

"It ain't permanent, so don't get comfortable," Coin said, her brown face glistening with sweat.

She threw several leftover branches into a pile by the fire and stretched her hips from side to side. She'd been working on building shelters all day. I felt sorry for her. She was the only Builder among our women. Although we still outnumbered the shelters she'd constructed, it was better than not having any at all.

"Dibs," Franklin said, plopping herself down into a hammock that hung between two mighty branches. Above it was a banana leaf canopy that hung on an angle, sheltering the hammock entirely.

Coin had used branches to create solid nets covered with huge leaves. Most of the canopies were positioned against tree trunks, roughly six feet in the air, and the others were above the three hammocks she'd built.

Women began scurrying in all directions to claim their spots.

"Get lost, Lisa Simpson, this is my spot."

Two women were standing in front of an empty hammock.

"Your attitude is completely unnecessary."

"Piss off!"

The calm, lanky one stepped back with both hands flat open at shoulder's width. "We're all in this together. I don't understand why you're being so—"

The one who'd told her to back off—a woman of average height with sun-damaged skin—grabbed her by the neck and pinned her against the nearest tree. She raised a fist midair, but Fisher's hand caught it.

"Enough," Fisher said. "Hammer, this spot's yours."

Hammer looked at everyone and stepped forward awkwardly.

"Johnson, Proxy," Fisher said, eyeing them both one at a time, "you two can sleep on the ground."

"That's unfortunate," said Proxy—the lanky one with ratty, unkempt ash-brown hair. She looked at her bully, but only briefly. Aside from her generous height, Proxy did remind me of Lisa Simpson if Lisa wasn't a yellow cartoon character in her 98th season: smart, nerdy, and emotionally stable. It was evident that she was well-educated by the way she spoke, and had she been wearing glasses— which she probably did before being dropped off on the island—she'd have likely pushed them up her nose with her index finger just then.

"Whatever," said Johnson. Everything about her was average—her looks, her weight, her age. She had more freckles across her shoulders than I'd seen on any woman. Her frizzy reddish-brown hair was split in the middle on her head and hung loosely over her ears, touching right above her shoulders.

"We may not live in the Village anymore," Fisher said, her voice loudening, "but we're still more civilized than this." She shot a calculated glare at the women around her. "If we're going to survive, we need to stick together."

"Zat's not a problem for me," Everest said, her saggy face barely moving as she spoke.

"Rules don't change just because Murk isn't here right now," Fisher said. "If you turn on your own, you're out."

I remembered seeing women banished from the Village for having attacked one of our own. I didn't want to imagine what they'd gone through following the banishment. Had they survived? How did they eat if they'd never been taught to hunt?

"What makes you think Murk's still alive?" Franklin kicked her feet into the air, her hammock swinging back and forth.

I was instantly nauseous. Had the Northers killed Murk, our Chief? Was she hiding? Was she with some of the Hunters? I couldn't imagine a society ruled by anyone other than Murk. She was a gentle woman with strong values and a lifetime of experience surviving Kormace Island. Without consistent, solid leadership, women would begin to rebel. It was in their nature.

"Even if she ain't alive," Coin said, her biceps bulging underneath her skin, "what Fisher says, goes."

Franklin scoffed. "Calm your pom-pom, Gold Tooth, I was only askin' a question."

Coin glared at Franklin but bit her tongue.

"What will happen when we find others?" Proxy asked. "We don't have enough space in this location. Realistically, our capacity will reach its maximum if we locate—"

Fisher sighed and pinched the bridge of her nose with her thumb and index finger. "We're not staying here. Like Coin said, it's not permanent."

"Where we going then? What's the plan?" Franklin asked. "You gonna ditch us like you did Mia and Impa?"

I stood up, my fists clenched. "Fisher had nothing to do with that," I said, remembering Mia's cold, sweaty body lying underneath the warmth of a wall torch inside the waterfall.

She'd been shot at during the Northers' attack, and Fisher had carefully dislodged the arrowhead from her belly. When we finally left the inside of the Working Grounds' waterfall—Murk's old quarters—her friend refused to follow us. She merely lay there, her arm wrapped around her best friend's dying body.

"She's in charge, isn't she?" Franklin said. "She could've told Impa to leave Mia behind."

"She's also not a dictator," I said, eyeing Fisher. "Impa wanted to stay with her friend. That was her choice and hers alone."

"Well, they're both as good as dead now." Franklin stroked the skull tattoo on her shoulder.

"Would you shut up, Frank?" Fisher said.

"What're you gonna do, Fish? Slit *my* throat, too?" Franklin pressed.

Fisher's nostrils flared and she inhaled a deep breath.

Coin stepped toward Franklin. "What's your problem?"

"No problem here," Franklin said. "But if someone's gonna be in charge, they'd better do it right."

Coin crossed her arms again, stiffened her back, and cocked a brow. "You sayin' Fisher ain't doin' a good job?"

"I'm sayin'"—Franklin's voice took on a mocking tone—"we need more answers than what we're getting."

My heart raced—not because I was afraid, but because that familiar rage was rising within me. I'd felt it before I jumped Hammer and beat my fists into her face. I was tired, sore, and starved, and the last thing I wanted was to hear someone complain about Fisher's leadership capabilities when the only reason we'd even made it this far was because of her.

I stared at Franklin, imagining how quickly she'd shut her mouth if I had an arrow pointed at her face. I was sick of people causing unnecessary conflict. We already had enemies lurking on the island. We didn't need any more.

A high-pitched whistle pulled me out of my state.

I followed the sound and spotted Fisher walking away with a hunting spear. "Come on, Brone."

Everyone had gone quiet. I hopped over the stream of flowing water and caught up to her.

"I need to get out of here before I kill her," Fisher whispered, "and by the looks of it, you were having the same thought."

I smirked.

We stepped through a bush of narrow leaves, disappearing from Redwood's view.

"You think it's safe to leave her alone with everyone?" I asked. "She's got a big mouth."

Fisher shrugged. "Not my problem. I may be in charge right now, but I'm not a mother. Honestly, I don't know how Trim does it."

"How she leads?" I asked.

Fisher nodded. "I don't know how much of this I can handle. It's like dealing with kids, and I don't like kids."

"Trim's—"

Without warning, Fisher slapped a hand against my chest. Right at the tip of my toes, a red-and-white serpent slithered in and out of decomposing leaves.

"You need to watch the ground as much as anything else," she said. "That one's poisonous." She jabbed her spear into the snake's head. Its long body wagged several times before it stopped moving.

"Plus," she added, sticking out her leaf- and vine-protected foot, "these aren't gonna hold for long."

I looked down at my own. They were snug with my old shoelaces wrapped around them, but I knew it was only a matter of time before they'd start to fall apart.

Fortunately, Hammer had agreed to work alongside one of the Needlewomen to build us actual boots for hunting. All she needed was skin—preferably from something large. I couldn't wait.

"You know where you're going?" I asked.

She appeared so confident, almost as if she'd spent her entire life in this part of the jungle.

"No clue," she said, her voice lowering. "But

that's the whole point... We need to scope the place out."

"You think the Northers live nearby?" I asked.

She shook her head. "I haven't seen any human traces around here."

"You're telling me some women have been here for decades, and there are still areas that haven't been explored?" I said, brushing past scratchy branches.

She stopped walking and turned to stare at me. "I think most women would prefer to stay where they're comfortable." She wiped a big patch of glossy sweat off her forehead. "Why go out exploring unfamiliar territory if everything you need is right where you are? Life on this island is dangerous enough as it is. Heck, I don't even know how big Kormace Island really is. I've only heard that it's huge."

That was something I'd wondered ever since stepping foot on the island. Sure, I'd seen Kormace from a distance—that is, before those military bastards threw me out of the helicopter—but I didn't know its actual size.

"All I know"—Fisher jabbed her spear into the ground—"is that I'm not going far north."

"Ever?" I wasn't sure why I asked that, but the word had slipped out. The idea of never avenging our people pissed me off beyond words, but at the same time, I knew we didn't stand a chance against the Northers.

She smirked, her eyes squinting maliciously. "I didn't say that."

She spun her spear upside down, its shaft pointing toward the sky, and pressed her index finger into its sharp point.

"See this?" she said. "This'll be shoved right through Rainer's mouth and out the back of her skull when I'm finished with those goddamn, motherfu—"

"Fish!" I hissed, and she immediately stopped talking. "Did you hear that?"

Her round eyes shot from side to side. "Hear what?"

It had been a trumpetlike sound.

"This way," I whispered, rustling through a multitude of bushes with small blooming bulbs. At the other end of the thick verdure was a bright light coming from a wide-open space. Had we reached the other end of the island? Had we already hit shore?

With my arm, I swept aside a branch full of leaves to form a path, but they only flew back into place the moment I let go, slapping Fisher across the face.

"Jesus, Brone!" she said.

Streaks of yellow light brightened the leaves around us as we continued toward the sound. I pushed aside one last bush and stepped forward, but Fisher caught me by the back of the shirt. Pebbles and debris trickled down a steep cliff inches away from my toes, drawing attention to us.

Dozens of heads turned our way, but we stood there like statues in absolute awe.

"Holy mother of..." Fisher muttered.

CHAPTER 3

A few hundred feet below us was a treeless open space the size of several football fields. At the center was a peanut-shaped body of brown water surrounded by dozens of creatures.

A handful of massive, clay-colored elephants had gathered and stood halfway in the water, their long, wrinkled snouts digging into it in search of something. Their bellies were wet, giving off the appearance of being black in comparison to their dry heads and backs. Underneath them were two calves, not much bigger than ponies, pressed up against their mother's legs. Most of them had long, ebony-colored tusks, except the largest one, whose right tusk was missing entirely, and its left was cut in half.

A bit farther away were dozens upon dozens of wild dogs. At first glance, I'd thought these to be hyenas, but they were scrawny, had puffy white-tipped tails, and didn't have any rising fur on the backs of their necks. Their ears were bearlike—round and pointed upward. Their fur was a patchy combination of black, brown, and white, resembling a jumbled version of a German Shepherd. I knew what they were only because of a fifth-grade school project I'd done specifically on wild dogs in Africa. What elephants and hyenas and the like were doing here on Kormace was a mystery.

To the right of this pack was a handful of antelopes, their curved, ridged horns pointing straight ahead as they bent down to drink water. They had white bellies, which were stained brown, and black stripes running along their sides.

Three zebras unexpectedly walked out into the open, their vivid, black-and-white-striped coat creating an illusion—blending the three of them together as one large animal.

There were also boars, one orangutan, a few lemurs, and a pack of deer.

Unbelievable.

"You're seeing this, right?" Fisher said.

I turned to look at her. She was smiling from ear to ear.

"Yeah," I breathed.

The numerous heads that had turned our way returned to their drinking water. I could tell by the large body of dry sand surrounding the water that the bay had once been fuller.

"You think that's rainwater?" I asked.

Fisher nodded. "They probably haven't had a

good drink in a while."

We stood in silence, admiring Mother Nature's magnificence. One of the antelope's heads perked up all of a sudden. Another head followed, and another, and another.

Within seconds, all the animals scattered in opposite directions and vanished into the jungle. We immediately dropped into crouched positions, anticipating the worst, but what came running out of the forest was neither Norther nor Ogre.

A young woman sporting a blue hoodie and a pair of torn jeans came jolting out into the open in a frenzy. She appeared disoriented, swaying from side to side and rubbing her eyes with the back of her hand.

"Is that a drop?" I asked.

Fisher slowly stood up straight. "Looks like it."

"I thought drops only came from the west," I said.

Fisher's jaw muscles popped out. "I thought so, too."

The woman fell flat on her face right before reaching the water.

I blinked. "Did she just die?"

But the woman's hands came up over her head, and she clawed her fingers into the sand attempting to drag herself toward the water.

Fisher sighed. "Come on."

We ran along the edge of the cliff, which

gradually descended. As I moved down, I grabbed onto baby trees that were sprouting from the rocky terrain, careful not to miss my step. We hopped down onto the flat surface and ran toward the woman.

She'd made it to the water, her face soaked and her stringy hair full of clay.

"Hey!" Fisher said.

The woman didn't look up. She sucked in as much muddy water as she could, gasping for air every few seconds.

Fisher glanced sideways at me, then moved in closer.

"Hey," she repeated.

The woman took a deep breath, rolled onto her back, and closed her eyes.

Fisher walked up to her, casting a shadow over her face. The woman's yellow-brown eyes shot open.

"You real?" she asked with a thick Australian accent.

Fisher nodded. "Real as you. Come on."

She reached down, grabbed the woman by her sweat-stained arm, and helped her to her feet.

"How long have you been here?" Fisher asked. "I mean, since the drop?"

"The—the drop?" the woman stammered. She squinted at Fisher, the sun reflecting in her eyes.

She was completely disoriented. Did she even

know where she was? Did she even remember being dropped by the government?

"How long have you been on Kormace Island?" Fisher said, her face almost touching the woman's.

The woman missed her step, nearly pulling Fisher to the ground with her.

"Whoa, easy." Fisher yanked her back up, and I came around to help her by pulling the woman's other arm around my neck.

One of her legs gave out again, forcing Fisher and me to share her dead weight.

"She needs food and water," Fisher said.

"Ins—" the woman mumbled.

"What?" I asked.

"My insulin..." she said.

My eyes met Fisher's. A diabetic?

"She needs to eat something, now," Fisher said, her pace quickening.

We scurried across the open land, following the water's edge. The woman mumbled a few more times, but I couldn't make out what she was saying.

"How the hell is she supposed to survive without insulin?" I asked.

Fisher shook her head. "You'd be surprised by how many health problems are reversed on Kormace Island."

I stared at her.

"What?" she said, noting my stare. "Everything here's raw and organic. You really are what you eat."

I tugged harder, my muscles burning and my lungs aching. I was already feeling the nasty effects of inadequate caloric intake—I could only imagine what it was like to be diabetic.

"If you see any fruit, grab it," Fisher said. She pulled upward and grunted, but the woman's head just swayed from side to side. "Come on, wake up. You need to help us out a little here."

I gazed up at the slope we'd come down. It looked much steeper from the bottom.

"I think she passed out," I said quietly.

"She's in critical condition," Fisher said. "Feel her skin—she's cold."

"We can do it," I said, eyeing the uphill path.

We took a few steps up the slope when my grip loosened and the woman's arm fell off my shoulder.

"Hold on," I said. I wrapped my arm around her waist and pulled up as hard as I could. Her arm flapped around my neck and her head fell back.

"She's out cold," I said, my attention turning to the woman's face.

Her lips were blue and her face a translucent white. But what made my stomach sink were her eyes—they were open.

CHAPTER 4

"What do you mean, she died in your arms?" Franklin asked.

Fisher rubbed her forehead and paced back and forth. "Diabetic crash, I'm guessing. She was far gone. Her heart probably stopped. Don't know how long she'd been wandering around on the island."

Everyone circled us, hoping we'd brought home a carcass to feed on. The sickening part was that the thought of dragging the woman's dead body to Redwood had crossed my mind. I was starving—I wasn't thinking straight.

"Here," Everest said, handing me a red mango. I quickly grabbed it with both hands and bit through its skin, its juices squirting on either side of my face.

"Ve found plenty of fruit," she said, her Ukrainian accent still thick as usual. Inside one of Redwood's tree hollows was a pile of fresh fruit—bananas, mangoes, oranges, pineapples, avocados, kiwis.

Hammer sat on a log with a coconut squished in between her two bare feet and some tools in her hands. It was apparent that she'd cracked open coconuts many times before.

"You said she came from the east?" Proxy asked, tucking her ratty hair behind her ear.

"Northeast," I said, slurping my last few pieces of fruit.

"Interesting." She rubbed her pointed chin with her thumb and index finger.

Everyone stared at her.

Johnson, the woefully average-looking woman, stepped forward the way an egotistical man does—fists closed, shoulders pulled back in exaggeration, and chin raised high.

"Well spit it out already!"

Proxy quickly glanced her way but didn't react. She was so cool and collected I wondered if that was the reason Johnson didn't like her—because they were complete opposites.

"All of our drops have always been picked up on the island's western shore," Proxy said.

"Maybe she's a recent drop." I let the skin of my fruit fall to the ground and continued eating. "Maybe the pilot saw *The Dead Zone* and decided to drop her on the other side."

Fisher scoffed. "No way they'd give a shit."

Franklin crossed her arms. "The helicopters rarely fly over the island. Besides, we'd have heard it. Any of you ever think that maybe she's from a different part of the world?"

Everyone looked at each other.

"You're saying Kormace Island is being used internationally?" I asked.

Franklin shrugged. "Why not?"

"She did have an Australian accent," Fisher said, almost in the form of a question.

Franklin shook her head. "That doesn't mean anything. Look at White Mountain over here. She's from the United States."

Everest glared at her, lines forming underneath her old eyes.

There was an uncomfortable silence. How big of an island were we talking?

"That's concerning," Proxy said. Everyone stared at her, waiting to hear what that oversized brain of hers had concluded. "I'm sure this woman wasn't the first to come from the northeast, and she won't be the last. That also means there isn't only one drop location."

I knew what she was getting at, but Hammer, being more of an all brawn and no brain type, stood up with two coconut halves in either hand. "What's your point?"

"My point," Proxy said, "is that we have no idea how many women have actually been dropped on Kormace Island. Nor do we know how many of these unknown women were dropped on the northern shore."

"Goddamnit!" Fisher shouted. She threw her spear into the ground and circled around us.

Were the Northers recruiting more women without our knowing? Was the north receiving drops?

"What're we supposed to do now?"

"We don't even know how many of them there are!"

"I don't care. I'll kill them all if I have to."

Everyone bickered back and forth until Coin raised two solid fists in the air and whistled.

"Guys!" she said. "Ain't nothin' we can do about that now. We need to focus on findin' our own."

I felt a gentle hand against my back.

"Coin's right," Ellie said. "It's out of our control. Fighting about it isn't going to fix this."

Coin sucked on her tooth and nodded, her hands resting on her waist.

Ellie grabbed my hand and tugged. I followed her to one of the hammocks Coin had built. She sat down and pulled me next to her, my body falling against hers.

With her index finger, she drew circles on my thigh. "You okay?"

I looked up at her. Where was this coming from?

"I'm fine," I said.

"You just dragged a dead woman's body," Ellie

said.

I thought back to the dead woman's face—her purple lips, her chalky freckled face, and her wide-open eyes. Although disturbed by the image, I wasn't scarred by it. Was I losing my sense of reality? Was I losing myself? Any other rational human being would probably have vomited and later suffered post-traumatic stress disorder. But I couldn't feel anything. Was I in shock? In comparison to the horrible things I'd seen over the last few months, a woman's dead body fell to the bottom of the disturbance scale. She was another nameless face I'd find in my nightmares.

It didn't affect me, I kept telling myself.

I forced a smile. "I'm fine."

She sighed. "Okay. Well, if you ever need to talk…"

I grabbed her hand. "Thank you."

But I wouldn't want to talk. There was nothing to talk about. Words wouldn't take me away from this wretched place, nor would they allow me to unsee the things I'd seen.

A crooked smile curved her lips, and she patted my lap before climbing out of the hammock. I slid off my bow and quiver then stretched my aching legs and leaned back, the hammock's stringy material wrapping itself around my body.

Just a few minutes, I thought.

"Brone."

I stared at the trees overhead, wanting nothing more than to pretend I hadn't heard her.

"Sleep's for the dead," Fisher said.

I turned my head sideways and looked at her. She was standing beside Coin, her face resting against the stone head of her hunting spear.

She made her eyes go big as if to say, "Hello?"

I grumbled and sat upright.

"Coin's coming with us," she said.

"Where?" I asked, an involuntary tone of apathy in my voice.

"We need to hunt," she said.

"We were just out there," I said.

"Yeah, and we didn't come back with anything, did we? Coin here'll make sure we don't get distracted this time."

Coin stared at me, her lips flat and her dark eyes glued to mine. It was apparent she was all about business.

I lazily stood up, feeling like the bottoms of my feet were on the verge of peeling off, and grabbed my bow. My leaf boots were completely falling apart. I could see my big toe sticking out at the tip of my left boot.

"Besides," Fisher added, eyeing my feet, "we need leather."

I joined Coin and Fisher as they made their way out of Redwood. I glanced back one last time at Ellie, but she was chatting with Everest by the stream. Instead, my eyes met Franklin's.

"Don't worry, ladies," she said, raising a stiff tattooed arm in the air. "I'll hold down the fort."

"That girl's nothin' but trouble," Coin said, hacking away at the never-ending webs of vegetation.

"Franklin?" I asked.

Coin nodded. "Used to train with her—you know, on the Grounds."

Fisher scoffed. "Wasn't she the one always bragging about how strong she is?"

"Yep," Coin said. "Arrogant little sh—"

"Guys," I whispered. I set my bow and pointed up. Leaves rustled and a branch cracked overhead.

But Coin's hand reached for my wrist. "I don't know about you, but I don't think monkey meat'll get us real far."

"How do you know..." I tried.

"Little guy's been following us since we left," Coin said. "White-faced capuchin."

"Why weren't you assigned the task of Hunter?" I asked, appreciating her unique skill set.

"These things," she said, pointing at her ears, "work better than these." She pointed at her eyes.

I remembered Murk's stance on Hunters. The

only reason I'd been assigned the task of Archer was thanks to my perfect vision. But in my opinion, a heightened sense of hearing was as important as good eyesight.

"You think there're any Ogres around here?" I asked, scanning every inch of greenery around me. It was much harder to see up ahead on this part of the island. The trees, shrubs, bushes, and vines were twice as plentiful as those that had surrounded the Village and the Working Grounds.

Coin hacked away at two oversized leaves and turned to face me. "Girl, them crazy cannibalistic twits could be anywhere. That's the problem with 'em—you don't see 'em until they've got you hanging by your intestines... And at that point, well, heck, you can't see 'em at all."

Fisher nudged Coin in the ribs. "You don't have to be so vulgar."

"You know," Coin went on, ignoring Fisher's comment, "being that you probably wouldn't have any eyes left eith—"

"Kay, Coin, we get it," Fisher said.

"It's the truth!" Coin's dark eyes widened.

That's when I thought of Sunny—my first friend on the island. She'd been unusual yet charming despite her mouth full of rotten teeth. I wanted to remember those sunny-yellow eyes and the way they lit up as she talked about the most ridiculous of things, but all I saw was a swollen face and eyes so cold they looked like stones. She'd been left to hang upside down above an altar of sorts, her throat slit by an Ogre.

And although I tried to focus on her bubbliness and greater-than-life persona, all I saw—whether in my mind or in my dreams—was that swollen face. How could anyone be so barbaric? And then I remembered Mr. Schumer—my History teacher. He'd always been so confident with his smooth jet-black hair combed to the side and his soft cotton knitted sweaters. Several of the girls in my class had a crush on him, but I'd never paid much attention to his looks. I preferred to listen to him. He was eccentric: unfiltered and direct. Somehow, that made him my favorite teacher.

* * *

"At least eleven million people," Mr. Schumer said, slapping a wooden ruler against the chalkboard.

In cursive writing, he'd written, "Adolf Hitler."

"How does one man lead an entire civilization—over eight million card-carrying Nazis—to turn against their own kind? Against humankind?" He walked across the front of the class, his bristly chin raised high and his stiff back almost curving backward. "Eight million..."

Artie, the classroom know-it-all, raised a hand.

Mr. Schumer stared at him for a moment, almost assessing whether Artie was worthy of answering such a question. He wiggled a loose finger at Artie, granting him the right to speak.

"He hated Jews," Artie said, matter-of-factly.

Mr. Schumer nodded slowly, continuing his back-and-forth pace. "That's true," he said. "But that doesn't answer my question."

Everyone stared in silence.

He smacked his ruler against the chalkboard again, and my shoulders jerked forward.

"Because we're all human," he said, "and human beings are weak."

I glanced sideways at Melody, my best friend. She was staring at me with a convoluted look on her face that said, "Are we in tenth-grade History class, or in Psych 101?"

"Human beings are nothing but civilized animals," Mr. Schumer went on. He reached for his mug of coffee, took a sip, and added, "capable of monstrous things..."

* * *

"Pay attention, Brone," Fisher hissed.

We'd reached a riverbed surrounded by tall slanted grass. I pointed the head of my arrow at what appeared to be a fat otter. It was perched up on a rock in the middle of the brown murky water.

"Shoot him," Fisher said. "What're you waiting for?"

I pulled back on my arrow, but slowly lowered my bow. "It's gonna jump in the water to get away after I shoot it. We'll never catch it."

Coin let out a long breath. "Man, that sure is a lot of meat, but Brone's right."

Fisher looked like she was contemplating punching me square in the nose. She bit down, the veins in her neck popping out on either side, her wide eyes scanning the river.

"We can't keep eating fruits and nuts," she said. "We need something to sustain us if we expect to trek across the island to search for Trim and the other Hunters."

"Let's keep moving," I said.

I could tell that hunger was getting the best of her. And I didn't blame her—I was starving, too. Normally, the idea of shooting an arrow through a cute, whisker-faced creature would have broken my heart. But I didn't care. I'd have ripped off its silky, furless legs myself if it meant eating an actual meal.

I stared into the water at the silver-backed fish swimming with the current.

"Hey." I pointed into the water. "Think you can spearfish here?"

Fisher scoffed. "With current like that? I don't know."

Why was she being so difficult? Was she not starving? Was it not better to at least try? I stared at her, imagining how upset she'd be if I pushed her in the water. I didn't do it, but I was furious.

"Look," Coin said, pointing upstream at what

appeared to be a small bay along the edge of the river. "That should work."

We trudged along the edge of the water, our feet sliding in and out of the soft soil and slimy mud. Fuzzy brown reeds tickled my arms and shoulders as I moved forward. A soft splash caught my attention, and I quickly turned around; the river otter was gone. As we approached the bay—a wide pool of murky brown water surrounded by drooping lush grass and sharp-edged stones—Fisher walked passed Coin and made her way to the front of the line.

She glanced back at us, grinning from ear to ear like a child being told Santa Claus was going to be at the shopping mall. "Jackpot."

I hopped over a meadow of wildflowers, scaring away several oversized dragonflies, and joined Fisher in the bay. She was up to her knees in water, swinging her arm back at us to tell us to be quiet. I waded through the water, careful not to ripple the bay and frighten the fish. There were dozens of them swimming in figure eight motions, slipping right past our shins. Most of them had silver backs, but there were a few exotic-looking ones with wide gills and multicolored scales.

That's when I remembered one of the rivers we'd visited several months ago—the one with a massive school of piranhas swimming with the current. Disgust and anxiety overwhelmed me. I couldn't see anything farther than my own two feet. The water was too dirty: dark green and full of floating seaweed or algae.

Fisher walked even deeper into the water, her spear up in the air in a two-handed grip, and her eyes wild like those of a feral cat. She quickly stabbed her spear into the water, its sharp tip sliding through so easily it barely made a sound.

She growled and repositioned herself.

Another jab.

"Got you!" she said, though not loud enough to frighten the other fish.

She turned her spear upside down, plucked the fish off its point and swung it across the bay by Coin's feet. It flapped from side to side, but Coin picked it up by its tail and smacked it hard against the nearest tree.

Clunk.

Coin tossed the fish onto the pebbled ground at her feet and grinned. She wiggled all her fingers with palms faceup as one would do to provoke a street fight. "That's it. Keep 'em comin', girl."

I turned back toward Fisher, now excited at the prospect of eating fresh fish, but what I saw next made my stomach drop.

Several feet away from Fisher, who was now smiling and full of confidence in her spearfishing skills, was a dark green—almost brown—lumpy mass slowly swimming toward her. It had a V-like shape to it, with two big bumps evenly positioned on either side. Its eyes, I knew. Behind its head were sharp ridges poking out of the water, its body swaying from side to side.

I'm not sure how long I stood there staring at it in shock before my throat finally loosened.

"Fisher!" My voice cracked.

She swung her head around at me, completely pissed off that I'd frightened away a good portion of our meal. I couldn't say anything else. It was as if my vocal chords had stitched themselves together. I simply pointed, my eyes wide.

She slowly turned around—the kind of stupid movement you'd expect to see in a horror movie—but the moment she saw it, she bolted in the opposite direction. Her arms flailed from side to side as she tore through the water, creating big splashes and ripples of white foam.

I ran out of the water and stood by Coin's side, an arrow drawn and my eyes fixated on the crocodile. I pulled back on the elastic, but I couldn't get a clean shot—Fisher's frantic movements kept getting in the way.

"That ain't gonna do anything," Coin said, quickly eyeing me. She stood as stiff as a pole but seemed to be in a panic—her nostrils flared and her fists clenched so tightly, I thought her fingers might puncture through her own hands.

I glanced at the tip of my arrowhead and back

up toward the oncoming reptile. Coin was right. *What was I thinking?* An arrow wouldn't penetrate its thick skin. *But what if I hit its eye? What if it opened its mouth, and I shot straight into its throat?*

Fisher finally reached shallow water, her pace quickening, but something threw her off balance. A slimy rock? Shells? Both legs came out from underneath her and she fell on her side—*crack*. She grimaced and tried to stand, but the next thing I knew, she was violently thrashing around, attempting to free herself from the crocodile's monstrous jaw.

CHAPTER 6

A layer of cool water grazed the tips of my leafy toes as I stood motionless. There was so much blood that a dark pool of black swirled around my ankles. I couldn't remember what had happened. I was breathing heavily, my hands shaking like autumn leaves on the brink of letting go, and my legs trembling so badly I was certain my femur bones had somehow magically evaporated.

"Fish!" Coin shouted, but she sounded miles away.

I heard water splash behind me, and Coin was by my side, bending down to grab Fisher by the arms. Was she dead? Why couldn't I move?

"Yo, snap the fuck out of it!" Coin shouted. "Help me pull her out."

I looked down to see Fisher lying on her back, her upper lip curled over her teeth. She threw her frizzy wet-haired head back and growled in agony.

She wasn't dead.

That's when I saw the crocodile's jaw. It had scooped her up in one bite and clenched both her thighs in its mouth. At the center of its head, right in between both eyes, was Fisher's spear. Its shaft was sticking straight up into the air, wiggling from side to side as Fisher tried to pull herself out.

I immediately came to.

"Open its mouth," I told Coin. "I'll pull her out."

Coin did as instructed. She wrapped both hands around the tip of the crocodile's terrifying jaw, careful to slide her fingers in between the gaps of its teeth, and pulled upward.

I wrapped my arms around Fisher's chest and pulled her out. She yelled as the crocodile's teeth slid out of her hamstring muscles, and she breathed quickly through her clenched teeth. Her suede pants were stained a dark shade of reddish brown.

I slid my head underneath her arm and stood her up, her weight nearly forcing me down on my knees.

"Come on," I said, encouraging her every step.

"Goddammit," she growled.

There was a quick rip-like sound, and Coin appeared beside us with Fisher's spear in hand, its tip a bright red.

When we finally reached the edge of the bay, she collapsed onto a patch of dry dirt and lay down on her back. She slammed tight fists on either side of her, clearly fighting through an immense amount of pain.

"We need to see it," I said.

I wasn't sure where this was coming from. I wasn't a nurse. I wasn't a doctor. But I knew—whether because of instinct or common sense—that we could not overlook the graveness of her injury. Not on Kormace Island.

She quickly nodded and squeezed her eyes shut.

I knelt by her side and untied the suede strings at the front of her pants. I'd been about to start pulling them down when her clammy fingers clasped my wrist.

"Thanks," she breathed.

"For what?"

"Saving my life."

Now I remembered: her spear floating away from her, its tip sinking slightly into the water. I'd grabbed it, just like that, and ran up to the horrific scene. With its shaft held tightly in both hands above my head, I'd stabbed the spear's pointed tip as hard as I could in between the crocodile's eyes.

I'd been about to say, "Anything for a friend," but she let out another bellow.

I gently tugged on her pants. They were too wet to pull off, so I rolled them bit by bit until both of her bloody thighs were completely bare.

"Holy sh—" Coin said, clasping a hand over her own mouth and turning away briefly.

"Is it bad?" Fisher asked.

Coin shrugged and stretched a crooked smile as if Fisher could see her. "Ain't that bad…" she said.

"It's bad." I wasn't about to sugarcoat it. What was the point? They were her legs—it was only a matter of time before she saw them.

The water had rinsed off most of the blood, thankfully, but that wasn't what worried me. I stared at all the puncture wounds forming two squiggly lines across both her thighs—one near her knees and the other, below her hip. They were dark, but not perfectly round as one would expect from a crocodile's teeth. There were patches of skin missing; some wounds were circular, and others, almost square-looking. Only a few appeared to be deep, with purple edges and dark gooey blood.

"We need to get you back to Redwood," I said.

Fisher nodded. It was obvious she wanted someone else to take charge. She was weak, vulnerable, and in excruciating pain; the last thing she wanted was to be forced to start making decisions.

She slowly sat up, her eyes fixated on the prehistoric monster that had tried to eat her. "What the fuck is this? The 2069 remake of James Patterson's Zoo?"

Coin let out a laugh, but her face straightened when she realized neither one of us was laughing.

"Where are all of these goddamn"—she

grimaced and caught her breath—"animals coming from?"

"There was only one," Coin said, peering back at the crocodile as if she'd missed something, "and to be honest, I think that's a young female."

"What makes you say that?" I asked.

"Don't look no more than four feet long to me. And look at Fisher's legs. Ain't pretty, but a full-grown male crocodile would've torn her apart or left more holes than that." She placed both hands around her waist. "Now what other animals are you talkin' about?"

Fisher shook her head. "We saw a bunch of animals before we found that Australian girl. They were all drinking water. Wild dogs, zebras, elephants—"

"Elephants?" Coin blurted. "Zeb—" She scratched her head before widening her eyes at us. "Why the hell didn't y'all catch us somethin' to eat? And since when are there elephants on Kormace Island?"

"Exactly," Fisher grumbled.

Coin stared at her, waiting to hear more.

"I've been on the island for years," Fisher went on. "I've seen a gorilla"—she looked up at me—"with you, that one time... The usual wild boars. And a leopard..."

Everyone fell silent.

I knew what she was referring to. Several years

ago, she'd witnessed her girlfriend get mauled to death by a leopard. Rocket had been the one to tell me. The leopard had dragged her far up into a tree and the Hunters, including Fisher, heard the entire thing: the crunching through bone, the tearing through tendons, and the chewing of muscle.

"It's the fire," I said, breaking the silence. "Must've forced hundreds of animals to migrate."

Fisher glared up at me as if this reason wasn't good enough for all our sightings.

But there was no other explanation.

Coin leaned on Fisher's spear. "You know as well as I do that every time we leave the base, there're dangers."

Fisher shook her head. "I don't care. This is"—she inhaled a sharp breath through her teeth—"this is bullshit."

I agreed with her. But being upset with Kormace Island's wildlife was a moot point. It was what it was. We had no control over it. This place was crawling with vermin, critters, insects, and predators. We weren't camped out at an all-inclusive five-star resort. Things would never be comfortable.

"Guys," I said, breaking the unnecessary bickering. "We need to go back. Maybe someone has some kind of medical—"

"Brone," Fisher said.

I stared at her.

"Can you touch my toes?"

I tilted my head. Was she trying to be funny?

"Touch my damn toes!"

Her leaf boots must've fallen off during the attack. I stretched my arm and pinched her right foot's big toe.

She nodded. "The other one."

Pinch.

She nodded again. "No severed nerves."

I let out a relieved sigh, but my throat swelled. "You think we can treat this?"

I couldn't lose Fisher. She'd been my sidekick day in day out. The fact that I'd run toward a crocodile to save her life—even the memory was still a bit hazy—proved that I cared for her more than I'd realized.

Fisher squinted as she tried to sit up straight. "We need to clean it and wrap it up. But after that, I need Navi."

If only things were so simple. The odds that our Medic had survived the attack were slim to none. She was a healer, after all. Why run away when so many women were being injured? To flee the attack would have contradicted everything she believed in.

"I'll find her," I said. I was being delusional, but the words had come out nonetheless. Whether I'd said that to comfort her, or me, I wasn't sure. But I had to try. I had to.

"Help me up."

Coin and I scooped her up and she let out a soft yelp. I felt terrible. I should have been by her side, not standing out of the bay for safety. Maybe this could have been prevented.

"Wait," Fisher said, her curled toes dangling inches away from the ground. "Promise me something."

"Anything," I said.

"Promise me you'll come back here."

Coin cocked her eyebrow and shot me a dazed look. Fisher turned her head slightly, her eyes fixated on the bay. "That motherfucker tried to eat me. I want crocodile for supper."

CHAPTER 7

"What the fu—" Coin growled.

She raised her leg, her knee nearly touching her belly. Underneath the pad of her foot was a long, flat piece of brown feces.

"Are you kidding me?" she went off.

"Coin," I said, matter-of-factly. We didn't have time for this. Fisher's face had lost a shade of color, and her eyelids were becoming heavy.

"Why would someone shit so close to camp?" she continued.

"What makes you think it's human?" I asked.

"'Cause it is. I can tell. You wanna take a look?" she asked, her huge eyes glued to me.

"Because we didn't give the women a designated spot," Fisher said, her voice hoarse.

"That ain't good enough." Coin wiped her foot over and over against a broken piece of bamboo, shaking Fisher from side to side in the process.

"Coin!" I hissed.

She bickered for a few more minutes before we reached our new camp—Redwood. The sun had set, and women lay around a small, flickering fire. Some appeared to be sleeping; others chewed on pieces of fruit or vines for hydration.

"What happened?" someone asked.

Footsteps ran in our direction. There were a few moans as women woke from sleep, and in an instant, everyone was surrounding Fisher.

We placed her by the fire, careful not to touch her wounded legs.

"*Bozhe miĭ!*" Everest cried, quick-stepping her way close to Fisher.

I had no idea what she'd said, but I assumed, based on her disconcerted tone, that it meant something along the lines of "Oh my God" or "My goodness."

"What happened?" Ellie was the first to kneel by Fisher's side. She pressed a firm, comforting hand on Fisher's arm, but Fisher swung away and bared her teeth. She was in too much pain. Her forehead's shiny skin reflected the campfire's orange hue, and although difficult to confirm due to the lack of sunlight, she looked pale. How much blood had she lost? It wasn't like we had the tools or the knowledge required to perform a blood transfusion.

"We need to clean this up and stop the bleeding," I said.

Proxy walked away and quickly returned with what appeared to be a bamboo stick.

"May I see Fisher's knife?" she asked.

Fisher's hateful eyes rolled up at her. No way was she letting anyone touch her knife, even if it meant she'd die as a result. The knife had once belonged to her sister, who was also sentenced to serve time on Kormace Island. When Fisher first arrived on the island, she found her sister's dead body, stabbed multiple times, lying in a bed of dirt near the southern shore.

"Here," Franklin said, handing Proxy a small shiv.

Proxy pierced a hole at one end of the stick, her long frail arm muscles barely swelling in size as she forced the knife in.

"Use this." She handed Ellie the stick. "There should be clean rainwater in there. The inside of the bamboo stick acts as a filtration system."

Johnson—hating on Proxy as usual—scoffed, "And you couldn't think to tell us about this earlier, dipshit? When we were all dried up and cracking from dehydration?"

Proxy ignored her, which was probably the safest move. "I'll go try to find matico leaves."

"Mati—what now?" Franklin asked.

"I can't be certain, but I believe I may have seen them right outside over there." She pointed into absolute darkness. "Matico leaves act as an antiseptic. We can hopefully use it to eliminate or reduce her infection. It's also an antinausea herb, and it alleviates most digestive issues. It would be good to keep some around. If I find any coca leaves, I'll pluck them as well. We can use them as an anesthetic to numb her pain."

"How the hell do you know all of that?" Johnson asked.

"Who cares?" Franklin cut in. "Coca leaves? We have coca leaves on the island?"

"Observation," Proxy said, ignoring Franklin's excitement. "I was a big fan of Tegan's."

Tegan, I thought. If there was one person we needed most, aside from Navi, our Medic, it was Tegan. She'd been the herbalist, if you will, who concocted all sorts of soaps, lotions, and medicinal herbs. Fisher had relied on Tegan for years to alleviate her endometriosis pain.

But as I stared up at Proxy's lanky silhouette outlined by a dim orange glow, I knew she'd play a key role in our new society. If we couldn't have Tegan, we'd have the next best thing—a brainiac who, despite her awkward social skills, was incredibly intelligent and rather knowledgeable about the jungle's plant kingdom.

"I'll go with her," I said, plucking Fisher's hunting spear out of Coin's hand. I didn't want to; I hated the jungle at night. It gave me chills. Although moonlight illuminated some areas, others were entirely black. The last thing I wanted to see was a pair of big night creature eyes staring right at me. But I'd have done anything to save Fisher.

Ellie grabbed my arm. "Be careful."

I nodded and turned away, but she pulled me in and threw an arm around my neck. I wasn't sure where it was coming from. I stood stiff, my eyes shifting from side to side, feeling like everyone was watching us.

"You never know," she said quietly before letting me go.

I didn't respond. Not because I didn't want to—I didn't know what to say. I didn't know how to feel around Ellie just then. I cared about her, but something was off. Ever since that morning, I was numb. Was she right? Had the dead woman's body affected me? Franklin suddenly appeared beside me, holding a stick with its tip a smoldering red.

"Won't last long," she said, "but it's something."

I thanked her and followed Proxy's lead in between two giant trees, carrying Franklin's stick that barely cast any light.

What had I gotten myself into? I glanced back at Ellie's still silhouette as guilt set in. What was wrong with me? Why couldn't I feel anything?

"This way," Proxy said, slipping through a curtain of hanging vines.

I grimaced as I slid through, envisioning my face brushing against the fuzzy leg of a giant spider.

But I was Brone—an Archer, a Hunter. I'd killed a Norther. I'd survived a massacre. I couldn't possibly be scared of the jungle at night. I repeated these words in my head, creating a delusional sense of confidence.

I clenched my teeth with every step taken, anticipating a venomous snakebite or a trap of some sort. Then I realized Proxy was already way ahead of me, breezing through like she'd done this her entire life. How long had she been on the island, anyways?

"You done this before?" I whispered, my voice barely carrying over the loud static sound of insects and night critters.

She turned around, her mouse-like features illuminated from my fire-lit stick. A faint smile curved one side of her mouth. "I used to sneak out of the Village all the time."

Was she nuts? She could have been attacked or ambushed as I had been.

"For resources?" I asked.

"That's correct," she said. "I've gathered a few supplies for Tegan—you know, for her potions and what have you."

She was so straightforward, which wasn't something I was accustomed to on this island. Most women were fueled by their beliefs and emotions.

"And what did you get in return?" I asked.

I knew how the women of Kormace operated—everything came at a price. No one offered services simply out of the kindness of their heart. Tegan had once given me free soap in exchange for a promise that I'd someday help her somehow. I'd probably never get the chance to repay her.

"I got to learn," Proxy said. "She taught me things she swore she'd never share with anyone else. She said it made her valuable to the community. Indispensable."

Indispensable, I thought.

Horrific images flashed through my mind, almost as you'd see on the screen of a DSLR camera shooting in burst mode. The images were short-lived but vivid nonetheless: women raising their arms above their heads, pleading for their lives; half-masked faces with white chalk and bloodstains around their eyes; women throwing their heads back with their mouths wide open, screaming in pain; blood splattering through thick clouds of smoke; Fisher digging her fingers inside Mia's lower abdomen to extract an arrowhead.

Mia, I thought. She'd been too weak to follow us. I hoped she'd died peacefully and not at the hands of a predator.

"The polite thing to do when someone speaks to you is to respond," Proxy said.

I shook my head. "Sorry."

"Are you all right?" she asked.

"I'm fine," I lied.

"It's a silent killer, you know."

I stared at her. What was she talking about?

"PTSD," she continued.

I'd heard the term tossed around a few times, especially when people spoke of the military, but what did that have to do with me?

"Post-traumatic stress disorder," she clarified.

I knew what it meant.

"What's your point?" I hadn't meant to get irritable, but we were out in the middle of the jungle with barely any visibility and Fisher's wounds needed immediate attention. I didn't have time to receive a lecture about some disorder.

"I can see it in your eyes," she said.

This took me aback. Was she seriously insinuating I had PTSD? Sure, I'd seen a few horrendous things over the course of a year—a brief image of Sunny's swollen, naked body hanging upside down flashed in my head—but it was nothing in comparison to the horrors soldiers were subjected to.

Was it?

"It doesn't only affect veterans," Proxy said, almost as if reading my mind. "A single traumatic event can trigger PTSD. Most women on the island suffer from it. In America, seventy percent of people experience or witness a traumatic event at least once in their life, and out of that seventy percent—"

"Can we keep moving?" It came out as more of an order than a request. I didn't care about her statistics. I didn't need a mental disorder to get in the way of my survival—our survival. These women depended on me.

"No problem," she said, clearly unaffected by my harsh tone. "I believe I saw the matico leaves over here."

I stared at her slender figure as it slithered through colorless verdure, barely making a sound. Did she know what she was doing? Were these mati-something leaves actually going to help Fisher?

"Bring the light," I heard her say.

I moved closer and extended the fire-lit stick. There was barely any fire left to it, but its bright red tip cast enough light to see the grooves on the leaves. She slid her thumb against the leaf's flat surface and along its edges, assessing either its quality or its family class—I couldn't tell which.

The plant itself, a shrubby tree, measured at least several meters in height. I couldn't see the top of it because it blended into the jungle's darkness. The leaves themselves were lance-shaped and bigger than my hands.

Proxy plucked several of the oversized leaves from their stems and placed them against her ribs, underneath her armpit.

"This should do," she said.

As we made our way back, I began to see Redwood's campfire flickering from side to side. No way could our mission have been that simple. I clenched my teeth as we moved closer, expecting to hear a snarl nearby, but the only sound came from frogs and insects projecting a soothing orchestral hum. There were no monkeys screaming, no leaves rustling, no branches breaking—everything was peaceful.

It was too calm.

My eyes shot this way and that, and I anticipated the worst. Sick to my stomach, the thought of crunching down on one of those matico leaves now seemed like a good idea.

"Looks like everyone's still up," Proxy said, and I flinched at the sound of her voice.

Out of nowhere, I imagined a Norther's skull face appearing behind Proxy and a spearhead cracking through her rib cage and tearing out through her chest.

My heart raced and my hands became clammy, but nothing happened.

"You guys found it okay?" I heard, but there was a loud ringing in my ears, and I wasn't sure who'd spoken.

Proxy rushed toward Fisher with the leaves in hand, and a few women surrounded me.

"Find any coca leaves?"

There was laughter.

"Hello?"

I stared at Fisher, who was lying on her back beside the fire and at Proxy, who knelt beside her and prepared the leaves.

Although I felt like I was dying, I knew I should have been relieved—for the first time in a long time, something had gone right.

CHAPTER 8

"Is this about the kiss?" Ellie asked.

I stared into her soft eyes, even though I could barely see them due to nightfall, and focused my gaze on her lips.

This was definitely not about the kiss.

"Let's forget it ever happened," she went on.

Everyone was sleeping, except for Johnson who'd been told to keep watch overnight.

She lowered her voice even further. "Lydia, I'm sorry about that."

The sound of my own name took me aback. No one called me Lydia on the island—I was Brone. I automatically felt vulnerable.

"Say something," she whispered.

I didn't know what to say. I wasn't ashamed of what had happened. I'd kissed a girl. What was the big deal? In fact, I'd enjoyed it much more than I'd have thought.

"This isn't about the kiss," I said.

She perked up, resting her head on one hand and placing the other on my belly.

"I... I don't know how to feel," I tried.

"About me?"

I looked up at her.

"We don't have to make this a thing," she started up again. "I mean, I want—"

"I don't want to care about you," I said.

Silence.

I waited, expecting her to either scold me or to climb out of the hammock and sleep somewhere else.

"Do you care about Fisher?" she suddenly asked.

Where was she going with this? Fisher was only a friend. Was she jealous?

"Just answer me."

"Of course I do. She's my friend."

"And the Hunters?" she asked. "Trim, Rocket, Biggie, Flander?"

"Of course."

"This island is full of death, Lydia. There's no escaping that. As much as you hope to see your friends again, you might not find them."

Was she trying to spill salt into my wounds? A few days ago, she'd spoken to me about hope and now, she was being completely negative.

"Do you wish you'd never met them?" she asked.

"What?" I said.

"The Hunters—if you don't ever see them

again."

I stared at her.

"If you could go back in time and build yourself a little shelter by the beach… If you could live in seclusion on this island, would you do it? Would you be happier if you'd never met any of us?"

"Of course not," I said.

She brushed her thumb up and down my arm. "I've been where you are, you know."

I was getting tired of lectures, but as usual, I wanted to hear what she had to say, so I waited.

"Pulling away… distancing myself from others," she continued. "I've lost a lot of people on this island. Everyone has. But that doesn't mean we have to stop being human. If we don't have love for each other, we're nothing but a bunch of savage animals."

Why was she always right?

"You can talk to me, you know." She reached a warm hand up to my face, curving her delicate fingers around the back of my neck.

I wanted to tell her about the flashbacks—about the night terrors and the anxiety attacks—but I couldn't bring myself to do it.

"Hey, Ellie?" I asked.

"Yeah?"

"Why are you here? I mean… What did you do?" I knew that questioning someone's past was a big no-no on the island, but Ellie was one of the sweetest women I'd ever met. The thought of her murdering someone was unfathomable.

"You honestly want to know that?" she asked.

I did.

She let out a soft sigh. "I was heavy into drugs when I was eighteen. I used to party every night. A friend of mine had a house party on November seventeenth. I'll never forget the date even though I can't remember what happened. I guess I walked in on some guy raping her... All I remember is coming to in a police cruiser and seeing blood all over my clothes. Turns out I stabbed him twenty-four times."

My eyes went big.

"You really shouldn't ask people that question if you aren't ready to hear the answer," she said.

"No, no," I shook my head. "It's okay. I'm glad you told me."

She knew she'd freaked me out a little bit. Twenty-four times?

"I was a different person, Lydia. And I was under the influence. Drugs can turn you into something completely different, especially excessive use."

"How old are you now?" I asked.

"Twenty-six."

I grabbed her hand and pressed it against my lips. I wasn't afraid of her. I knew she was a good person despite what she may have done in the past.

"Thanks for sharing with me," I said.

"Yo, shut the fuck up!" someone said. "We're trying to sleep."

Ellie laughed like a kid caught playing games during nap time—a whispered giggle, almost. I wrapped my arm around her and pulled her against my chest.

"We should get some rest," I said. "I need my strength tomorrow morning."

Her hair tickled my chin as she pulled her head back. "Why's that?"

"I have to go pick up a crocodile."

CHAPTER 9

"It's gone."

"What do you mean, it's gone?" I asked, my anger misdirected at Coin.

"It's gone," she repeated plainly.

I couldn't believe what I was seeing. It had been right here—the crocodile—right atop river stones in the shallow end of the bay.

"Well, it didn't just float away," I said.

Franklin, who we only brought along for extra muscle power, jeered, "Maybe it came back to life."

I glared at her. Was this all a big joke to her? Aside from fruit and nuts, most of us hadn't eaten a solid meal in days. She wasn't a Hunter—she had no idea what it felt like to venture dozens of miles per day on an empty stomach.

"What?" Her eyes went big at me, and she shrugged, her palms facing up.

I grinded my teeth and bit my tongue. I wanted to tell her off—tell her she was nothing but a worthless waste of skin because all she ever did was complain or find fault in others—but if I did, things would only escalate; and if things escalated while I was in pain, starved, and exhausted, I'd probably black out again.

When I looked away, she said, "That's what I thought."

The muscles in my neck went stiff and I stretched them slowly, hearing a loud pop. *It's not worth it, it's not worth it, it's not worth it.*

The quiver on my back was instantly hot against my skin, and I wondered how fast she'd drop to her knees like the pathetic coward she was if I were pointing an arrow at her face.

"Yo," Coin said, slapping me across the forearm. "Ain't worth it."

I quickly glanced at her, realizing how psychotic I must have looked—clenched teeth, eyes wide, neck veins bulging out. I inhaled a deep breath through my nostrils and slowly released it.

Franklin wasn't even invested in what was going on—she was wandering around at the edge of the jungle, walking circles around Proxy, who stood as stiff as a nail board, her hands held together behind her back and her chin raised high as she observed our surroundings.

I hadn't been too keen on Proxy tagging along, but we'd agreed to four women lifting the crocodile, while also leaving a few women behind at Redwood who were capable of battle in case of an attack. Proxy wouldn't survive one minute on the front line.

That left Johnson and Ellie—which I also wasn't keen on, but Ellie was caring for Fisher—to guard Redwood. Everest was too old to fight, so she didn't count.

Fortunately, Proxy had constructed a flutelike mechanism out of a bamboo stick.

"If you blow here," she'd said, guiding Ellie, "it will emit a high-pitched whistle capable of being heard several miles away and we will quickly return."

"Looks like it's gone," Proxy said now, staring out at the river's current.

"No shit, Batman," Franklin said.

I closed my eyes again and inhaled slowly. God, I hated her.

"There goes our meal," Coin said.

"Doesn't make much sense, though." Proxy stepped forward, the tips of her toes soaking in the bay's shallow water. She had thick leatherlike slabs underneath her feet and dry meshing around her ankles and shins. I'd seen a few women wear these when I first landed on the island. I would much rather have had that instead of my deteriorating leaf boots. "Crocodiles can weigh over two thousand pounds."

Franklin crossed her arms and rolled her eyes like a teenager on the verge of receiving a lecture.

"It wasn't that big," I cut in. "A young female,

maybe."

Proxy rubbed her chin. "A leopard can carry up to twice its weight up a tree"—she paced back and forth—"and a large leopard can weigh up to two hundred pounds."

Everyone stared at her in silence.

"Then I suppose, mathematically speaking," she continued, "if the crocodile weighed less than four hundred pounds, which it wouldn't unless—"

"We get it," Franklin said.

"Does it matter who took it?" Coin asked, her patience thinning.

It did matter. What if a group of savage women were responsible? What if it wasn't a wildcat at all, but Ogres or Rogues or even Northers?

"Could be humans," I said.

Everyone's eyes shot up at me.

I glanced around, peering through the dark gaps in between the flourished trees and tall reed grass around the water's edge. "I mean, we don't know this part of the jungle very well. What if there are Ogres nearby? Rogues?"

"Rogues travel alone," Coin said. "One woman wouldn't be able to carry a crocodile."

"Ogres?" I repeated.

The thought of being in close contact with uncivilized, cannibalistic women was more frightening than the crocodile. My shoulders stiffened, and my eyes continued to scan every inch of thick greenery around us.

"Look," Coin broke the eerie silence. "It don't matter anymore. The damn thing's gone. Let's get the hell out of here."

Franklin threw her head back and moaned, her mouth loose and her eyes in the back of her skull. "God, I'm starving."

"We're all starving," I growled.

"You're the Hunter," she threw back, her eyes narrowing. "Get us some damn food."

In one swift movement, I pulled an arrow from my quiver, loaded my bow, and pointed its sharp tip straight at her face.

"Whoa!" Franklin said and raised two open hands by the sides of her face.

My heart was beating out of my chest and a sense of surrealism clouded my head—that familiar, adrenaline-induced, out-of-body feeling like I wasn't in control of my physical self, but rather, a spectator.

She stood there, a crystal-clear image, with panic in her eyes.

"Brone!"

The bow's string made a stretching noise as I pulled back, and the arrowhead's aim bounced up and down from her face to her neck, following my rapid breathing.

But before even being able to visualize letting go of the arrow, I was hit hard from behind and propelled into the water, over a bed of slimy stones. Water flowed around me, but not over me, and the next thing I knew, Coin was straddled on my stomach and I was pinned down with no weapon in hand.

"Just 'cause Murk ain't around, don't mean we get to lose control," she said calmly.

"Get the fuck off me!" I shouted, kicking water in every direction. Who did she think she was? This was between Franklin and me.

"You need to learn to control your anger," she said. "Ain't nobody happy about being here. I'm hungry, too. I'm exhausted, too. But we ain't goddamn animals!"

Her thick arms were too short and stalky for me to break her hold. She held both my hands firmly against my own chest and sat there, her triceps bulging out.

I finally dropped my head back and stared at the sky. It was no use. She was too strong.

"You done?" she asked.

I waited a minute or so before finally answering. "Okay."

"Okay." She let me go and helped me up.

I slapped a hand into the water to pick up my floating bow and a few of my arrows that had fallen out.

"Just 'cause you have a weapon," Coin said, "don't give you the right to play God. If you're gonna fight, at least be fair about it."

"There's nothing fair about this goddamn island," I said, whipping my arrows over my shoulder and into their quiver.

"We're all struggling, Brone," Coin said. "We need to stick together."

I knew she was right, but I didn't want to hear it. I was too angry—angry at myself, angry at the justice system, angry at everyone.

I hated this place.

"Let's go," I said, making my way back into the jungle.

As I passed Franklin, who I assumed would keep her mouth shut after I pointed an arrow at her, she smirked sideways at me. "You're nothing without that bow."

Without thinking, I swung a fist as hard as I could at her nose and there was a loud *crack*. She stepped back, completely disoriented with both hands over her bloody nose, but her wild eyes slowly rolled up at me, and I immediately regretted hitting her.

I didn't have the time to dodge her attack. She swung her long arm out, a curved punch to the side of my head. Everything went fuzzy, and I heard a ringing noise in my left ear. She grabbed me by the hair, dragged me down to the ground, and dropped her knee right into my ribs.

At that moment, I thought for sure she'd

cracked my ribs, even though I could barely feel anything.

Another hit to the side of my head sent pain through my skull.

"Guys!"

"Ohhh, this is not good."

I swung back as hard as I could and felt the impact, but I couldn't tell where I'd hit her. She tried to pin me down, but I kicked her in the stomach and she fell back a few steps.

Coin intervened and grabbed Franklin by the arm, but all it did was aggravate her. She swung a fist straight for Coin's jawline and came back at me and drop-kicked me in the chest, crushing both my arms against each other.

Another hit—a stomp-like kick to my face this time, and everything around me began to fade.

I waited for that final blow to knock me out, but nothing happened. I glanced back, my vision blurry, and witnessed something I thought for sure was a dehydration-induced delusion.

Proxy, whose face was completely emotionless, had her long bony forearm wrapped around Franklin's neck from behind. Her biceps showed minor definition but nothing worth bragging about. Franklin's face was beet red and her eyelids became heavy as Proxy slowly lowered her to the ground until at last, she lost consciousness.

CHAPTER 10

"Oh my God, Brone, what happened?"

Ellie rushed to me, her panicked eyes scanning my swollen face and bloody arms.

"A slight altercation," Proxy said.

"Slight?" Ellie retorted.

Sensation had finally kicked in—a sharp ache in my ribs and painful throbbing on my face, my arms, and my knuckles, which were scraped up pretty badly. My vision was still fuzzy, and I had a wicked headache.

"Who did this?" Ellie's eyes shot up at Coin and Proxy. "Where's Franklin?"

"She'll find her way back," I said. "Maybe. Hopefully not."

"She did this?" Ellie asked.

"As I said," Proxy said, "a slight altercation."

"They got into a fight." Coin rubbed her jaw where Franklin had clocked her.

"And you guys left her there?" Johnson asked, stepping into the conversation.

"I had to subdue her somehow," Proxy said.

"With the right amount of pressure on her carotid artery—"

Johnson laughed out loud. "You put her in a sleeper choke?"

For a moment, it looked like she was getting along with Proxy.

"I did," Proxy said.

"Quiet down," Ellie said. She glanced back at the farthest hammock in Redwood. "Fisher's sleeping."

"How's she doing?" I asked.

Ellie shook her head. The look on her face told me Fisher's condition wasn't improving. "I've cleaned her wounds twice this morning, but I think the infection's spreading into her bloodstream. She's feverish."

I clenched my teeth. I couldn't lose Fisher.

"Where's the crocodile?" Ellie asked, glancing around.

"Wasn't there," Coin said.

Ellie cocked an eyebrow. "How on earth did a dead crocodile disappear overnight?"

Proxy pointed a finger in the air. "There are several possibilities. It could have been taken by Ogres, by Northers, or, depending on the weight of the crocodile—"

"Ogres?" Johnson cut in, distraught by the very idea of them. "I thought we were far away from those psychotic bitches."

"We don't know what happened," I said. "It could just be a leopard."

Proxy cleared her throat. "Actually, the odds of it being a leopard are quite slim—"

"Are we even safe here?" Johnson continued. "What if we're on Ogre territory right now? What if there are Northers nearby? We have no defense in place. We're all starving. We're an open target. What the hell are we—"

But she abruptly stopped talking, and everyone's eyes followed hers.

At the edge of Redwood was Franklin, huffing and puffing as she walked in backward dragging something, her back curved and her neck glistening with sweat. She stopped pulling, stiffened her posture in a stretch, and glanced at us.

"Well, are any of you twits gonna help me?"

I didn't move. Coin ran to her side and together, they walked into Redwood backward, branches cracking and leaves crunching as they dragged through the dirt whatever it was they were pulling.

"Holy shit," Johnson said.

There was a loud thump, and at the very center of Redwood lay the crocodile that had attacked Fisher. Its short, dinosaur-like legs hung stiffly at the sides of its body, and its belly faced upward. But what took me most by surprise wasn't the fact that Franklin had found the crocodile, nor that she had somehow managed to drag it by herself—what took me aback was its beige belly. It was completely torn open and empty.

I hesitated. "You took out its insides?"

Her eyes rolled up at me. There was pink swelling underneath her right eye and a gash across her lower lip but nothing else. Clearly, I'd lost the fight.

She smirked. "Found it like this."

I clenched my fists. "Where? When?"

"When I woke up," she said. "You know, after Gentle Giant over here put me in a sleeper choke."

"My apologies," Proxy said, "but it was necessary."

"Whatever," Franklin said. "I'm over it. Anyways, I ended up walking in the wrong direction for a while, and I found this little bastard lying flat on its back—like this."

Proxy knelt by the crocodile's side, her index finger running along the smooth scaled skin of its open belly. "This was cut open. It looks like the shape of a triangle. A ritual, perhaps."

Everyone looked up at one another.

"Did you see anything else?" I asked. "When you found the croc?"

Franklin shrugged. "I'm not sure. I didn't look around. I just grabbed it."

"Think," I said. "Any weird markings on nearby

trees? Any altars? Anything unusual?"

Her eyes were glued to mine. "Like I *just* told you, I'm not sure."

I nearly lunged at her again, but Fisher was sleeping, and truthfully, I didn't want to get my ass kicked again.

"You think this is an Ogre's doing?" Johnson asked, a slight tremble in her voice.

"Could be," I said.

Franklin scoffed—the one thing she was good at. "Ogres aren't even a sure thing."

I glared at her. "Excuse me?"

"You heard me," she said. "No one knows for sure if they're even real. For all we know, it's some dumb myth Murk invented to keep us inside the Village walls. It's perfect, really—a bunch of crazy woman-eating savages."

"You were practically shitting yourself by the river when the word Ogre was mentioned!" I pointed a stiff arm in the direction we'd ventured earlier.

Another scoff. "I was only messing around."

Why did she feel the need to look so tough in front of everyone? So badass?

"My friend was killed by an Ogre," I said slowly, grinding my teeth. "And I saw one during the wildfire. So don't tell me they don't exist."

There were a few gasps and low-toned bickering, but Franklin kept up her appearances.

She rolled her eyes and crossed her arms. "Your *friend*? What *friend*? Or is this an imaginary lover you like to fantasize about when you touch yourself at night?" She laughed out loud. "I mean, come on—we all do it."

The image of Sunny's naked, beaten body and her swollen, balloon-like face instantly popped into my head.

The next thing I knew, I was mounted on top of Franklin with both my hands tight around her throat, squeezing as hard as I could.

"She attacked me," Franklin said, pointing a stiff finger straight at me. She rubbed her throat, which was covered in red markings.

"I don't care who started it," Fisher said, her tired eyes fixed on Franklin. "You're both adults. If you expect us to survive, you can't be turning on each other." She winced as Ellie slowly lowered her onto a wooden stump by the fire. She was paler than I'd ever seen her—a pasty cream color—and her eyes were sunken into dark blue circles.

I tried not to stare at the wounds on her legs, but it was nearly impossible. There was yellow crusting and clear liquid dripping from the deeper wounds—puss, I assumed. The skin of her thighs was bright red, a sign of infection, but if you looked closely, you could see that her legs had turned a grayish-blue due to severe bruising.

I quickly glanced up at Franklin, who was staring at me with such ferocity, and I wondered whether she'd still be alive had Fisher not yelled at me to let her go. I remembered feeling hands all over me, and fingers gripping my biceps in a desperate attempt to help Franklin, but I wouldn't let go of her throat—at least, not until I heard Fisher's voice.

"Almost ready," Everest said, twirling one of the crocodile's skinless legs over the little fire.

Hammer, who was as happy as a pig in mud, was sitting near one of the back hammocks with piles of crocodile skin at her side, along with its entire head. She'd promised to make me boots, and she was delivering on it.

"After I eat," I said, "I'm going to look for Navi."

Fisher didn't say anything. She looked away, and her jaw muscles popped. I knew she wasn't mad at me—she hated Franklin. In fact, had she not been in so much pain, she'd probably have praised me for jumping her. She was simply scared, frightened that I wouldn't find our Medic in time, or at all. There was a good chance that Navi had been killed during the attack on our Village, but I had to try. Without proper medical care, she would die, and she knew it.

"I'm comin' with you," Coin said.

Johnson moved in. "Me too."

I wanted to smile, but my lips didn't move.

"We need protection here, too," I said.

Proxy stood tall. "I'll stay here."

Johnson burst out laughing, but the sound came to an abrupt stop when she caught my eyes.

I knew Proxy had more to offer than muscle—mind you, after having choked out Franklin, it was obvious she was stronger than she looked.

"I will build contraptions," Proxy continued, "along Redwood's perimeter to trap any intruders."

I gave a brief nod. "You guys should be safe from any Ogre around here, so long as you stay in Redwood."

Based on the Ogres I'd encountered before, I knew how they operated. They didn't attack merely to attack. They were nothing like the Northers. If you roamed their territory, however, that's when danger presented itself. So long as the women stayed inside the camp, they were safe—at least from the Ogres.

"You should have enough food here to hold you off for a while," I said. "Johnson, you stay here with the women. Coin and I can handle the jungle." I shot a quick glance at her muscular biceps. "I'd rather those muscles stay here to defend Redwood in the event of an attack."

She unfolded her arms and parted her lips to dispute my decision, but I looked over at Franklin, who was sitting against one of the massive trees carving a hunting spear, and Johnson went quiet. She knew my decision had nothing to do with protecting Redwood against an exterior threat—the only threat I was worried about was Franklin. Without Fisher in power, she'd try to take charge.

If anyone stood up to her, it would be Johnson.

She stared at me intently for a moment and nodded as a way of acknowledgment. For the first time, I viewed Johnson as an asset, rather than a nuisance who consistently provoked Proxy.

"Is ready." Everest raised the cooked piece of crocodile meat and straightened her rounded back.

Everyone gathered like a bunch of flies around a pile of dung.

Everest tore off a handful of meat and offered it to me before anyone else. I was a bit taken aback by this gesture. Was this a sign of respect? Was this her way of announcing to our society that she viewed me as their leader? Fisher was our leader right now—not me.

I peered back at Fisher, who'd lowered herself to the ground entirely, her chest bouncing up and down with every rapid shallow breath, and realized then that as an alpha wolf loses its position within its pack if injured, Fisher too, had lost her place.

Was I replacing her? It wouldn't have been the first time I was forced to lead.

I took the piece of meat and thanked her, but instead of biting down into it, even though I was starving to the point of pain, I brought it to Fisher. There was a powerful silence throughout Redwood as I knelt by Fisher's side, offering her the first meal.

"Here," I said.

But she shook her head and grimaced.

I pushed the meat into her hand. "You haven't eaten properly in days."

She placed a hand on her belly and shook her head again. "I can't."

"Nauseous?"

She nodded, her sunken eyes gazing up at me.

"Okay," I said, "but you need to eat soon." I stood and faced the crowd of women who were hovering around Everest like vultures. "Make sure she eats at some point, please."

I gently plucked the meat from her hands and nearly swallowed it whole, only briefly tasting its tender and juicy chicken-like flavor.

"I'll watch her," Ellie said, appearing beside me. She chewed a mouthful of meat, and added, "You'd better come back, otherwise, I'll have to go out there and find you. And truth be told, I probably wouldn't survive the jungle on my own."

She was trying to be silly—playful, but I could tell by the quiver in her bottom lip and the gloss over her eyes that she was doing everything in her power to avoid becoming emotional.

I nodded slowly and forced a smile. "Don't worry. I won't leave you behind."

My throat tightened at the sound of my own words. What if I did leave her? What if I died trying to find Navi or the Hunters? What if something happened to her while I was gone? I wanted to ask her to come with me, but I knew she wasn't equipped or trained to be out in the jungle. She'd admitted it herself. She was safer staying in Redwood, where she'd be able to attend to Fisher's wounds.

"I'm gonna miss you." I cleared my throat and looked away, but her arms came swinging around my neck and she pulled me tight against her. She combed her fingers into the back of my hair and held a firm hand behind my head, and we stood there, holding onto each other.

"Just come back, okay?" she whispered.

I nodded again, my face buried in her neck. I didn't want to let go. I didn't want to say goodbye. A profound guilt kicked in. Why had I pushed her away? Why had I been so distant? What if this was the last time I'd ever feel her skin against mine? Hear her soothing voice? Look into those beautiful, reassuring eyes of hers?

I brushed my cheek against hers until we were face-to-face. I looked down at her bright red lips and back up at her eyes, then slowly moved in and pressed my lips against hers. She pulled me in tighter, her hot breath blowing out of her nose and onto my face. I finally pulled back, knowing that if I didn't, I might decide not to leave.

"I'll come back," I said, but I couldn't shake the sinking feeling in my stomach—that something terrible was going to happen.

CHAPTER 12

They weren't Hush Puppies, but they were sturdy and guaranteed to protect my feet.

"Try to take them off as often as possible so they can dry," Hammer had told me, handing me my new pair of crocodile skin boots. She'd somehow managed to put together ankle-high boots with slabs of wood underneath to form soles. "I tried to clean off as much blood as I could, but there might still be some on the inside. And for the record, despite what you might think, they're not waterproof. If they're too wet, too often, you'll damage them."

Any anger I may have felt toward her in the past for having robbed me of my pearls when I first landed on the island was gone. She'd gone above and beyond to ensure that I was not only safe during my venture, but comfortable. She'd also carved new spears for Coin and me and crafted several new arrows to fill my quiver.

But what blew my mind was the protective crocodile scale vest she'd managed to put together. She'd used the crocodile's back—the toughest part of its body—and built something similar to a bulletproof vest, only it was dark green and completely scaled and lumpy due to its hard scutes, which offered a shield-like plate over my chest and back.

"This should protect you from arrows and other weapons," she'd told me.

I knew it was unfair that Coin hadn't received the same treatment as me, but at the same time, I was the one on the front line. If anyone were to get killed first, it would probably be me.

I owed Hammer everything.

"You honestly think Navi's still alive?" Coin asked, sliding her way in between two closely grown banana trees.

I didn't want to answer her. I didn't want to speak the words aloud, fearing they might come true.

"I don't know," I said.

"And the Hunters?" she pressed.

"They're out there," I said, remembering one of Coin's friends, Thompson, who'd assured us she'd seen Trim and several other women after the attack.

"Which way we goin', anyways?" Coin asked. "How do you know where to look?"

"I don't," I said, my patience thinning. I wasn't in the mood for chitchat. My friends were out there, possibly in need of help, and Fisher was back at Redwood, in need of immediate care.

If only Kormace Island had a hospital, I thought.

* * *

"Sweetheart, I think it's best you wait in the waiting room," the nurse said.

I scanned her name tag—Alice.

"She's my mom, Alice," I said. "I need to know she's okay."

I craned my neck to peer over her shoulder, but all I saw was my mom's blanket-wrapped feet pointing upward as they rolled her away on a gurney.

"She suffered a severe concussion and a dislocated jaw," Alice said. "The doctor needs to set it and scan her neck and spine for any damage to her spinal cord. He'll come see you as soon as she's stable."

She was about to walk away, but she froze and turned around on the heels of her sneakers. "The police will want to talk to you," she said, eyeing the two uniformed police offers standing in front of the reception desk. "Your mom told the doctor she fell down her apartment stairs. If there's something else you know," she paused, staring at me as if she could see right through me, "you should tell the police."

I nodded, even though I knew I'd stick by my

mom's story. This wasn't the first time Gary had beaten her, and every time it happened, she threatened to stop talking to me if I ratted on him.

"It's not his fault," she'd say, and every time, I imagined killing him.

* * *

Another memory flashed in my head—me, holding the cast iron frying pan and swinging it hard against the back of Gary's head to stop him from strangling my mother to death.

For the first time, I had no guilt about what I'd done.

I was glad I'd killed that son of a bitch.

I waited for the guilt to set in—for my moral compass to tell me that the thoughts I was having weren't real; they were the result of misdirected anger. But nothing happened. I felt no guilt, no remorse, nothing.

"Yo, Brone, check it out," Coin said in a whisper.

I followed her pointed finger to a woman's body curled up in the mud. Her freckled skin was pale and her lips a gray blue with bits of dry skin peeling off. Her bloody hands formed a cup over her stomach, covering what appeared to be a spear wound.

"She's one of ours," Coin said, pointing out her suede leather attire.

"She's not too far from Redwood," I said. "I wonder how many other women came out this way."

"Don't know," Coin said. "They sure as hell didn't go south. Ain't nothin' but the Dead Zone out there."

I sighed and scratched my eyebrow. I knew we were in way over our heads. Who was I kidding? How on Earth would I find the Hunters on Kormace Island? They could be anywhere. I'd probably never see them again.

"Just keep marking," I said. "Let's keep moving."

Coin used her spear and carved a groove in a thin, moss-covered tree that reached several hundred feet into the air. I stared upward for a while, realizing how much I missed sunlight. With the forest's dense vegetation and tightly closed canopies above, I was lucky to get a few inches of yellow warmth.

A familiar anger surged through me. This was all because of the Northers. Our sunlit home, our people—everything was gone because of them.

I had to find the Hunters. We needed to rebuild our strength.

I hacked a Swiss cheese-looking leaf out of my face and tackled my way through an array of palm plants. Coin followed quietly, continuing to mark trees as we pressed through the jungle.

We traveled for hours, aimlessly wandering in hopes of running into a few of our people. We did come across our people—three more of them, in fact—only they were dead.

Two of them had had their throats slit, which meant the Northers had traversed this area of Kormace Island, and the other suffered from what appeared to be dehydration, or a disease.

"Here," Coin said, handing me one of the dead women's knives.

We took what we could off the bodies—clothes, weapons, and even a pair of leather boots, which fit Coin's feet. I didn't like the idea of taking from the dead, but they weren't going to be using the items anymore. It would have been wasteful to leave them behind.

"We should try to find fresh water," I said, remembering that our best bet in finding our people would be to move toward water. Although Fisher had advised against drinking any water on the island without proper filtration, most women weren't aware of the dangers of contamination, which meant they'd drink any water they could find, even if it killed them. And if by chance they were aware of this danger, they would still gravitate toward water for cleansing purposes.

"If you hear any flowing water, let me know," I said.

Coin nodded.

My feet had already begun to chafe inside the crocodile skin boots. Fortunately, my skin was completely callused, which helped with the pain, but it would take a while for me to adjust to these new kicks.

"Goddamn it!" Coin hissed, dodging a full five feet to the side.

I swung around, prepared to scold her for having spoken so loud when I saw the intricate web crafted in the air between intertwined branches. Right below it hung a hairy spider the size of a tennis ball, its lanky legs flicking below its belly as it spun its web.

I smirked. Although it disgusted me, I'd seen so many of these little guys during our hunts. They were harmless, and for the most part, friendly.

"Doesn't bite," I said.

Her eyes went huge—bright white gumballs in comparison to her dark skin.

"Doesn't bite? Man, I wouldn't care if it did bite! I don't want that thing touchin' me!"

It was funny to see Coin—a short, tough-looking woman with arms the size of baseball bats—cower away at the sight of a bug. Granted, it was a big bug, but it was still funny.

I thought back to when I'd first landed on the island. Even the thought of a spider web had been enough to throw me into a panic attack. Desensitization was key.

She scurried underneath the web as fast as possible and ran her hands roughly over her head as if it had somehow spat webs at her.

I shook my head and smiled. "There'll be way more. And until you've seen a Goliath, that's nothing."

"Goliath?" she asked, her voice almost a croak.

"Tarantula," I said. "About the size of guinea pig." I held an invisible ball with my hands at eye level. "Some are bigger, some smaller. The ones I've seen are orange. They have beady little black eyes and a bunch of little hairs—" I pointed at invisible hairs along my arms.

"Yo! Okay!" Coin said. "I get it. Jesus."

"Wish you'd stayed behind?" I said, amused by her panic.

She parted her lips, but a nearby sound caught her attention and her eyes narrowed.

CHAPTER 13

I sat in a crouched position, listening to the sound of someone, or something, rustling nearby.

Coin's eyes met mine, and her knuckles lightened in color as she gripped her hunting spear with both hands. I prepared my bow and slowly crept toward the sound, adrenaline pumping through me.

With my arrow's head, I pushed aside a handful of bush leaves and peered through the opening.

Coin's face appeared beside mine, our cheeks almost touching. "What is it?"

But I couldn't answer.

Coin immediately pulled away and placed a hand over her mouth to prevent vomit from coming out. I'd have done the same, but car crash syndrome set in, and I couldn't stop staring no matter how disturbing the sight was.

A young woman—maybe in her early twenties—was lying flat on her side surrounded by a pool of blood. The first thing that caught my attention, aside from her dark eyes slowly meeting mine, was a pile of intestines and other small organs resting in front of her belly, which was torn open from her pelvic area all the way up to her chest.

She tried to crawl, but all she did was rake rotten leaves and collect mud underneath her fingernails.

"That's Maria." Coin held her face between both hands, drool dripping from her lips, and vomited stomach acid onto the jungle floor. She wiped her mouth. "She was one of the Builders. Worked with me in the Village."

"She's alive," I said. I wasn't sure why I'd said it. We both knew she was alive—torturously so. I simply didn't know what to do.

Coin burst through the bush with one hand over her mouth, and Maria's tortured eyes met hers.

"Hel...help..." Maria tried.

"Shhh." Coin grabbed her hand and stroked strands of clumpy, bloody hair behind her ear.

I couldn't believe what I was seeing. Why wasn't she dead? Who had done such an awful thing to her? How long had she been suffering? I stayed behind, not wanting to aggravate the situation. Coin knew her—it was better she look up at a familiar face.

"Who did this?" Coin asked.

"N-n-n..."

"A Norther?" Coin said.

She tried to nod, but instead coughed up globs of black blood and bared her teeth when her organs moved. I hoped for her sake she would die, but her eyes kept rolling in the back of her head and up at Coin.

Coin shot me a look through the bushes as if to say, "We have to do something."

What were we supposed to do? Put her out of her misery like a rabid dog? She was a human being and one of our own.

But as I stared at her pleading eyes, I couldn't even begin to imagine the tremendous pain she must have been enduring—and for how long? How long had she been suffering out here?

I quickly drew back on my arrow, its head aimed straight at her heart, and released it without any further thought.

Coin lunged back in a panic. "What the fuck!"

Maria's features hardened before her head collapsed onto the jungle floor and a long, heavy breath came out through her loosely open mouth.

As I stared at Maria's restful face, my bow still in position, my mind began racing in every direction imaginable.

What had I done?

I killed her—murdered her.

No.

I saved her.

Saved her from what?

From unfathomable pain.

But who was I to play God?

Who was I to decide who lived or died?

Coin closed Maria's eyelids and gently kissed her forehead. Her glossy eyes met mine, and she nodded slowly, a gesture of gratitude.

I stared at the pile of pink, blood-coated guts on the ground and clenched my jaw.

This wasn't my fault. I wasn't the one who'd slit her open like a pig. The Northers were to blame. They were nothing but a bunch of soulless monsters. What kind of a human being did this to another? What kind of a beast was capable of torturing someone so horrifically all because they were taught to hate their enemy?

Every muscle in my body stiffened as I stood straight, my hateful stare fixated into the jungle's intertwined branches and dense vegetation.

I'd kill them—every last one of them.

PART TWO

PROLOGUE

I couldn't believe it.

"Brone!"

Rocket ran straight toward me, her piercing green eyes blending with the jungle's surrounding vegetation. She had the same hair she did when I'd last seen her a few weeks ago—chestnut dreadlocks tied back at the base of her skull.

She lunged over a fallen tree and whisked through the jungle with a grin on her face. Her speed hadn't changed one bit.

"Rocket!" I shouted, beaming with joy.

Were the rest of the Hunters nearby? I shot an anxious glance behind her, but colors began twirling together like mixed paint on a palette.

"Brone!" Her voice warped and dropped an entire octave.

"Roc—" I tried, but her figure began melting away into the twirling greens and browns of the jungle.

Where was I? What was happening? Where was Rocket?

There was a blow to my ribs, and I was suddenly propelled into the air.

A soft prickle brushed up against my elbow, and then another, until I realized I was lying directly atop a bed of hairy-legged spiders and dry, yellow-skinned snakes. They crawled and slithered across my chest, and I flailed my arms in a panic.

I screamed and kicked, praying for the nightmare to end.

I slapped myself repeatedly until I found myself lying in an open field. There were no spiders, no snakes—only absolute silence.

I slowly stood and gazed out toward the horizon. The sun was coming up, creating a cotton candy-like look.

In the distance, dark figures formed a straight line of black silhouettes. I took a step forward, the tips of my fingers brushing against the tall, sharp-tipped grass on either side of my legs. But then, as if by magic or being dragged through the air at an incredible speed, I was standing right in front of these figures—only, they weren't figures at all.

In a perfectly straight row were five bloody pikes pointing upward in different directions. Atop them were pale, lifeless heads—the heads of my friends, the heads of the Hunters.

My eyes shot open and I was now lying on banana leaves amid the melodic sound of the jungle's nightlife—frogs, insects, owls, and other creatures I knew I'd probably never lay eyes on.

It wasn't real. None of it had been real. I shivered, my body drenched in cold sweat.

"Yo. You okay?"

I stretched my neck back and looked at up Coin. She was sitting against the base of a tree with her hunting spear resting on her crossed legs.

No, I wasn't okay.

CHAPTER 1

"You have nightmares often?" Coin asked, carving a small marking into the nearest tree.

I wasn't in a talkative mood.

"It's normal, you know—"

"Can we please keep moving?" I asked.

She didn't say anything. Instead, she regripped her hunting spear and slapped her way through a curtain of hanging leaves.

"Maybe Maria wasn't traveling alone," she said. "Maybe she had others with her. Maybe they know where Navi is. Or, where the Hunters are."

"That's a lot of *maybes*."

"You got any better ideas?" she snapped.

I sighed. No doubt, Coin was as stressed out as I was, if not more. She'd found one of her friends lying in the dirt like a slaughtered pig.

"I'm sorry," I said, realizing how harsh I sounded. She was grieving—she didn't need my attitude on top of it.

She didn't say anything. Instead, she wiped her sweaty forehead with her forearm and pointed at a river up ahead.

"Let's walk downstream," I said. "Should lead us to some survivors."

Coin nodded and we made our way along the edge of the river. There were small river stones along the water lying around the edges of grass, bushes, and tall palm trees that extended higher than any regular palm tree I'd ever seen. Some of the trees were slanted over the river, casting shadows along the edges of the water. It was slow-moving and a dark muddy brown—almost green—which made me think of crocodiles, and ultimately, of Fisher. The whole purpose of our journey was to find our Medic, Navi, to tend to Fisher's wounds. Her pain and the fear she must have experienced while a crocodile thrashed her around in the water were unfathomable.

I shivered at the thought.

"Watch the other side," I said, sticking my nose out in the direction of the river.

It was difficult to see beyond the trees, which put me on high alert. The last thing we needed was to be followed by a camouflaged enemy. If we were successful in finding other survivors, we'd be leading our enemy right to them.

"Jesus," Coin said, staring into the water a few feet below her. "Look at those."

I gazed into the water. Although barely visible, you could see a massive shoal of medium-sized fish swimming with the current. I would have recognized these silver-backed red-bellied fish anywhere—piranhas.

"Are those—" Coin tried.

"Piranhas? Yeah."

She looked terrified.

"They're not as dangerous as you'd think," I said.

Biggie had once hung me inches away from a river full of piranhas. She'd thought it hilarious. I, on the other hand, ended up jumping her for having scared me half to death.

After the tension had diminished, Biggie explained to me that piranhas get a bad reputation because of Hollywood movies—that most of their prey consists of dead or dying animals.

That revelation was a relief, especially since I'd always believed piranhas possessed the ability to strip one's skin and muscles from their bodies in only a few minutes.

But now I knew this was extremely far-fetched.

"Still wouldn't swim in there," Coin said.

I smirked. "Me neither."

The silence returned, and we walked for what seemed like hours. The morning cotton candy sky above us turned a bright yellow, and then finally, a clear blue as the afternoon crept in. If there was one thing I hated most about Kormace Island, it was sleeping in the jungle at night. It was cool, damp, and noisier than daytime—or at least, it seemed like it.

After some time, whether due to boredom or curiosity, Coin cleared her throat.

"Can I ask what you did? You know, to get here?"

I side-glanced at her and hesitated. Why was everyone so nosy? It wasn't the first time I'd been asked how I landed myself on Kormace Island, and it sure as hell wouldn't be the last time. Did it matter what I'd done? I was here, and I wasn't going anywhere.

"I'll go first," she said, almost inquisitively.

I nodded.

"Got into a fight by one of the clubs in downtown San Francisco. I wasn't the type to cause trouble or anythin'. I was out with some friends, goin' through the Castro District, when some pricks started harassing a lesbian couple. There were two of them—one was a tall, scrawny white boy, and the other, some Latino around my height. They were sayin' stuff like 'Fucking dykes' and 'Disgusting pieces of shit,' so I told 'em to back off. So then, they started givin' me shit." She swung her hands back and forth as if trying to paint an invisible image in the air. "We got yellin', until finally, the short one came after me. Said if I wanted to act like a man, I'd have to fight like one. He punched me in the face before bringin' me down to the ground. I had a knife on me at the time." She paused, her eyebrows slanting in a guilty way. "I was from a bad neighborhood. Never knowin' whether or not someone would bust into our house when we were sleepin'. So, I used it. I lost my mind and I used it."

I didn't know what to say, so I didn't say anything. How was I supposed to respond to that? *I'm sorry?* This wasn't the first time someone explained to me how they took another person's life, and every time it happened, I was left speechless.

"Thirteen times in the chest," she said. "There was blood everywhere. You ever have the feelin' where you can see what you're doing, but you can't actually feel it? Almost like you're not even in your own body?"

I looked at her. I knew the feeling.

"That's what it was like. Took me years to remember what even happened. Only remembered after comin' to Kormace Island. After hearin' other stories like mine. I know there's a bunch of crazies on this island... Women who aren't ashamed of what they've done. Women who are proud of their kill count. I don't get it, man. I ain't proud of what I did. I think a lot of women regret what they've done. Those who don't are a different breed, and if I didn't know any better, I'd say those are the kinds of women who go lookin' for Rainer… That wanna be part of the Northers."

I pondered this for a moment. I'd never thought of it that way. Was Rainer recruiting women and brainwashing them, or were the crazy, sociopathic women ending up on her side because they wanted to?

"Your turn," she said, revealing her gold tooth.

"My story's not impressive or anything," I said.

"Weren't you listenin' to anything I said? Ain't no pride in murder."

I wasn't proud of what I'd done, but I didn't regret it, either. Did that make me a bad person? Had I finally become the woman I hoped I'd never be?

"Come on," she pressed. "Deal's a deal."

"My mom had an abusive boyfriend. He had her by the throat one night, and I swung a cast iron pan at the back of his head."

Coin grimaced. "Youch."

I shrugged. "He could have killed her. What else was I supposed to do? The man was three times her size."

Coin patted a firm hand on my shoulder, and unusually enough, I was comforted.

"I'd a done the same thing."

I smiled. "Thanks for sharing with me," I said, and for the first time, I viewed Coin as a friend.

She stared at me, her dark, sweaty face glistening under the sunlight and a smirk on her thick lips. "You too." She stopped walking all of a sudden. "Check it out." She pointed at our feet. Right at the edge of the river was a messy footprint smudged into the mud, almost as if someone had slipped while walking in this direction.

My gaze shifted downstream. "Looks like they were going this way."

"Question is," Coin said, "are they one of ours?"

CHAPTER 2

It was hard to make out the footprints now that we were walking on the grass. But every few hundred feet, we found a partial print pressed into the mud.

"Must be one of ours," Coin said.

"What makes you say that?" I asked.

"Only seems to be one person. Ain't no way a Norther would travel on their own. Goddamn pussies."

Although this was mostly true, the Norther I'd killed with my bow had been traveling alone. Anything was possible. On the bright side, if we were in fact following a Norther, they were outnumbered two to one.

We followed the river around its bend, keeping a lookout for more prints. The river's smooth flow almost masked the sound of our feet crunching river stones and flattening grass. Every few seconds, there was a gentle splash, and if my eyes were quick enough, I'd see shiny scales disappear into the water.

That's when I noticed something.

"Wait," I said. "Look."

There was another print, but it wasn't going straight—it wasn't following the river. Instead, it turned off the path and disappeared into the jungle.

"Should we follow it?" Coin asked.

I hesitated. What did we have to gain from following someone's footprints? What if we were walking straight toward an enemy? What if it was an Ogre? A knot formed in my stomach. Were Coin and I truly cut out for this? I'd always traveled with the Hunters—women who specialized in tracking, camouflaging, and killing. But Coin and me? Sure, I was good with my bow and Coin had astounding auditory senses. But what good would that do us if someone attacked us from behind? If we were cornered or forced into melee combat?

Thoughts of Franklin and how she'd attacked me with her bare hands came to mind. I'd taken quite the beating, which meant I was pretty useless when it came to fighting.

Oh God, what were we doing?

Coin smacked me on the arm, the sound of impact bouncing off nearby trees.

"This is time sensitive, Brone."

"I know, I know," I said impatiently. I needed to think.

"I know what you're thinkin'," she said. "But I have a hunch it's one of ours."

I wanted to believe her, but in the end, we wouldn't know unless we followed the prints. And if it was one of ours, maybe they needed help. Or, better yet, maybe we could team up with them and increase our odds of surviving this hellhole.

"Okay," I said.

"Okay," she repeated, and without discussing it any further, she walked into the jungle. The prints were staggered and short in distance. They were of average size, which didn't help whatsoever in trying to determine who they belonged to.

"This way," Coin said, pointing her spear into each print she found.

We went around an oval-shaped boulder covered in moss, and I crashed into Coin's muscular back.

"What're you—" I started, but she raised a stiff hand.

I peered over her shoulder. At first, it looked like the dead carcass of a gorilla or a bear. A big ball of black and gray fur was curled up in a pile of leaves, its long hairs wiggling with every gentle gust of wind. Was it alive?

Coin looked back at me, her eyes big and her lips curved downward like a bad circus clown with too much makeup. She wasn't cut out for this.

I yanked her hunting spear out of her hands and used the end of the shaft to poke the creature. I jumped back when it shuffled away from us and vanished behind the rock.

What the hell was that thing? And why was I provoking it? Maybe it was dangerous. But I needed to know because the prints we'd followed were human.

I gave Coin her spear back and she grimaced, almost as if wanting nothing to do with this. But it had been her idea to follow the prints, so she'd have to suck it up. I pulled an arrow from my quiver and set it in place, then moved away from the rock to create space between the creature and me. My back hard and my arms stiff, I sidestepped through dry leaves until I had the creature in sight.

But it wasn't a creature at all.

It was a young woman, maybe in her early twenties, curled up with her legs pressed against her chest. She wore a big piece of fur over her shoulders, assumedly gorilla skin, and a necklace made of what appeared to be human teeth. She glanced up at me, her dark eyes tired and her face drained of life, then curled her lips over her bloody front teeth like a rabid dog.

She made a sound I'd never heard before—a bubbly growl originating somewhere deep inside her stomach. The fur around her neck was soaked in blood. That's when I noticed it—a deep gash underneath her right ear and down the side of her neck. From the looks of her chalky white skin, she'd already lost a lot of blood.

I slowly lowered my arrow, and Coin, who was still hiding behind the rock, looked at me with her big eyes and shook her head as if to say, 'Don't do it.'

I returned my arrow to its quiver and raised both hands beside my face.

"I'm not here to hurt you," I said.

Her eyes were dark and wild. It was like staring into the soul of an animal. I wondered if she even spoke a word of English.

"Are you hurt?" I asked.

She released a hiss-like growl, a combination of saliva and blood spritzing on her bottom lip and chin.

"Yo, let's go," Coin said in a whisper. She was leaning in toward me, her hand pressed up against the boulder for support, but her body was completely out of sight.

This wasn't what I'd have expected from Coin. What was the point of having such big muscles if she didn't even use them? Only a few days prior, she'd jumped Fisher thinking she was a Norther. What had changed? I supposed most people were terrified of Ogres and with good reason.

I hated Ogres. A group of them had taken away a friend of mine and slaughtered her for sacrificial purposes. I had every right to despise them. There was certainly a part of me that wanted to kill any one that I saw, but as I watched this young creature whose bony legs were folded underneath her belly, ready to pounce at any moment, I asked myself—how did she become like this?

As much as Ogres gave me the chills, I knew they were still living beings. I remembered the old woman I'd run into when fire was spreading across the island. Her naked body pressed up against a tree, she'd sat staring at me with so much fear in her eyes. I remembered thinking, *She's just as scared as I am.*

"I want to help," I said.

Again, she hissed.

"Did anyone else walk this way? Who did this to you?" I pressed.

Her eyes flicked toward Coin, even though she couldn't see her. She must have heard her breathing or stepping down in the leaves.

"It's okay," I said. "She's a friend. She won't hurt you." I nodded at Coin. "Get over here."

She reluctantly stepped away from the boulder and walked a half circle toward me, her posture as awkward as an extremely introverted kid trying to blend into a crowd. The Ogre's eyes shot from side to side, and she retreated even farther.

"Who did this?" I asked, pointing at my neck.

She slowly reached up to her wound, her fingers dipping in the blood.

I then pointed to myself and at my clothes. "Was it one of us?"

She shook her head, and her matted hair shook from side to side. It was as dark as the fur she wore over her shoulders, only much longer and more damaged.

We were finally getting somewhere.

I grabbed Coin's arms and pointed a finger at her skin, watching the woman's reaction. "Dark skin?"

She shook her head. I then pointed at my skin, and she quickly nodded.

I eyed Coin. "White, and not one of ours. That much we know."

Coin stepped forward, to my surprise, and knelt on one knee. "Was there only one?" She stuck out one finger.

The Ogre stared at her.

"Two?" She uncurled her middle finger, revealing two fingers.

No response.

"Three?"

The Ogre nodded, and Coin stood up with a sigh. "Leave it to three white bitches to do somethin' like this."

I cocked an eyebrow but didn't entertain her comment.

"She *is* an Ogre," I said. "Maybe she tried to attack them. We don't know what happened."

"Did you"—Coin pointed a finger at the Ogre—"try to attack anyone?" She role-played by clawing at me, her mouth open and her eyes wide.

I rolled my eyes. "Stop it. What happened doesn't matter."

"Hell, yeah it matters! I wanna know what we're up against!" Coin said.

The Ogre remained seated, her eyes darting between Coin and me.

"Which way did they go?" I asked.

No response.

"Goddamnit," I said. "They could be out there killing our own right now!"

Coin briskly made her way toward the Ogre, her shoulders drawn back and her spear held tight. "Where did they go?" she asked. It had come across as more of a command.

But the Ogre swung her hand—a veiny, brown fingernailed thing—at Coin's leg. Coin hopped backward and let out a screech—the kind of sound you'd expect to hear from a five-year-old girl on Christmas morning.

I burst out laughing.

Coin straightened her posture and punched a pink-knuckled fist in the air, obviously embarrassed by her lack of bravery.

With a huge smile on my face, I let out a deep belly laugh—something I hadn't done in a long time.

"Shut up," she said.

"I don't think giving orders is the way to go

about this." My lip twitched as I held back a smile.

She paced back and forth. "Yeah, yeah, laugh it off."

I regained composure and lowered myself to the Ogre's level, my arms resting atop my knees. "Do you speak English? Or at least understand it?"

Nothing.

"Please," I said. "If you do, please tell us which way they went. These women are dangerous, and they're trying to kill our friends."

She looked at me intently, almost as if calculating my every word.

"Please," I begged. "We need your help."

Coin sighed behind me, clearly prepared to tell me to forget this whole thing, when the Ogre parted her lips and a croak-like sound escaped her mouth.

"D-d-ey went d-down-r-r-iver."

CHAPTER 3

"Can you believe that?" Coin scoffed. "She could'a opened her rotten-tooth mouth instead'a wastin' our time like that."

I waved a hand as a breath-saving way of telling her to shut up. Coin had a big mouth when she had an opinion about something, and her voice was the last thing I wanted to hear right now. In fact, her loud voice would probably get us killed out here.

"Look," I said, pointing ahead.

"Shit," Coin muttered.

Straight ahead, maybe half a mile down the river, was white foam spitting onto the surface of the water.

"Rapids?" Coin said.

I nodded but didn't respond. The less noise we made, the better. I pointed my chin out at the rapids as if to say, 'Let's go,' and we started jogging. Three Northers, I thought. I knew we were stupid for chasing after them, but at the same time, they were looking for survivors, which meant they were trying to kill our people.

I couldn't sit back and do nothing.

As I moved swiftly through the palm trees and tall grass, my crocodile-skin boots chafing against the skin of my calves, the most unexpected song popped into my head—a memory of my old life—Nancy Sinatra's "These Boots were Made for Walkin.'"

My mom used to sing it at Joe's Restaurant on karaoke night. It was always her favorite. She'd strut back and forth with her cheap no-name pleather boots, pretending they were worth hundreds of dollars.

I smirked down at my boots and envisioned one pressed into a Norther's bloody face. I'd walk all over them, all right.

Thank you, Hammer, I thought. I'd beaten her to a pulp after the attack on our Village (in my defense, she deserved it), and she'd made me a pair of boots along with a dozen arrows for our trek.

Apparently, punching people in the face earned you some respect. I licked my scabby lip—okay, maybe not. Attacking Franklin hadn't been the best of ideas. But she was such a hotheaded woman with a stupid mouth you'd swear was run on Energizer bunny batteries (keeps going and going and going), that anyone would have done the same as I. If only I'd actually won the fight.

I needed to learn how to fight.

"Yo, check this out."

Coin had stopped running and stood at the edge of the river with one hand wrapped around a palm tree's trunk for support.

I peered over her shoulder and at the arrow that was protruding from the ground.

"Is that one of our arrows?" I asked.

Coin plucked it out of the grass and pointed its head upward.

"Nope." She twirled it several times. "See these?" She wiggled her fingers through the arrow's fletching—a pair of long green and red feathers. "Not our feathers... And look at this." Flipping the arrow around, she pressed her thumb into the head's point. At first glance, it looked like carved stone, but it wasn't long before I realized what she was trying to show me.

"What the—" I snatched the arrow out of her hand and brushed my finger along the point's smooth texture. It was cool to the touch and softer than any arrowhead I'd ever touched.

"Is this—" I started.

Coin nodded. "Some kind of metal."

"How the hell are they making arrows with metal?" I blurted. "There's no metal on an island."

Coin shrugged. "I don't know, man. Maybe they melted old jewelry or somethin'."

I stared at the arrow, then at the ground, attempting to recreate the scene in my mind.

"Where was it?" I asked. "Here?" I pointed at

the hole in the grass.

"Yep."

"And it was pointing this way? Downstream?"

She nodded again.

"So, someone was being chased this way," I said.

Her big brown eyes rolled up toward the rapids ahead. "Let's keep movin' and we'll find out."

I hurried along the edge of the water, careful not to miss my step. The last thing I wanted was to fall in and relive my seventh birthday.

* * *

"Lydia, honey, stay close to Perry if you want to use the tunnels," my mom said, flipping through a tabloid magazine in her plastic lounge chair.

Perry, a twelve-year-old friend of a friend, was the oldest in our group, so the adults always put him in charge. The last thing I wanted to do in the Bermuda Triangle, a giant indoor water park, was to follow anyone. I wanted to roam the area, pick and choose any slide I wanted, and venture through the park on my terms.

But I wasn't the type to disobey rules, and I wanted to go into the tunnel—the Bat Cave. For the most part, it was a slow-moving ride that brought you through dark tunnels with indigo-blue walls. All you had to do was bring a tube and sit still.

It was creepy, which is why I liked it. It got my adrenaline pumping.

So, I followed Perry and a few of my other friends—Adam, Lesley, and Briana—toward the Bat Cave. We waited in line for a good half hour or so, which was to be expected at the Bermuda Triangle. It was always so busy, especially during the summer holidays.

The biggest downside to waiting in line for so long in a water park is that by the time you get into the water, you've completely dried off, which meant you had to force yourself into the water all over again.

I followed the lifeguard's instructions and plopped myself down into the water, my butt cheeks clenching as they touched the cold water.

"Just hold on to the handles," he said, tapping the black rubber handles on my circular-shaped tube.

I gripped my fingers around the plastic bars and stiffened up as he pushed me toward the dark tunnel, my tube gently rocking from side to side. Perry was right behind me, wiggling his toes in the water and chatting away with the lifeguard.

"Anyone younger than ten shouldn't be allowed in here! It's way too scary!" he said.

I knew he was trying to freak us all out. But it wouldn't work. I'd been in the tunnel more than once. I lay my head back against the inflated plastic and closed my eyes. The sound of water trickling down walls surrounded me, and a cool breeze kissed my skin.

"Scared?" Perry said, floating beside me. His eyes were dark, as was most of his skin, and the only reason I could see him was because of small pod lights under the water and along the tunnel floor.

"I'm not scared," I said.

"It gets faster," Perry said.

"I know that."

He smirked at me and kicked his feet into the water to speed up ahead. There was a narrow opening coming up—an entry big enough to fit one or two tubes at a time—that led to a quick drop around a bend.

But instead of floating through the entry, Perry swam ahead of me and a few other kids, his hands and feet dangling until he stuck his legs out to block himself from going through.

"Hey!" someone said, and their voice carried throughout the entire tunnel.

There was a bump, then a splash, and Perry managed to create a jam. What was he doing? A few other tubes crashed into him, and he laughed, amused by the roadblock he'd created.

"Come on!"

"Move!"

I bumped into the growing crowd of tubes and glared toward Perry, even though I was unable to see him behind all the heads and flailing arms.

"Careful!" I heard.

I glanced back right in time to spot a young mother sharing her tube with her son. She was coming fast—much faster than I'd expected in the Bat Cave. I didn't have time to move. She bumped right into me and my tube squished, before flipping upside down.

The first thing I felt was cold, and then a sharp pain on the skin of my back as I crashed against the tunnel's cement floor. I kicked off the floor, but my head hit something hard: a tube with someone sitting in it.

I tried again, but no luck. Then the panic set in. I was trapped. There were tubes of people floating above me, forming a ceiling. I stretched my arms in a desperate attempt to reach out of the water as my lungs burned.

This was it. I wasn't getting out. I wanted to scream, but I didn't want to swallow a bunch of water.

Help me, I pleaded.

I thought for sure I'd die of a heart attack caused by panic when someone grabbed me by the back of my swimsuit. They plucked me up by my armpits and pulled me out of the water.

It was a tall man who was standing by his daughter's tube.

"You okay, kiddo?"

I gasped to catch my breath. I wasn't okay—I

was terrified.

* * *

I never did return to the Bat Cave, I thought to myself. I'd been crippled by fear—fear of harm, fear of entrapment, fear of reliving that traumatizing day.

But as I gazed into the white foaming rapids that spat mist into the air, I realized that allowing fear to cripple me was precisely what would get me killed on this island.

The most crippling thought of all was my death. I was too young to die. The idea of it was surreal—an unpleasant lucid dream in which you try to wake up, but you can't. I kept telling myself that one day, I'd make it off Kormace Island. One day, I'd have a normal life again.

Who was I trying to convince? Deep down, I knew my chances of ever returning home were slim to none.

This life—my friends, the Hunters—were all I had left.

I'd do whatever was necessary to find them.

Out of nowhere, something grabbed my arm and pulled me into the jungle. Coin's hot, rancid breath blew against the side of my face.

"Look, right there." She pointed at a figure standing at the end of the flowing water. I didn't know how far the waterfall dropped, but I knew it was there—it sounded like the Working Grounds:

bubbly, hissy, and most of all, incredibly loud.

She was a Norther; that much I knew. I observed from a distance, my body pressed against one of the river's palm trees. She wore brown fur around her shoulders, and although her face was hidden, I could only imagine how filthy it was based on her matted hair and dirt-stained hands.

She held a bow in her left hand and a feathered arrow in the other. I recognized it immediately—it was the same arrow we'd seen along the river.

What was she staring at?

Her hunched figure swayed from side to side as if she was contemplating some important decision. I took a step forward, and Coin grabbed me by the arm, her big eyes warning me not to get any closer.

But I didn't care to listen.

The only thing on my mind was Coin's friend—Maria—and the Ogre we'd spotted in the jungle who'd been attacked. The woman standing at the edge of the waterfall was no different from the rest of the Northers—a soulless monster. She wasn't human. She was an animal.

I moved quickly through the tall grass, one hand wrapped around my bow and the other reaching over my back and into my quiver. Coin stayed behind, partially hidden from view in the darkness of the jungle.

I knew the Norther couldn't hear me. She must have been concentrating on something—even an idiot would have known that standing out in the open like that was equivalent to wearing a target sign. The rapids and the waterfall were far too loud. At any given moment, she could turn around.

But I didn't care. I welcomed it. She was probably the one who'd gutted Maria. An indescribable rage filled me almost instantly, and the only thing I could think about was killing her. I tiptoed even closer over the river stones, my nostrils flared and my muscles tense.

I'd wanted to tear her to shreds, make her suffer for all she'd done.

My heart was beating out of my chest, but for the first time, my hands weren't trembling. Everything was so vividly bright, and the only thing I saw was the monster in front of me.

There was no doubt in my mind—I'd kill her.

As I took one final step, her head turned to the side, her dark eyes spotting me from their peripheral. Her body stiffened, almost in slow motion, and she reached for what appeared to be a blade, or a stake, clipped to the side of her belt.

Yet I didn't give her the time to fight or even turn around. In one swift movement, I snatched as many arrows as I could from her quiver and front kicked her as hard as I could in the back, right in between her shoulder blades.

A loud breath came blasting out of her lungs, and she screamed for her life as she was thrown over the cliff. I inched toward the edge and watched as she fell several hundred feet before landing on her back against the ground, her body contorting upon impact.

"Jesus!"

I glanced back at Coin. She rubbed both hands against the grain of her shaved head, and then through her hawk—approximately two inches of woolly brown hair that was already growing out. Her eyes looked like they were on the verge of popping out, and she rushed over, craning her neck far enough to see the dead body on the ground.

It looked so small from this distance, like a shriveled ant under a scorching sun.

"Yo... how... what the..." she ranted, waving her arms.

"What?" I asked.

Was I supposed to feel guilty? Remorseful? I didn't. She didn't deserve to live—not after everything she'd done.

"You killed her," Coin said.

I cocked an eyebrow. "Was I supposed to shake her hand?"

She punched me playfully on the shoulder then clapped her hands together, a grin stretching her face. "Yo, Brone, you's some badass shit."

She raised a flat hand in the air at face level and stared at me, waiting.

I grimaced. "Are you seriously trying to high-five me right now?"

Her smile quickly evaporated and she dropped her hand. "Nah, man. I'm just proud of you."

I threw my bow over my shoulder and loaded my quiver with my new set of arrows. I didn't know how to respond to her, so I didn't. This wasn't some game. I didn't earn points every time I killed someone. I wasn't ashamed of what I'd done, but I wasn't proud of it, either.

I did what had to be done.

"Brone," Coin said.

I'd nearly ignored her again, but she nudged me in the ribs. Her thick lips were parted, and she was staring down below, but not at the dead Norther—at something farther ahead. She squinted her eyes and raised a hand over her brows to block out the sun.

Her vision wasn't great, I knew. But mine was, and I could see it.

I could see her.

"Is that who I think it is?" she asked.

I was speechless. Was I hallucinating?

Down below, on the right side of the bay, was the tall, frizzy-haired outline of a woman I'd have recognized anywhere: Trim.

CHAPTER 4

I stepped off the last rock at the bottom of the waterfall, careful not to trip. Trim was kneeling in the tall grass, hovering over something out of view.

"Trim!" I shouted.

She got up and swung around, her eyes wild and thirsty for blood, but the moment she saw me, something in her softened. For the first time since I'd met her, she looked happy to see me, even though she wasn't smiling.

But the smile on my face vanished when a spear came whistling through the air, missing my face by less than an inch. I stopped midrun and turned toward my attacker—a four-foot girl with red markings across both cheeks and hair wilder than Trim's. Her mouth was open wide, letting out a bloodcurdling scream, and she ran at me with a blade above her head.

Elektra?

"Whoa, whoa, whoa!" I shouted, two hands by my face. "Elektra, it's me!"

As Elektra sped closer, I realized she wasn't

coming at me, but at Coin, whose eyes looked like golf balls. She didn't know anything about Elektra. In fact, I'd never told her the story; I'd never explained to her that we'd found an eleven-year-old girl on the island during one of our hunts.

I stepped out in front of Coin, shoulders drawn back, and raised a stiff hand. "Elektra!"

She stopped, her feet sliding through the grass, and stood there looking dazed.

"I know you," she said.

"Yeah, you do. And this is Coin. She's a friend." I patted Coin on the shoulder to show Elektra she was on our side. Coin flicked her index finger in the air as a way of waving hello.

Trim stepped over the tall grass and grabbed me by the forearm, pulling me in for a one-armed hug.

"I can't believe it's you," she breathed.

I'd never imagined the leader of the Hunters would one day be hugging me. I hugged her back, feeling at home.

"I can't believe it's you, either," I said. "Where is everyone?"

She pulled away and averted her gaze. Where were the rest of the Hunters? What wasn't she telling me? Was someone hurt? Was someone missing? Was she not with them at all?

"You look taller," Elektra said, her orange wire hair bouncing up and down as she moved closer to me. She threw her arms around my waist and hugged me. She still looked like a sweet kid with her tiny nose and eyes spread wide apart, but the red markings all over her face and her torn clothes made her look like someone who'd been raised in the jungle.

I'd once found her to be extremely annoying, viewing her only as a liability (or a disability), as someone who would only slow us down, or worse, get us killed. But by the looks of her, she'd taken her role of *superhero Elektra* rather seriously.

"You look shorter," I teased.

"Brone!"

My eyes shot up, but just in time, because through the abundance of soft grass came Rocket bursting out into the open. She lunged at me and the air in my lungs came blasting out. I fell flat on my back with her arms wrapped around my waist.

"Oh my God, it's you! It's really you! Sorry. I didn't mean to—"

She climbed off me when I tried to say "Rocket," and I sounded more like a house cat being accidentally stepped on. She gave me her hand and helped me back up. "I never thought I'd see you again," she said.

It was hard to believe she was here, right in front of me. She still looked the same—bright emerald eyes, small build, and dreadlocks tied back into a knot at the base of her skull. She smiled from ear to ear, her eyes darting from my eyes to my lips, to my hands, and to my toes, as if seeing an illusion.

The image of the Hunters' heads on pikes flashed into my mind, but I shook this horrific nightmare away. It hadn't happened. I had to stop dwelling on it.

"And who's this?" she asked, looking at Coin.

"Coin," I said. "She's a friend. Listen, guys, Fish—"

"Ain't nobody told me we was havin' a party!"

From the thick of the jungle came Biggie, waddling her way across the field. She looked like a giant beside Flander, who was limping and holding on to her for support. I was so thrilled—so indescribably happy to be seeing the Hunters' faces, but for some reason, the only thing I could think about was the next step. As much as I wanted to sit down with my friends to talk about everything that had happened, there was no time to waste.

Fisher needed us, and to help Fisher, we needed Navi.

I parted my lips to try again, but Biggie's arms came swinging around me. She lifted me into the air, and I thought my lungs might explode.

"Je-Jesus!" I let out.

"Yo, Brone! Am I hallucinating?" She gave me a big kiss on the cheek, then dropped me back to the ground.

"Are you guys okay?" Rocket asked, her eyes narrowing and her smile disappearing. "Where have you been? Where did you go? Did you see anyone else? Who else survived?"

"Hold your horses, Speedy Gonzales!" Flander said, the loose skin of her arms jiggling as she waved a hand. Her silver hair had grown out a bit, and it hung to the sides of her face. Her skin was darker, if that was even possible. She'd always been so suntanned to the point of looking like a giant piece of leather. She clasped me by the shoulders, a gentle smile on her lightly wrinkled face. "Good to see you, Brone."

I smiled back. I'd missed them all so much.

"Yo! Give the girl some space," Biggie said, using her body as a human shield. She then reached for Coin's hand and shook it hard. "I remember you. You were one of dem Battlewomen, right?"

Coin nodded. It was evident she felt out of her element. Maybe she was intimidated, too. The Hunters had always been so highly thought of. And now, she was standing in front of them as if this was some high school reunion.

"Where's Eagle?" I asked, peering over Biggie's shoulder and toward the jungle.

Everyone went quiet. I didn't need verbal confirmation to know that she was gone.

"Eagle saved me!" Elektra let out, and Rocket quickly turned away, digging her face into Biggie's chest.

They held onto each other, a heavy silence weighing down on us.

"I-I'm sorry," I said.

Trim stepped forward and raised her chin, but she didn't make eye contact. "Don't be," she said. "At least she's in a better place than we are."

I knew she was hurting, but she'd never show it.

Flander cleared her throat and patted me on the arm. She pulled a bow from around her chest and handed it to me. It was carved of cherry wood, and the bowstring was green—something pulled off, or out of, a plant. There was an engraving on the handle that read, "E." She grabbed my arm and placed the bow in my hand. "Make 'er proud, girl."

I rubbed my thumb against the engraved initial. E, for Eagle, I knew. This was her bow. This was the bow she'd used to defend the Village when the Northers had first attacked us—when she'd been maimed.

Eagle had always been regarded as the best Archer in all of Kormace. To carry her bow was the biggest honor anyone could ask for.

"I will," I said. I pulled my old bow off my back and gave it to Flander.

"We should head back," Rocket said. "The

women are unprotected right now."

"The women?" I asked.

Biggie let out a loud scoff. "We ain't the only ones who survived, Brone."

"How many more of you are there?" I asked.

"Twenty-eight," Biggie said. "Two are hurt pretty bad, but we managed to get the others out in time."

"We're camped out in a cove," Rocket said. "Shore's not too far from here. Come on, we'll take you there."

She reached for my wrist, but I pulled back. She looked like a kid who'd been given a gift, only to have it taken away.

"We can't," I said.

"What's going on, Brone?" Trim asked, her dark eyes narrowing on me. She knew something was wrong.

"It's Fisher," I said, and her eyes lit up like a Christmas tree.

"You saw her? Where is she? Is she okay?" she rambled, and I was taken aback. I'd never seen Trim express so much emotion before. But then again, Fisher wasn't only her right hand; she was her best friend.

"No, she's not." I bit down hard, and my jaw popped.

"She was attacked," Coin said, finally getting involved in the conversation.

"Attacked!"

"By who? When?"

"Who the fu—"

Everyone circled around me, their eyes popping out of their sockets like something out of an old Tim Burton movie.

"It was a crocodile," I said. "Bit her pretty bad."

"Where is she now?" Trim asked.

"She's in Redw—" but I cut myself short. They wouldn't know what Redwood was. "She's in a camp we set up. A few of us. Ellie's with us, too. We have a brainiac who's been trying to heal her with plants, who's great, don't get me wrong, but I don't know if Fisher will pull through. We came out here looking for Navi."

Trim pulled back, her posture straightening. "Navi," she repeated.

"You didn't tell her?" Rocket hissed.

I glared at them. "Tell me what?"

Rocket shook her head, a solemn look in her eyes. But she didn't say anything. Instead, she turned around and walked toward where Trim had been kneeling earlier. She pushed aside a handful of grass and looked back at me with slanted eyebrows and an upside-down smile.

Navi's pale body was lying in a bed of broken plants, her bare arms crossed over her bloody chest and a peaceful blue smile on her face.

CHAPTER 5

"Brone, calm down."

I paced back and forth, slipping my fingers through my hair and pulling hard and cursing under my breath.

Someone touched my shoulder, but I slapped it away. What the hell were we supposed to do without our Medic? How were injured women supposed to recover? A few medicinal plants weren't enough. We needed someone who knew what they were doing. We needed Navi, and now, she was dead.

This time, a pair of solid hands grabbed me by the wrists. Without thinking, I pushed back as hard as I could, only realizing my mistake when Trim fell back against Biggie.

No one said anything, and for a moment, I thought Trim might kill me. I'd pushed our leader. She stepped close to me, her breath making its way into my mouth.

"Fisher's my best friend," she said. "So, trust me when I say we're going to make this right."

I let out a sigh. She was right. There was no use panicking over what we couldn't change, and if there was one person who'd risk everything to save Fisher, it was Trim.

"You good?" she asked, resting a hand on my shoulder.

I nodded.

"Now," she said, repossessing her role as the leader, "we split up. You guys head back to the Cove, and Brone and Coin will lead me to Fisher. We'll gather up the women over there, including Fisher, and bring them to the Cove."

"I'm not letting you guys go alone," Rocket said.

"Rocket—" Trim tried, but Rocket pulled a blade out of the holster on her belt and came by my side.

"No one's gonna go looking in that Cove," she said. "It's safer there than it is back in the jungle, and you guys need all the help you can get."

Trim nodded. "All right. Flander, Biggie, you guys head back to the Cove and let the women know what's going on."

Biggie wrapped an arm around Flander, nearly knocking her over. "You got it, boss."

Trim glanced at me briefly. "Lead the way, Archer."

I led them out of the open field and back toward the waterfall, along the steep, rocky slant we'd come down. A mass of thoughts rushed through my mind. Was Fisher still alive? Would she even make it all the way to the Cove? Would I remember how to get back? Coin had left markings on the trees—hopefully that would suffice.

"Is that your doing?" Rocket asked, tilting her head toward the dead Norther's body.

Coin slapped both hands together. "Damn, you shoulda—" but she stopped talking when I shot her a *leave it alone* sort of look. This wasn't the time to celebrate.

"Yeah, it was," I said plainly.

"Were there any others?" Trim asked. Her body was hunched forward as it always was in a constant predatory state. Her eyes never rested, and she was always inspecting every inch of space around us. I was happy to have her by my side.

"Didn't see any," I said. "But we came across an Ogre who said—"

"An Ogre?" Trim cut me off. "It spoke?"

I nodded.

It was hard to tell if she was intrigued or disgusted at the idea we'd had any kind of communication with an Ogre.

"What'd she say?" Rocket asked.

Coin scoffed. "Not much."

Neither one of them bothered to look at Coin. Gaining the respect of the Hunters wouldn't happen overnight.

"We had to force it out of her," I said. "She was injured. Looks like three Northers did it. And if that one"—I pointed in the direction of the body at the base of the waterfall—"was part of that group, there are only two left."

Rocket regripped her blade—a loose twirl in her hand. "Let's keep our eyes open." She hopped over two rocks at once like she had springs for knees. "You should be proud, Brone. I think you avenged Navi."

I looked back at her. "What're you talking about?"

"Navi came from this way," Rocket said. "We found her in the field with an arrow in her back. Whoever shot her did it from over here."

Had Navi been with Marie, Coin's friend? The one we'd found lying dead with her intestines pulled out? It made sense. Footprints trailed alongside the river. Navi must have tried to escape, only to be shot by the Norther at the top of the waterfall—the one I'd kicked down. Then, maybe the Ogre came across Marie's body and started pulling out organs, only to be attacked by another group of Northers.

It was all speculation, but it added up.

Maybe if I'd run faster... I thought. Maybe if I'd kicked the Norther off before she fired at Navi...

Rocket must've sensed my guilt. She pressed her hand against my lower back. "Navi was dead way before you came down."

I nodded. I wasn't so sure this was true, but the

thought eased my guilt, so I did my best to convince myself that Rocket was right. Once we made our way back up to the top of the waterfall, I followed the footsteps we'd been tracking earlier, but in the opposite direction toward Redwood.

I stepped inside the crowded jungle, moving past the trees and gliding through shrubs. It was better to move through the wilderness than to travel alongside the river where we were basically walking targets.

Trim clicked her fingers. It had to be Trim; she was the only one who ever did that. It was a quick and easy way of telling everyone to stop moving and be quiet.

I glanced back. Her eyes looked like little black slits and she was scanning the area like a hound dog, her nose in the air and her head moving from side to side.

"What?" I mouthed.

She pointed at her ear, and I listened. Through the jungle's static, never-ending orchestra, I heard it—the sound of hundreds of flies buzzing in unison. And then the smell hit me, and I threw a hand over my mouth.

Trim pointed a few meters away from us toward hanging vines and a rotten tree stump, but Coin quickly grabbed her shirt.

Trim swung around, an alien rage in her eyes. It was evident that being the leader of the Hunters, she wasn't accustomed to being pushed around by anyone, especially not by a complete stranger.

"Ain't worth it," Coin whispered.

I understood where she was coming from. Why inspect a dead body? Why set yourself up for heartbreak? For all we knew, it could have been an Ogre or a Norther or even an animal. I exchanged a look with Rocket, and although neither one of us wanted to inspect a dead body, it was better to be subjected to a traumatic scene than to forever wonder whether it was one of ours and whether we knew her.

"What if it's Murk?" Rocket whispered.

Trim lowered her eyes and bit down hard. "We need to check."

She pushed aside a curtain of banana leaves and disappeared into the greenery. I listened to the sound of her footsteps—the sound of vegetation crackling and popping—and followed close behind. The smell was vile—a mixture of sour, rot, and a sickening sweetness. It was enough to make me slap a hand over my mouth.

I nearly bumped into Trim when I stepped out into open space. She stood stiff with her arms on her waist and her muscular back leaning backward.

"Looks like they're at it again," she said.

The moment I peered over her shoulder, I wished I hadn't. I turned away quickly, but the image kept flashing in my mind, almost like a painful pulsation. It was a woman lying in the dirt, her body positioned in the shape of a crucifix—her arms were spread out on either side of her, and her head hung loose to the side, her tongue sticking out. Her head had been shaved, leaving only patches of hair and a bloody scalp. I didn't recognize her face, and because she was naked, there was no way of telling whether she was one of ours or a Norther.

Gashes and cuts covered her body, and right down the middle of her abdomen was a slit so wide it looked as though she'd been gutted, as though there was nothing left inside. These cuts, though... I'd seen these marks on a Norther before.

But it didn't matter who the woman was.

I shook my head and words came spilling out. "This isn't the first time..."

Rocket, whose face was so distorted she looked like a Mrs. Potato Head left in the hands of a two-year-old child, rubbed her forehead and started pacing. "What're you talking about, Brone?"

Coin knew what I was talking about.

"The crocodile," Coin said. "Marie..."

Trim slowly turned around, and it was hard to tell if she felt any emotion at all. Her eyebrows were flat and her lips remained the way they always did—in a straight line. How was she always so calm, so matter-of-fact about everything?

"In Redwood," Coin continued. "The crocodile that attacked Fisher... We found it again. Well, Franklin did—"

"They don't know Franklin, Coin. Get to the point," I said.

"When we found the crocodile again, it had been gutted," Coin said. "And Marie..." and then her eyes glazed over. I knew what she was picturing: her friend who'd been slit open and left to die with her intestines all over the jungle floor.

"Then we found another woman," I cut in. "One of Coin's friends." I looked at Coin, but she turned away. "She'd been cut open and gutted."

Trim's eyebrows slowly came together; whether out of rage or thought, it was impossible to tell. Everyone watched her, waiting for her to guide us in the right direction. But I couldn't wait— couldn't stand around and watch her try to make a decision when I knew precisely what had to be done.

"We have to hurry," I said.

Trim's dark eyes rolled up at me, but not in a menacing way—she was receptive, prepared to listen to what I had to say.

I plucked an arrow out of my quiver and set it into my bow. "I think Redwood's in dead center of Ogre territory."

CHAPTER 6

"It's right through here," Coin said, brushing her fingertip over an engraving she'd earlier carved in a tree.

I was surprised to know that Coin had been assigned the task of Builder in the Village when she had outstanding hunting skills. She knew how to track, follow, and blend effortlessly into the jungle. The only downside was her poor vision, but Hunters needed other abilities that were as crucial as sight. Had I been in charge of the group, I'd have asked Murk that Coin join our crew.

"Who's there?" someone shouted.

I stepped through a wall of giant, silk-textured leaves to find Johnson at the edge of Redwood, her knees bent, holding a spear over her head. Her eyes were wild above her freckled cheeks and her thick eyebrows came close together. She was ready to attack, her teeth bared like a dog hovering over a fresh carcass, but it was obvious the way she kept shifting and repositioning her spear that she'd never fought before.

I slipped my arrow back into my quiver and raised a hand to my face. "It's me."

Her big eyes shot behind me as Trim, Rocket, and Coin stepped forward, rustling through the jungle's vegetation. She regripped her spear and bit down on her bottom lip, obviously confused by Trim and Rocket's presence, but at last, she must have realized who they were.

"You're the Hunters," she said, lowering her spear.

Trim didn't respond, but instead, nodded and stepped into Redwood craning her neck back to take in the view. She looked mesmerized, like a kid seeing a snowman for the first time. It made sense—she'd most likely never traveled this far. It was astonishing to think that the Village and the Working Grounds were only a fraction of a massive piece of land. But something else caught her attention—her best friend.

"Fisher," she breathed and ran to Fisher's side.

I let out a long breath, relieved to see Fisher was still alive, but she looked terrible. Her skin was blanched, almost mistakable for porcelain skin, and her dark eyes were closed at the centers of sunken blue bags.

"I've cleaned her wounds at least a dozen times," Proxy said, straightening her frail figure. "Unfortunately, I do not believe this to be enough. It would appear that the infection has spread—"

"Who's this?" Trim asked, throwing a thumb in Proxy's direction.

I didn't blame her for being so aggressive about it. Proxy was an acquired taste with her formal speech and brainiac comments.

"The person who's been keeping Fisher alive," Johnson said, crossing two thick arms over her big chest. "And who are you?"

Trim cocked an eyebrow and glanced at me. I was surprised to see Johnson come to Proxy's defense, but I was even more shocked by her inability to recognize the leader of the Hunters. Everyone knew Trim.

"I'm Trim—" she started, but Johnson cut her short.

"I know who you are. I meant, what's your role in all of this? You may be the leader of the Hunters, but you aren't the leader of us."

Franklin stepped forward now, stretching her lanky, tattooed arms and resting her hands on her hips. I glowered at her. I hated her as much as I'd once hated Hammer. At least she hadn't destroyed Redwood during my absence. I worried her big mouth might have caused a fight. Everest was the next one to join the crowd, her fluffy white hair bouncing on her head as she limped her way over.

"Old rules don't apply here in Redwood," Johnson said. She was now standing face-to-face with Trim, who towered over her, but Johnson didn't back down. Instead, she jerked her head sideways toward me. "Brone's the leader here."

If I hadn't been paying attention, I'd have thought someone punched me in the gut. Me? Their leader? I almost burst out laughing.

Proxy raised a straight arm into the air. "I believe a vote is in order."

"Shut up," Johnson hissed.

"I vote Brone," Proxy said. "Her intelligence is rather useful, and she is fair."

Then Everest raised a wrinkled, veiny hand and said, "Zat's my decision too. She saved our lives."

Trim slowly turned toward me, and I swallowed hard. Was she going to challenge me? Trim was a beast. She'd snap me like a twig. But she didn't do anything.

Instead, a sly smirk crept across her lips and she shrugged her muscular shoulders. "If Brone's proved herself as a leader, then I have no objections."

What was she doing? I didn't want to be the leader. I wanted Trim to take charge. I didn't want the stress of having to please everyone, of having to ensure everyone's survival. This wasn't a task intended for a nineteen-year-old.

Then, from behind the hammocks at the far back of Redwood came Ellie and Hammer carrying handfuls of bananas and coconuts. Hammer's fat face stretched into a grin, and Ellie dropped her bananas.

"Lydia!" she shouted. She ran toward me and threw both arms around my shoulders.

"Ellie," I breathed, pressing my face into the warmth of her neck. "I told you I'd be fine."

She drew back, her chocolate-colored eyes analyzing every inch of my face. "I was worried sick."

"All right, all right," Johnson said, flicking a hand in the air. "Get a room."

But then, I remembered the woman we'd found—the mutilated body positioned in a crucifix—and I pulled out of Ellie's hold.

"We need to leave," I said.

"Leave?" Ellie said, and everyone started chiming in.

"Leave?"

"We're finally getting settled."

"Why are we leaving?"

"What's going on?"

I raised a stiff arm into the air, and everyone went quiet. I wasn't accustomed to receiving this much respect, but it was nice—definitely something I could get used to.

"We're on Ogre territory," I said, matter-of-factly.

Franklin's eyes nearly lunged out of her head. As much as she tried to act tough all the time, she was probably the most fearful of us all when it came to Ogres. But when she caught me staring at her, she pulled her shoulders back and made her eyes go flat.

"Ogres?" she scoffed. "You expect us to buy into that?"

Trim stepped forward with a fist closed so tight, her knuckles looked like little knives. "You'd better put a filter on that trap of yours. When the leader gives an order, you obey it."

Franklin rolled her eyes.

Was she insane? Trim could take her out with one punch.

"What're you? Her guard dog?" she sneered.

In one swift motion, Trim grabbed Franklin by the throat. Prepared to make the blow, she raised her balled fist into the air, but Franklin didn't budge. She stood still, her face swelling and darkening to a crimson color, a sly smile curving her lips.

"Trim," I said, and she immediately released her grip. I didn't want any more violence, especially not among our own. And there was no winning with Franklin. Even if Trim handed her a whooping, Franklin would eventually open her mouth again, or she'd attack when Trim wasn't looking.

And what was going on, anyway? How on Earth did I have the ability to tell Trim what to do? To get her to stop? Trim turned around, her nostrils flared, and she stepped beside me. She leaned in, her hot breath hitting my ear.

"If you don't teach them to respect you, they'll walk all over you."

"I get it," I said, glancing up at Franklin who was still smirking. "But some people can't be taught with violence. There are other ways."

Trim nodded. I knew she understood—she'd banished women from the Village before. If anyone knew how to hurt a woman without violence, it was her.

"We're leaving whether you like it or not," I said, staring Franklin in that pointy-nosed, square-shaped face of hers. "You can either join us, or you can stay here and rot. And by rot, I mean most likely be gutted by an Ogre. Personally, I'd rather you stay here because it's what you deserve, but I'm giving you the choice because I'm *fair*."

Her narrow eyes shifted between me and everyone around me, evidently contemplating how best to approach the situation. But for the first time, she didn't scoff or roll her eyes. She didn't let out some snarky remark about how this Ogre thing was some fabricated story. Instead, she bit her bottom lip and nodded, looking like a kid who'd been given the option to either eat their vegetables or go to bed with an empty stomach.

I turned around, my eyes meeting Coin's. "Can you build us some kind of gurney?"

"Gurney?" she blurted.

"A transportable bed," Trim said. "For Fisher."

Coin crossed her arms, and with her right hand, rubbed her jaw. "Y-yeah. Sure. I can put something together. Won't have wheels though. We'll have to pull her through the jungle."

"I'll help pull," Hammer said, stomping her way over to us. Her belly jiggled and the flab of her arms flapped against her sides.

I was beginning to admire Hammer for her hard work. Aside from having made crocodile-skin boots and a vest for me, she'd already crafted us a handful of weapons including stone-carved arrows. Surviving Kormace Island without her was unimaginable.

"How much time do you need?" I asked, returning my attention to Coin.

She shrugged, placed two veiny black hands on her waist, and said, "Few hours, at most."

I nodded. The sooner we left, the better were our chances of returning to the Cove unharmed. The last thing we needed was to travel at night, surrounded by nothing but darkness and unseen predators. And the last thing I wanted to do was sleep here one more night, knowing all too well it could be my last.

"Vell zat's just great..." Everest mumbled. "I don't know how much more my poor hips can handle."

She limped her way to the small creek at the

center of Redwood and slowly lowered herself onto a log by the campfire.

"I could help you with that," Proxy said, pointing a straight finger in the air—something she seemed to enjoy doing every time she had a solution or an idea to offer.

"I don't vant any of your drugs," Everest said, sounding somewhat like Dracula.

"Well," Proxy said, "you should know that the term drug is often utilized in a negative context when drugs are, in fact and for the most part, natural prior to being synthesized by money-grabbing organizations."

Everest looked unimpressed. Her eyes resembled two balls of clay and she shook her head from side to side. Either she didn't understand a single word that came out of Proxy's mouth, or she didn't care—it was hard to tell which, but I assumed it was the latter.

"But if you would simply allow me," Proxy went on, "I would be happy to—"

"Yo, Lisa Simpson, let it go," Johnson said. "White Mountain already told you no."

I watched Everest as she stared into the unlit fire pit. She chewed on her lips over and over, her wrinkly chin moving back and forth. I knew she'd never talk to me—never open up about her past—but it didn't take a genius to figure out that drugs bothered her on a deep level. Maybe she'd lost a loved one to drug abuse, or maybe she had messed up her life because of addiction. I would have loved to know her story, but I didn't ask. She'd probably tell me to go fuck myself. Everest may have been old, but she was fearless; either that or extremely depressed.

"Look," I said, breaking the back-and-forth bickering between Johnson and Proxy, "I know it sucks. I get it. I know everyone's stressed out. I wasn't planning on relocating again. I thought we'd be here awhile, but it isn't safe. Trim here, and Rocket"—I pointed at my fellow Hunters—"found a safe space off the coast."

Rocket nodded and stepped forward, her chest puffed out with pride, obviously attempting to make herself look bigger than a thirteen-year-old girl. "There's a lot of space, and we're right by the water. We have an endless supply of fish, and we're protected by a barrier"—she craned her neck back, analyzing every inch of Redwood—"unlike this place." She then cocked an eyebrow at me and curled her lip up over her front teeth. "Honestly, this place is pretty dangerous. I mean, really dangerous. You're wide open everywhere. You could be attacked from any direction. Brone, what were you thinkin—"

"I get it, Rocket." I extended my arm, palm facing her. "But we didn't have a choice. We didn't exactly have our pick. We needed a place to camp out. We were tired and starving."

I received a few nods of approval around me.

"Brone's right," Hammer said. "We wouldn't have made it another day."

Franklin forced a cough into a closed fist and quickly said, "You would've."

Hammer's round nostrils flared and her mouth turned into an upside-down moon, revealing a chipped front tooth. "Got something to say, you fuckin' walkin' stick?"

Franklin let out a loud laugh. "Walking stick. Is that supposed to be insulting?"

"Yeah," Hammer said. "You look like a fuckin' twig insect with your bony little arms and your big-ass head!"

I'd been about to tell Hammer to calm down, but I didn't. Instead, I caught myself smiling. Franklin *did* look like a bug, though I'd never noticed until now. I'd read about walking sticks online before—insects that literally look like a twig with tiny arms.

"Oh, real mature," Franklin said, waving an open hand in my direction. "And you call yourself a leader? Laughing at someone who's being called an insect? How old are you, anyway? Fifteen?"

My smile stretched into a full grin. What was happening? It wasn't *that* funny. But at the same time, it was. Was it stress? Fatigue? All I could picture was Franklin standing there with big bug eyes and little insect legs flailing from side to side.

"Sorry, Frank," I said. "But Hammer's right. You do sort of look like a bug."

Everyone around me laughed—a magical sound I hadn't heard in a long time, and Franklin let out an irritated grunt before turning around like a kid throwing a tantrum.

"What's so funny?" someone moaned.

"Fisher!" Trim shouted. She rushed down to her knees, grabbing Fisher's hand into hers. She kissed it, then pressed the back of her hand against Fisher's forehead.

"Trim?" Fisher asked. "Rocket? Am I hallucinating?"

Trim squeezed her hand even tighter, and for a moment, it almost looked like her eyes were watering. I'd never mention it though, and even if I did, Trim would deny it.

"No, you aren't," Trim said. "It's us. We're here. Right here. We're getting you out of here."

Fisher's colorless lips formed a soft smile, and she placed Trim's hand over her heart. "Oh God, I missed you guys so much." But that sweet look in her eyes disappeared almost instantly, and she lay there, her eyebrows slanted and her lips drooping down.

Her dark eyes rolled up to meet Trim's. She let out a choppy breath, then said, "Don't waste your time, Trim. I'm dying."

CHAPTER 7

"That gonna hold?" Johnson asked, tugging at the vine ropes around the bed-like structure Coin had finished building.

It almost looked like an old bamboo sled or sleigh—the kind you'd see in history books or the ones you'd find in vintage shops—only without a curve at the end. Coin had somehow managed to fasten long pieces of bamboo together, and on top, she laid out ridiculous amounts of banana leaves to form a flat bed.

"She'll hold," Coin said, wiping a line of sweat from her forehead.

I made a rushed come-hither signal with my hand. "Let's get Fisher up on it."

Hammer was the first to bend down by Fisher's side, and Trim followed, wrapping Fisher's frail arm around her neck.

"Guys..." Fisher tried. "It's only. There's. Come on. Where am—"

She wasn't making sense. She was probably running a fever. What were we going to do? Even if we took her to the Cove, what then? Navi was dead, and my hope of ever finding Tegan was slowly fading. I'd have to rely on Proxy—hopefully, she'd learned everything Tegan knew. I could only pray she'd pull through.

"Proxy," I said, "do you know how to help her?"

Proxy nodded, her rat's nest hair barely moving on her head. "I do. We need to bring down her fever; however, I cannot seem to locate—"

"We're leaving," I said quickly. "Can you find whatever plant you need deeper in the jungle?"

"Yes, of course," she said. "The easiest plant to find should be a cocoa tree; however, I have not seen—"

"Everyone," I said, "keep your eyes open for a cocoa tree."

"Cocoa tree?" Johnson said.

Proxy pointed a stiff finger in the air. "Cocoa contains flavonoids—"

Johnson let out a sharp sigh. "I don't give a shit what it contains. What am I lookin' for?"

Proxy, with her finger still pointing toward the sky, averted her eyes toward Johnson and said, "Ah. A cocoa tree is rather hard to miss. Although it is small, reaching a maximum of twenty-six feet—"

"Proxy!" I said.

Proxy cleared her throat, her glossy hazel eyes darting between Johnson's and mine. "Big orange or yellow balls."

"Everyone got that?" I said, and everyone nodded.

Fisher suddenly let out a loud moan.

"Almost there," Trim said, lowering Fisher's upper body onto Coin's handcrafted bed.

Hammer, who was at the other end, gently let Fisher's legs fall onto the bamboo, and Fisher let out another groan. I stared at Fisher's thigh and grimaced—it was swollen and red. But I wasn't complaining; I much preferred red over white. If it weren't for Proxy having cleaned her wounds religiously, Fisher would probably be already dead.

"Let's go," Trim said, reaching down to grab one of the ropes.

Hammer did the same, and together, they dragged Fisher on the jungle floor.

"Everyone ready?" I asked.

Rocket patted me on the back and joined Trim's side. It wasn't like her to be this quiet. And it wasn't because of the new crowd, either. Rocket wasn't shy. She talked more than anyone I knew, and she'd always been so chipper. Yet the way her bright green eyes kept watching Fisher showed she was scared—terrified beyond belief to lose her friend.

I'd seen those two go at it many times before, but in the end, they were like any other dysfunctional family—a family filled with an imbalanced ratio of love and hatred. Even if they fought, they cared about each other in a way that words couldn't describe.

I turned on my heels and made my way to the front of the crowd with Coin by my side. We'd ventured this way before and we could do it again. It was best to retrace our steps—to follow Coin's markings—than to attempt to find an untraveled path to the Cove. Besides, the path alongside the river was smooth and unbroken, which would make the trip much more endurable, not only for Fisher but also for Trim and Hammer who were exerting themselves to pull her. The last thing they needed was to carry Fisher over their heads only to step over uneven terrain.

"You okay?" Ellie asked, appearing by my side.

Why did she feel the need to check up on me, anyway? Of course I wasn't okay. I'd seen countless dead bodies over the last year, most of them the result of unnecessary and gruesome violence. If women weren't being slaughtered by women, they were being attacked by an animal or decomposing from an illness that Navi had been unable to cure. Maybe deep down, that's what I was waiting for— an illness. Why hadn't I gotten sick?

Rocket once told me that at least a quarter of the women who are dropped on Kormace Island end up dying within one week of being there. So why was I spared? Why couldn't I have caught some foreign virus? I wouldn't have ended up here.

I wouldn't be leading a group of women through a jungle filled with threats all around us.

And what did the government do? Release goddamn zoo animals to increase our likelihood of dying? Because that's what this was about, wasn't it? Saving on tax dollars. And what better way to do that than to permanently eliminate us. Honestly, I'd rather have the death penalty: the standard electric chair version, not this one.

I thought of Mr. Milas, the Attorney General of the Department of Justice. I remembered seeing him in an interview once when he was asked about this new approach to criminal convictions. With his crisp, white suit and his blond hair pulled back into a small bun, he'd looked smugger than the president himself. "Our primary goal," he'd said, "is to ensure public safety while also improving our economy by eliminating unnecessary costs that go into our penal system."

The interviewer, a young man wearing a carrot-top button up who'd probably only recently graduated from University, pulled his notes up underneath his glasses and asked, "And speaking of this approach, Mr. Milas, we've recently discovered that there are several islands currently being considered for this project. Can you tell me more about that?"

Mr. Milas smiled a set of perfectly white teeth, undoubtedly the result of an expensive dental procedure, and said, "Yes, Greggory, that's correct." He fixed his tie and stiffened his posture. "We are currently considering four islands, three of which will be reserved for the male population of prisoners convicted of first-degree murder. The fourth will be reserved for women only. While I can't divulge the whereabouts of these islands, I can assure you that the government is taking every measure to ensure these islands are safe and livable and allow for a prosperous life."

Greggory crossed one leg over the other. "You mention the island being safe and livable. Is this to say that the government will be playing a role in cultivation on these islands?" He leaned forward, his voice taking on a more serious tone. "What I mean is, are they designing these islands? Will they be adding wildlife?"

Mr. Milas smirked and ran his fingers over the golden scruff of his face. "Some wildlife will be brought to the islands for feeding purposes, yes."

That's all I remembered. I'd turned off the TV after getting sick of looking at his cocky smirk. I didn't realize it then, but he knew more than he was letting on. He knew exactly what the government was doing, and that was setting us up for failure. Why couldn't the women of the island see that? Why weren't we banning together as women, rather than turning on each other?

"Lydia?"

My eyes shot up at Ellie. Had she been staring at me this whole time?

"You okay?" she asked again, this time reaching for my arm.

I considered lying to her and forcing a smile, but I'd tried the same thing before, and all it did was push her away from me. I didn't want that. If there was one person I wanted by my side, it was Ellie. She understood me like no one else.

"I'm tired," I said, stepping through a pile of decomposing leaves. What I truly wanted to say was, *I wish I were dead*, but I didn't want to upset her. If she knew my thoughts, she wouldn't look at me the same. I wanted it all to end.

She squeezed my forearm and her plush lips curved at one corner.

"What about you?" I asked, suddenly realizing that our conversations were always about me. Why didn't I ever take the time to see how she was doing? Because she was always smiling? That didn't mean anything.

She shrugged, and for the first time, I saw a glimmer of doubt in her eyes—something that told me I had to be strong for the both of us.

"This Cove," I said, grabbing her hand, "we'll be safe there. Things will go back to the way they used to be and we'll build a home for ourselves, okay?"

She nodded, but she wasn't convinced. I'd never seen her this upset before. She was always the strong one—always the one who, despite our horrific circumstances, told me to hold on to hope.

"What's wrong?" I asked.

She shook her head, but I didn't release my stare. Something was up, and I wanted her to know she could talk to me.

"You can tell me," I said.

She laughed—an uncomfortable chuckle that I knew was the result of her trying to mask her emotions. "It's probably hormonal," she said.

"What?" I asked.

She shrugged again. "I don't know... You're gonna think I'm neurotic."

I stopped walking and tugged on her hand. "I'd never think that."

She pulled a loose strand of hair out of her mouth, brushed her wavy hair back, and said, "It's this feeling I have. But it's only a feeling, you know? Feelings aren't real."

"What feeling?" I asked.

Her dark eyes rolled up at me, almost pleading. "A nasty feeling that keeps telling me we won't make it to the Cove."

CHAPTER 8

We won't make it to the Cove.

We won't make it to the Cove.

Why had I kept pushing? I wished she hadn't told me what she was thinking. The last thing I needed as the newly voted leader of this crew was to have even an ounce of doubt about my decision. I may have wished for death a few minutes prior, but not death to the people I was leading—especially not a violent one.

Why would she feel this, anyway? It wasn't like she was psychic. So why did I believe her? Why was my heart pounding against the leather of my shirt? And why were my hands clammy around my bow?

I bit down hard, attempting to focus on the hazy path in front of me. I could hear Rocket and Trim talking to each other and nearly swung around to tell them to shut up.

But I wasn't that person. They weren't doing anything wrong. It was me. I was panicking.

"Yo, you good, Brone?"

I glanced sideways at Coin. She'd cocked a

brow and her dark lip was pulled over her gold tooth.

"What?" I said, almost in a snap.

"You're lookin' a little pale. What's up?"

I shook my head. "Nothing. Let's keep moving on the same path we took earlier."

I regripped my bow, feeling it slip inside of my palm, and started imagining what it would feel like to have an arrow penetrate my chest—crack through my ribs and tear out through my back. Why couldn't I stop thinking? And then another image flashed through my mind—the sight of a young woman screaming amid hot flames, the side of her face melting into her clothes.

"Brone!"

My heart nearly jumped out of my throat.

Coin was staring at me, her eyes wide open—two big white balls at the center of a black head.

"Snap out of it. Whatever you're thinkin' about, think about it later. You ain't even lookin' around for predators, and my eyes ain't good enough. I got ears, that's it."

She shot a glance back toward the crew, almost as if ensuring they hadn't heard anything. I was thankful for that—I didn't want them knowing I was off my game.

She made her eyes go big again until I finally nodded. "Sorry, you're right."

I cleared my throat and stared straight ahead.

The sound of the river's flow filled the air, as did the scent of fresh cool water, and I knew we were nearing the waterfall. Now, it was only a matter of following the river down to the waterfall without being ambushed or hunted by anyone or anything.

* * *

"Mom, I don't want to go," I said, repositioning my candles and mirror on my shelf.

"Honey," she said, "you've been excited about this for months. What's going on?"

I looked back at her. How was I supposed to explain to her that it simply didn't feel right? That I had a big ball of anxiety in my stomach and it felt like I was going to melt into the floor. My seventh-grade teacher had organized a school trip to a local zoo called Paprica Habitat.

Yeah, I'd been really excited about it. I loved animals. But that morning, it felt like my entire world was falling apart. It was as though I knew something others didn't. Maybe the school bus was going to get into a major accident, or maybe, one of the caged animals was going to get out and attack someone.

Either way, I didn't want to go.

"Just don't feel good," I said, and I could tell by the way my mom tilted her head of curly blond hair that she wasn't buying it.

But she didn't push. Instead, she leaned in with her red-stained lips and kissed my forehead.

"You're old enough to make your own decisions. I'll call Mr. Trume and let him know you're sick."

Embarrassed, I barely made eye contact. But at the same time, if something *did* happen, I wouldn't be in harm's way. So, I stayed in bed reading a book that day, constantly wondering if my classmates were okay.

I even went to bed that night and dreamed that the school bus had been in a horrible accident on the highway, leaving nothing but pieces of seats, crushed metal, and a disassembled engine. Then the next morning, the sun came up and the birds chirped beside my bedroom window. I rubbed my crusted eyes, sat up, and grabbed my phone to read the news.

There was no bus crash nor any outrageous zoo story to be told.

I got dressed, ate breakfast, and made my way outside to the bus stop. At exactly 7:45 a.m., the black-and-silver-framed school bus appeared at the end of my road as it always did, the morning sun glistening off its tinted windows.

The bus driver reached for the door's release button, and the glass doors swung open with a swoosh. She smiled down at me from underneath her baseball cap.

Everything was the same as it was every morning. So why had I felt that way the day before?

"Lydia!" Steven called out.

Steven was my bus buddy. He always wanted to talk about the latest and coolest video games released for the new PlayStation Infinity.

"Where were you yesterday?" he asked. "It was so much fun. You should've seen the green lions and the hairless pandas!"

I'd heard about these genetically modified animals. Although I didn't agree with the process, I agreed with the cause, which was to save endangered animals. I still wished I'd been there.

"Sorry, Steve, I didn't feel good."

He slouched his shoulders and let out a playful sigh. "Too bad. You missed out."

I had missed out, I thought. All because of a feeling—a feeling of anxiety that hadn't even meant anything.

* * *

We will make it to the Cove.

We will make it to the Cove.

Maybe if I repeated these words enough times in my head, we'd be okay. I glanced back at Ellie, who was walking along the river's edge with Trim and Hammer, checking in on Fisher every few minutes. I wasn't a fan of standing out in the open like this, but it was the smoothest path to the waterfall, and with Fisher grasping to life by a thread, it was important she be at least somewhat comfortable throughout the trek. The more she slept, the better.

Proxy walked in a zigzag motion, raising her long legs over giant leaves to get through the jungle. She brushed her fingers along the surfaces of leaves, across branches, and around little berries.

"How much longer?" Franklin said.

I resisted the urge to tell her to keep her mouth shut. Instead, I glanced back briefly and said, "Keep your weapons up and your eyes open."

Franklin rolled her eyes again, but she listened. She turned her head from side to side, the tip of her hunting spear following her movements.

Johnson, looking almost overweight beside Franklin's bony structure, clutched her stick with both hands and twirled her palms around it a few times, her brown eyes wide and never resting.

Everest wasn't much help, but I couldn't blame her. She was using her stick as a walking staff more than anything, trying to ease the pain in her hips as much as possible.

"You guys okay?" I asked, turning toward Trim and Hammer.

Trim let go of the ropes, placed her hands in the arch of her back, and stretched.

"She's heavier than I thought," Trim said, and for a moment it almost looked like she'd been about to smile.

Hammer, on the other hand, was as red as a

tomato. She had big blotchy patches running down her neck and across her chest. The skin on her face looked like it was melting—shiny and drooping.

"You okay, Hammer?" I asked.

She bent forward with her hands on her knees, and saliva came stringing out of her mouth. She raised a hand in the air as if to say, "I need a minute."

But we didn't have a minute. We needed to keep moving.

Rocket must have noticed my wheels turning. She nudged Hammer in the shoulder and said, "I got this, big guy."

Hammer nodded, her round face jiggling as she took Rocket's spear and traded positions.

"I'll help, too," Ellie said, and she reached for the rope by Trim's feet.

Trim hesitated, noticeably unaccustomed to accepting help from anyone.

"It's okay, Trim," I said. "I'd rather have you up here with me."

She nodded, grabbed the hunting spear Ellie was carrying, and came to my side, her heavy footsteps crunching over small twigs and river stones.

"You think Proxy will save her?" Trim asked, her dark eyes rolling toward Proxy who kept disappearing behind curtains of vines and intertwined plants.

I glanced back at Fisher—with her pale, slimy body, she could easily be mistaken for a corpse. She already looked dead and it was as if we were taking her body someplace that allowed for a proper burial. I didn't want to think that way, but I couldn't help it.

What if she did die? I kept telling myself she'd be okay, but there was no way of knowing for sure.

I shifted my attention to Proxy, who now appeared to be talking to herself.

"I think Proxy knows what she's doing," I said, staring Trim in the face. I'd never seen her this worried before. "If anyone can save Fisher, it's her."

Trim nodded and looked away, seemingly on the verge of shedding a tear or two. She swallowed hard, then pulled her thick round shoulders back and slapped the spear in her hands.

"Well the best thing we can do for Fisher is make sure she gets to the Cove in one piece," she said.

The ironic part in all of this was that had anyone else been attacked by the crocodile, Fisher wouldn't have allowed us to construct a bed for transportation. She'd have left the woman at Redwood, explaining to us that one person wasn't worth the risk of getting us all killed.

While I admired Fisher for her matter-of-fact ideologies, I didn't necessarily always agree with them. Maybe it was a good thing these women had elected me as their leader. Maybe I'd save more lives—then again, maybe I'd get us all killed.

Everything about Kormace Island was a gamble.

"How big's this Cove?" I asked, my eyes remaining straight ahead. "Is it big enough for—"

But Coin's hand swung sideways and slapped me across the chest. Everyone stopped walking, and Coin's big golf ball eyes were glued on me. "Did you guys hear that?"

CHAPTER 9

"Stop tryin' to scare us," Franklin said, moving past Johnson and making her way to the front.

"I ain't tryin' to scare nobody," Coin hissed. "I heard somethin'."

"Yeah, like what?" Franklin said, jabbing her spear toward the jungle. "A bird? A monkey?"

Coin looked at me, then at Franklin. "Didn't sound like no animal."

I scanned the jungle to our right and across the river. There was nothing but giant walls of greenery—massive leaves and tall grass making it impossible to see beyond the jungle's perimeter.

"If ve stopped for every sound ve heard," Everest said, her tired eyes rolling toward Coin, "ve'd never make it to da Cove."

I could tell the women were anxious to keep moving. And it was no better to practically stand still like a bunch of ducks. Although we were doing our best to stay within the jungle, we were still following the edge of the river, which meant we were easy to spot.

I jolted my head sideways, signaling everyone to keep moving.

"Keep your eyes on the jungle," I said.

I took one step forward, and the sound of something scraping was enough for me to swing back around with my arrow pointed straight ahead.

"Whoa!" Rocket said, raising a flat hand against her forehead and squinting her eyes. "Easy, Brone. It's Fisher's bed. It's stuck."

She tugged on the rope, and that same scraping sound overpowered the river's heavy flow. Ellie gave another tug, but all it did was send her tripping back a few steps. Trim lowered her spear and took a step toward them, but Rocket raised a stiff hand and said, "It's okay. Just stuck on a tree. We got this."

She bent down at one end, her small back curved, and wrapped her fingers around one of the bamboo supports. Ellie rushed around to the foot of the bed and did the same thing.

"One, two, three," Rocket said, her third word sounding more like a grunt.

Together, they raised the bed to their waistlines and stepped over the fallen tree. At the same time, Proxy appeared beside Fisher, her scraggly head moving from side to side as she examined her wounds.

"In one hour's time, I'd like to reapply some

cleansing herbs to reduce the swelling in her leg," she said.

"How're you gonna know it's been an hour, genius?" Franklin asked. "Got some magic watch we don't know about?"

Proxy closed her eyes and pointed at the sky. "Actually, by studying the sky, one is capable of—"

But I didn't hear the rest. All of a sudden, it was as though I were being sucked into a lucid dream—a nightmare, to be more precise. Across the green-watered river, standing hunched on a boulder underneath a canopy tree, was a woman with red markings across her eyes, a half-skull mask on the bottom of her face, and hair so wild she looked like an animal.

I didn't have the time to comprehend what I was seeing because I heard something at the same time. The sound hadn't come from across the river where this woman stood—it had come from beside us—from within the jungle. Quickly turning around, I spotted three more shadowed faces with bright red markings around their eyes.

All sound around me vanished, and the jungle's greenery began to blend into one massive swirl, spinning around me like a tornado as it had in my dream.

Jesus Christ, Brone, focus.

I was thinking so fast, it felt like everything around me had somehow transitioned to slow motion. Rocket and Ellie were still carrying Fisher's bed; Ellie's face was all red and her mouth was half-open as she spoke with Proxy, but I couldn't hear anything.

I could sense Trim and Coin beside me, but I knew they hadn't seen the figures; they hadn't spotted the Northers. I glanced into the jungle one more time, noting the handcrafted bows fastened to their fur-lined backs.

They were all Archers.

We were surrounded.

Then, I did the only thing a strong leader could have done. Without thinking, I lunged toward Proxy, shoving her as hard as I could against Fisher's bed. In one chaotic motion, Proxy's head whiplashed back and everyone's arms flew into the air as they attempted to catch their footing.

But they didn't stand a chance. I'd pushed hard enough to force Fisher's bed into the river, bringing along with her Proxy, Rocket, and Ellie.

They fell backward, eyes widened in confusion by my betrayal. Ellie's arms slapped the water around her, her thick wavy hair becoming black and glossy, and she gasped to catch her breath, her mouth and nostrils wide open.

If this was the feeling of heartbreak, I'd collapse any moment. Ellie kept looking back at me, not understanding what was going on. I watched her wet head float away into the rapid current, and the three of them attempt to stabilize Fisher's bed. I knew they were heading straight for the waterfall, but I'd had no other choice. Had I not done anything, they'd have been killed or captured; and if they'd been captured, Fisher would have died.

The sound of angry voices exploded around me, and a sharp point jabbed me in the chest; only, this wasn't a Norther's doing, it was Trim's. She was staring at me with ferocious eyes underneath bushy eyebrows that led me to believe she'd be the one to end me.

Her nostrils were flared as wide as her open, rotten-toothed mouth, and the skin on her forehead formed rolls between her eyebrows. Her jab turned into a painful prod. But I didn't have the time to explain myself because the sound of a whistling arrow zoomed by Trim's face, landing in between two river stones at our feet.

Then, from inside the jungle came three women pointing metal-tipped arrows at our faces. The biggest of them all, a woman wearing a leather combat vest, a skull mask, and a necklace with what appeared to be a massive shark tooth, stepped forward. She had a small blond bun at the top of her partially shaved head, and her hands were veiny and muscular—almost enough to mistake her for a man.

She aimed her bow at all of us, one at a time, then pointed it down toward the slimy rocky surface, the mask on her face sliding up right below her eyes.

"On your knees!"

CHAPTER 10

Their leader—the one with the small blond bun at the top of her head—circled us, her hollow, animallike eyes scanning us from above her half-skull mask. It covered the bridge of her nose, cheeks, and face down to the top of her neck and almost looked like burned wood, its surface dry with black stains and cinder ash spots around the teeth.

She kicked aside our weapons, and I watched as my bow—Eagle's bow—landed inches away from the flowing river. My quiver rolled down a slant and several arrows fell out.

I shifted from side to side, and a sharp rock jabbed into the skin of my knee.

"Hands behind your back," the leader ordered, her voice muffled and raspy from behind her mask.

I looked at Trim who was glaring up with a crease in the middle of her forehead. What was she thinking? Was she planning to attack? Was it better to fight for our lives? My eyes shifted to two other Northers who stood farther back, their arrows pointed at our chests. We didn't stand a chance.

There were five in total—I hadn't seen two of them until I craned my neck to see behind the leader. If we tried to fight, they'd release their arrows and kill us instantly. What were they planning, anyway? Why hadn't they killed us when they first saw us?

My heart pounded hard, and my face was so hot it was probably red and blotchy.

This was it, I thought.

I was going to die.

As long as Ellie was okay... That was all that mattered, wasn't it? That was the reason we were here, and they weren't. Who was I kidding? There was no way of knowing if they'd even survived the waterfall drop. I shook these thoughts away. It was better to have given them a chance to survive than to let them stay in this position—at the mercy of the Northers.

"Tie them up," the leader said.

Two of the Northers stepped forward. One of them had a similar skull mask while the other wore a bandana-like cloth over her face. It was brown, though I was certain it used to be white—most likely a sheet of cotton.

I watched them as they moved in, wondering if they had any shred of humanity inside. These were the monsters we'd been fighting for so long, and they were precisely that: monsters. They moved with such confidence, their shoulders drawn back and their arms swaying from side to side. It was almost like they weren't even human, like robots programmed for battle.

"What do you want with us?" Johnson shouted, her face distorted in anger.

Everyone looked at her, including the leader of the Norther clan. She slowly tilted her partially covered head, her soulless eyes narrowing to two black lines. "You can ask Rainer yourself."

Rainer? So, they weren't planning on killing us? Why? What did Rainer want with us? Wasn't she satisfied enough already? She'd proven herself to be the most powerful leader on Kormace Island when she massacred Murk's people—my people—and burned our village to the ground.

So why were they still hunting us if they weren't trying to kill us?

Two strong hands grabbed my wrists, pulled them behind my back and wrapped a rough, stringy material around them until my palms were stuck together.

Trim was next.

For a moment, I thought she might jump to her feet and start bashing some faces in, but she didn't budge. I could tell it was eating her alive. All she wanted to do was kill these pieces of shit.

I didn't blame her—I wanted the same thing.

Had they not been pointing arrows at us, I'd have taken my chances and fought without a second thought. But if I got up, I'd be killed. It was better to wait and see where this was going.

I glanced at Franklin who looked like an injured baby donkey, her eyes big and fearful, her jaw twitching. For the first time, I felt sorry for her. She may have trained as a Battlewoman, but that was equivalent to training a pilot in a simulator and throwing them into a multiengine jet to fly solo. She'd never been in battle—at least, not on Kormace Island.

Her badass tattooed exterior was now unnoticeable. All I saw was a girl on the verge of death—a girl who didn't know what to think, feel, or believe. She bit down on her lip, and her eyes caught mine. She didn't glare or scowl. She almost looked like she was going to cry.

I tightened my lips and nodded as a way of saying, *We're going to be okay.*

I didn't know whether that was true or not. There was a good chance we weren't coming out of this alive, but she needed reassurance and it was my job to give it to her.

"Vatch it!" Everest shouted when one of the Northers grabbed her wrists.

The leader stepped forward, her tall leather boots crunching over small river stones.

"Something wrong?" she asked, slowly bending

down to meet Everest in the eyes.

"I'm old," Everest said. "Vat do you expect?"

The leader straightened her posture and slowly turned to the other Northers.

"She's right," she said. "She *is* old. And if she's old, what does that mean?"

"Can't produce," said one of the other Northers, baring a set of brown crooked teeth. "Useless."

She sounded like a cavewoman, or worse, someone who'd been raised here on Kormace Island with no education whatsoever.

In one swift movement, the leader reached down and slapped two hands on Everest's shoulders, her fingers clasping hard. Everest let out a yelp, but the leader didn't stop. She picked her up and dragged her across the river stones.

"Stop it!" I shouted, but no one listened.

"Let me go!" Everest yelled, slapping a weak hand against the Norther's padded shoulder.

The leader grabbed her by the back of her colorless hair, and Everest grimaced in pain, the folds of her face multiplying. What was the Norther doing? Why was she dragging her toward the river?

"Let her go!" Trim growled.

Everest tried slapping her attacker one more time, but the Norther didn't flinch. She bent her knees, tightened her grip around Everest's shoulders, and threw her into the river with a loud splash. Everest's wet white head resurfaced, and she croaked and flailed her veiny arms in every direction possible trying to stay above water.

But then, the Norther standing beside me—the one who'd spoken like a cavewoman—drew her bow, pulled back, and released an arrow, the string of her bow making a snapping noise. I barely had time to see what happened, but the silence that filled the air told me she hadn't missed her mark.

I looked at Everest as she floated away in silence, an arrow protruding from her neck, a pool of murky red water forming around her.

"What the fuck?" Johnson snapped, and she tried to get up.

But the Norther behind her smacked a solid hand on her shoulder and she fell back to her knees.

The leader slowly turned to Johnson, her eyes squinting with pleasure. "She wasn't of any use to us."

"She was a human being! What the fuck is wrong with you?" Johnson spewed.

My heart was beating so hard I felt it in my throat. Why was she doing this? Was she trying to get herself killed?

The leader dropped into a crouched position in front of Johnson—a condescending stance that exuded dominance—and dug a shiv against her throat. She slid the blade up her neck, along her freckled jawline, and across her lips.

"One more word out of you, and I'll slice those pretty lips right off," she said.

Johnson winced and pulled away from the knife's sharp point, and the leader laughed. She stood up tall, her leather belt making a chafing noise with her movement. I wished I could see her face—see the monster behind the mask. But the Northers—all five women standing before me—were covered from head to toe. Even their arms, despite Kormace Island being hot and sticky all year round, were covered with a beige meshing that made it almost impossible to see their skin.

I felt a dull pull on my arm and the Norther behind us let out a grunt. "Get up!"

I struggled to my feet, doing my best to maintain my balance with my hands tied behind my back.

"Get in line," the leader ordered, waving a black fingernailed hand at each of us.

Johnson stood at the front and I stood between her and Trim. Beside Trim was Coin, then Hammer, with Franklin at the back of the line. There was so much emotion in the air it seemed as though electricity was pulsating through all of us. I could sense Trim's anger—her wanting to torture these women. I, for one, wished I could rip off the Norther's mask, plunge my hands into her mouth, and snap her jaw in two.

I'd never felt so much hatred in my life. At least when Greg attacked my mother, I'd been able to do something about it. It was my decision to swing that iron pan. But now, I was at their mercy—at the mercy of these filthy, horrid excuses for human beings. How much longer would I be able to keep my mouth shut? The idea of killing one Norther became appealing, even if it meant I'd be killed immediately after.

But it was too late now. My hands were tied and my bow and arrows were too far away.

The leader paced back and forth across the line we'd made, twirling her shiv in the palm of her hand almost tauntingly.

"Who's the leader of this little group you have here?" she asked.

Leader? I swallowed hard and my heart skipped a beat. What did they want with the leader? Did they expect me to give them information on something? On someone? Would they torture me for it?

But I didn't even have time to step forward. Trim raised her chin, her dark frizzy hair falling and masking the back of her neck, and said, "I am."

I parted my lips, but Trim turned to me and didn't say anything. She'd never looked at me like that before. It wasn't a look of pride, but rather, one of purpose. She pulled up one corner of her lips and her eyes softened above her acne-scarred cheeks.

If I'd had to guess what she was trying to tell me, it would have been: *Let me do this.*

At once, her features became distorted—her lips drooped, eyes went wide, forehead wrinkled—when the leader grabbed her by the hair and pulled her to the ground. Trim landed on her hands and knees, a loud *crack* filling the air around us as she hit the rocks.

"That's going to be a bit of a problem," the leader said, and she front kicked Trim straight in the ribs, propelling her onto her back.

"No!" Johnson shouted, but one of the Northers moved forward with her arrow drawn at Johnson's face.

"Leave her alone!" I shouted, and a sharp prod jabbed me in between the shoulder blades.

"You see," the leader said, leaning her weight on her knees, "there's only room for one leader on this island."

Trim's vengeful eyes rolled up toward the Norther and she spat a glob of dark blood at the ground. "And what?" she said, blood filling the gaps of her teeth. "You're it? You're the almighty leader? You fucking piece of sh—"

Crack—the leader kicked her thick boot at the side of Trim's head, knocking her back down.

"Stop it!" someone shouted.

It was impossible to tell whose voice was coming from where anymore. My adrenaline was through the roof, and it felt like I was dreaming again.

I couldn't let Trim do this.

"I'm the one you want!" I said, or at least, I think I did. It hadn't sounded like my voice.

But the leader threw her head back and laughed, the bun on her head wiggling. "How noble... Your little sheep are trying to take your place."

The other Northers joined in on the laughter, but all it sounded like were demons speaking in tongues. And then, the leader bent down and wrapped her fingers in Trim's hair and pulled up as hard as she could, exposing her neck.

Trim's teeth were sealed tight and she breathed rapidly through her nose, her pink nostrils moving quickly.

"This is what happens when you try to be a hero!" the leader shouted, her voice carrying above our shouts.

And in one swift movement, she swung her arm in front of Trim's face and everything went silent. I didn't understand what had happened. When the Norther's arm moved out of the way, Trim's eyes rolled back in her head and she made a choking sound.

And then I saw it—the red gap. There was a

small a slit in Trim's throat, but it grew wider and wider, until finally, it burst open, resembling a bucket of gooey red paint being poured out.

This wasn't happening.

It couldn't be.

Trim gurgled, and bubbles of blood splashed from her throat and into the air. Then, almost as if the volume of a muted TV had been turned on, everyone started screaming.

I let out a shout as loud as my lungs would allow and lunged straight toward the leader, my hands swinging from side to side behind me. I'd tear out her jugular with my fucking teeth if I had to.

I'd kill her.

I'd fucking kill her and then I'd kill all of them.

That's when something hard hit me against the head, and everything around me went black.

PART THREE

PROLOGUE

His eyes rolled from side to side as he puffed on his cherry-flavored cigar. It filled the room with a sweet smell I'd come to hate. He ran his thick oil-stained hand through his curly brown hair and coughed out a cloud of smoke.

I despised him.

What did my mother see in him?

He was a complete drunken waste of skin who was good for one thing: helping my mom pay her bills. Even then, he only did it when it suited him, although he was always at my mom's place, leeching off her electricity and stuffing his face with the little bit of food she had. What kind of man leeched off a woman who received less than $2,000 per month through disability insurance? I averaged $3,000 per month working minimum wage.

Some days, I wondered if maybe she was scared of him—terrified to talk back to him or to make any demands. I'd asked her time and time again if she felt afraid, and all she'd say was,

"Sweetheart, Gary's a little rough around the edges... But you don't know him like I do."

A little rough around the edges... That was one way of putting it.

He was a piece of shit, that's what he was.

I stared at him, wondering if he'd forgotten that it was the first of the month, and my mom hadn't been able to pay her cable bill last month because he'd gone ahead and rented a dozen specialty programs—wrestling or something.

He got up with a loud grunt and a swing in his upper body, stomped his way into the kitchen, and went digging inside the fridge. The sound of beer bottles clanging against each other filled the apartment, and my eyes rolled toward my mother's.

She smiled at me, almost apologetically, but all I saw was cowardice. I loved her, but it was so hard not to be mad at her. I glanced toward the kitchen at the pile of dirty dishes and a dozen empty beer bottles against the wall.

That was the other thing I hated about him—he never helped my mom or gave her any emotional support. She suffered from fibromyalgia, a chronic pain illness often referred to as a suicide disease. Some days—because there were good days, and bad days—getting up to do the dishes was excruciating for her. Yet there he was, piling it all up.

I tried to visit her as often as possible to help out around the apartment. On her bad days, though, she couldn't even get out of bed. She'd described her pain to me: like venom slithering through her body and eating through her muscles, bones, and tendons, or like being prodded with thousands of knives over and over again.

She'd even asked me if I thought the hospital would amputate her legs so the pain would stop. If the hospital couldn't even give her pain medication when she came in by ambulance—because she was on opioid medication and they viewed her as a junkie—they sure as heck wouldn't waste their time with any surgical procedure to ease the pain that was *in her head.*

Gary was never sympathetic to her pain, either. When she'd moan or rub her legs, he'd roll his eyes and tell her to have a beer or take one of her pills, if he hadn't already gone through the bottle.

He dropped back down into his spot, took a chug of cold beer, and let out a bubbly burp.

I watched my mom as she rubbed her inflamed fingers together, obviously trying to figure out how to ask him for money. She shifted from side to side, her brown eyes bouncing between Gary and me.

I wanted to speak up, but I knew if I did, I'd probably upset my mom more than him.

"What's up with you?" he asked, more annoyed

than anything.

His bottom lip was slobbery, and his eyes couldn't stay straight. He'd gone through half a bottle of vodka and a dozen beers already. There was no use talking to him when he was this drunk.

"It's... it's the cable bill," my mom said, playing with the tips of her chestnut hair.

"Ca-cable bill?" he blurted. He leaned forward and smashed his beer bottle onto the coffee table, causing my mom's shoulders to jerk forward. "Is that—is that all I am to you?" he slurred. "Money?"

"No, of course not, sweetheart," my mom said quickly. She was trying too hard to be sweet to him. "It's just that—"

"It's just, it's just, it's just," he sneered, his lips drooping down into the shape of a horseshoe. "If you have somethin' to say, spit it out!"

His voice, now a growl, shook the apartment walls and my mom slouched her shoulders forward in an attempt to make herself look smaller.

"I-I was just. Gary, please. I can't afford—"

"Can't afford?" he roared. He swung his hand at his beer bottle, and it flew across the living room and shattered against the television's entertainment unit. This time, I was the one who flinched.

"Is that all I am to you?" he repeated, his eyes now narrowing on my mom. "A d-dollar sign? I love you, Janet, I love you. And this is how—this is..."

"Gary, please..."

He swung the back of his heavy hand against her face and a loud crack resonated across the apartment. "D-don't you talk back to me."

I lunged to my feet, but his dark eyes rolled up at me. "You stay out... Stay out of this."

I couldn't waste any time trying to argue with him. I rushed down the hallway and into my mom's room, where I pulled out my phone with shaky hands and dialed 9-1-1. My mom would hate me for this, but there was no other choice. I couldn't stand around and watch him beat her.

"9-1-1, what's your emergency?"

"It's my mom's boyfriend," I said, my voice muffled with my hand. "Forty-five Victoria Street, apartment 305. He's drunk and he's"—my voice cracked—"he's beating her."

"Is he armed?" the woman asked, her voice calm and reassuring.

"Not that I know of," I said."

"We'll send police escorts right away," she said.

I'd been about to thank her when I heard glass shattering in the kitchen, followed by a scream.

"Mom!" I shouted, blasting my way out of her room and down the hallway.

But what I saw first wasn't my mom—it was him. He was facing the wall, his massive back rounded and the curly hairs on his head dancing from side to side as he struggled with something.

"I love you," he slurred. "I've done everything... Everything for you. You don't. You. I can't believe..."

That's when I saw her white socks. Her feet were dangling in between his legs, kicking back and forth. He had her pinned up against the wall by her throat.

"Mom!" I shouted again, this time running straight for him.

I jumped on his back, blasting my fists against him, but it was like hitting a stone wall. He wasn't even reacting. I wrapped my arm around his thick neck and squeezed as hard as I could—nothing. His massive hands were around my mom's throat, and her bulging eyes rolled in the back of her head.

"Stop it!" I yelled.

Her face was dark red, almost purple, and her lips were going blue. She slapped a frail, veiny hand over his to stop him, but it didn't do anything. He wasn't letting go.

I needed something—something hard. I considered picking up the television and throwing it at his back, but my eyes caught sight of something in the kitchen. I ran toward the cast iron frying pan, picked up the handle with both hands, and came charging at him with it over my head.

I let out the loudest scream I'd ever released and swung down as hard as I could. A loud clunk filled the space around us, and he took a step back, before dropping to his knees and onto his side, shaking the entire apartment. My mom fell to the ground, her bony hands clasped around her red and inflamed throat.

Her wild eyes shot from me to him as I stood there with the frying pan dangling at my side for what seemed like hours. As if being shaken from a trance, panic surged through my mom. She started shaking and muttering things I couldn't understand. She crawled toward Gary, cupping his big bearlike face in her hands.

"Gary?" Her wet eyes rolled up at me. "What did you do? What did you do? He's... he's not breathing. Lydia, what did you do?"

I stared at his motionless body, trying to understand what had happened. I couldn't think. I couldn't breathe. I couldn't talk.

What had I done?

A loud knock blasted against the front door, and I dropped the frying pan.

"Police, open up!"

CHAPTER 1

Was I even alive?

Maybe the Northers had killed me, too, and this was an alternate reality. Maybe my wrists weren't actually tied up with rope behind my back, and maybe, just maybe, we weren't being led toward the Northers' territory like cattle to the slaughterhouse.

This couldn't be happening.

I stared straight ahead, my eyes wide open, but all I could see were Trim's hollow black eyes staring at me from atop a pool of blood over unevenly shaped river stones. I remembered screaming until my voice became hoarse, but after that, everything faded away.

There was a throbbing pain in the back of my head, and I could only assume someone had hit me from behind to stop me from charging after Trim's killer.

"Where are you taking us?" Johnson asked, her voice like nails on a chalkboard.

But the Norther who was leading the way—the

one at the front with short, choppy brown hair and pointy shoulders—tugged on the rope that connected us all as a way of telling Johnson to shut up.

Coin's chin jabbed me in between my shoulder blades, and I fell forward, my chest hitting Johnson—who was at the front of the line—in the back. She almost fell flat on her face.

"Stupid bitch," Johnson muttered.

"What'd you say?" the choppy-haired Norther asked. She whipped a knife out from her belt and stared at Johnson with eyes too big for her face.

God, she was so ugly without her skull mask. Dirt stained her face, paint—which had assumedly once been a straight line—smeared underneath her eyes, a missing front tooth stood out amid all her decaying ones, and a scar ran from her chin all the way up to the eyebrow, deforming her nose.

Johnson didn't respond. She stared back, most likely contemplating whether running her mouth again was worth her life.

"That's enough, Rebel," the leader of the Northers said.

Rebel, which I assumed was the ugly one's name, pulled her nose up in a piggish way and raised two arched eyebrows.

"You heard Rainer," the leader went on. "She wants these ones alive." She stepped forward, the sound of her heavy gear chafing, and yanked the rope out of Rebel's hand.

Rebel slid her mask back on and looked either dumbfounded or pissed off—I couldn't tell which—as she stood still and stared at her leader.

"Go!" the leader snapped, her bright eyes popping out and the little blond bun on her head wiggling like an old bobblehead doll.

Rebel short-stepped her way past us, nearly blinding us with her hateful glare, and joined the other three Northers at the back of the line. They followed us closely, whacking sticks in their palms as a form of intimidation, as a way of saying, 'One wrong move, and I'll break you.'

"Keep moving," the leader ordered.

How far is this place? I wanted to ask. But I wasn't stupid. I wasn't suicidal. Besides, I didn't *want* to reach our destination. With every step I took, I prayed that Biggie or Flander or anyone I knew—even young Elektra, for crying out loud—would come swinging down from a vine like Tarzan to save the day.

Or, better yet, that we'd be ambushed by Ogres or saved by a Rogue. We'd been saved by a Rogue before—the image of a huge tiger swinging its massive paw at me automatically flashed through my mind. Maybe Rogues were decent human beings. If a Rogue could face a tiger to save a group of strangers, a Rogue could definitely be our knight in shining armor—well, leather—and save us.

I glanced up at the trees overhead, noticing for the first time how beautiful every break of sunlight truly was. There were all sorts of shapes... triangles, squares, rectangles. And each of these shapes shone a different hue of the sun's yellow light.

Why hadn't I ever taken the time to appreciate its beauty?

And why was I noticing it now? Was I having an end-of-life moment? Deep down, did I believe I was going to die?

I swallowed and my heart thumped so hard, I could barely breathe.

That's exactly what I believed, even though I didn't want to believe it. After everything I'd seen from the Northers (the attacks, the massacre, the fire), I knew there was no way I was coming out of this one whole.

I was either going to be strung up naked like a goddamn piece of meat and slaughtered in front of every Norther, or I was going to be tortured by Rainer's finest. I thought of the tools they'd probably use—shards of bones, rocks, rope capable of stretching one's limbs out of their sockets—and my stomach sank.

Remembering the metal arrowhead Coin found, I was instantly nauseous. How advanced were they?

My vision became fuzzy and every sound

around me was amplified. Every leaf that ruffled sounded like a plastic bag flapping in the wind; every insect that crawled sounded like nails falling on a concrete floor; and every twig that snapped underneath our feet sounded like a bolt of lightning striking the earth beside me.

"You!"

I wanted to cover my ears at the sound of the leader's voice, but my hands were tied. I cringed and turned my head to the side, hoping that the angle of my head might reduce the amount of noise my ears were taking in.

Footsteps became louder, shaking the ground under me, and a strong hand gripped my arm.

"Get it together before I send you along with that Bigfoot frizzy-haired friend of yours."

Frizzy... Bigfoot... What was she talking about?

Trim. I saw her face—her pointed nose, her acne-scarred skin, and her dark eyes that stared into me before she'd died as if she'd planned the whole thing, as if she knew she was going to die.

Why had she done that? Why had she announced herself the leader to save me? Trim should have been standing here. Maybe if Trim were alive, she'd find a way out of this mess.

But Trim was dead.

My throat swelled, and my vision slowly returned along with my sense of reality.

The leader's frighteningly beautiful eyes darted

from me to the back of the line, assumedly at her people.

"If this one collapses, cut her loose and kill her," she said.

My heart skipped before returning to a rhythmic pace.

I had to pull myself together. If not for me, then for Trim. Her death had to mean something. The moment the leader turned away, something hard kicked me on my heel. I swiftly turned around and found Coin's glossy brown eyes staring into mine. They were completely bloodshot and sitting in the middle of dark circles.

But she didn't say anything. Her eyes were wide as if telling me that everything was going to be okay. I didn't believe her, but I'd have to lie to myself until I did. I glanced past her and up at Franklin, who looked as terrified as the rest of us, if not more.

I'd never seen her like this. For the first time, I didn't hate her. I felt sorry for her. Despite her having been a complete pain in everyone's ass over the last few days, she was still one of ours, and she was still a human being.

Her eyes appeared over Hammer's short-haired head, her stare lingering in a pleading way. If I'd been a mind reader, I'd have concluded she was begging me to save her life. So, I mustered the bit of strength Coin had shared with me and forced a reassuring smile, even though all I could picture were our five lifeless bodies lying in a pile of dirt, our limbs crisscrossing overtop one another.

I tilted my head back and searched the trees overhead. At this point, I'd have accepted the help of chimpanzees, a tiger, an elephant—anything. Maybe if I made some noise, I could draw attention.

"Something interesting?" the leader asked, her crystal-like eyes hovering over her mask like two glow-in-the-dark balls.

A knot formed in my stomach.

Who was this woman? The spawn of Satan? Or maybe his wife—if he had one. There was something intimidating about her.

I shook my head. "Stretching my neck."

Her eyes turned into little slits. "Lie to me again and I'll gouge those eyes out with my fingers."

I swallowed hard.

Jesus Christ.

She was utterly barbaric—a feral woman capable of harming one in ways most people would never even consider. What had she done to get here? Murdered a bunch of people? Was she a sociopath? A serial killer? She looked like a goddamn sociopath.

She pulled a bone shiv out from her belt, rolled up her sleeve, and glared up at me with her shadowed eyes, but all I could look at was her arm.

Pink scars and half-healed wounds covered it. They looked like knife cuts, but I couldn't say for sure. Some of them were flat, and others, either bumpy or elevated like leftover glue found inside a dresser drawer.

She pressed the point of her knife into a white spot—a patch of skin without any scar—and slowly pulled back, leaving behind a narrow line of bright red blood. She glanced at me again. "That's for your frizzy-haired leader."

She had to be a lunatic. Who in their right mind would self-inflict a wound on a remote island? Had she never considered the risk of infection? What a moron.

But something else hit me. I realized what she'd done, and what she'd been doing, most likely for years. She was marking every life taken, and by the looks of it, there were dozens.

She slowly straightened her hunched posture and with the tip of her knife, raised her skull mask so that it sat on her forehead. I almost stepped back at the sight of her. She was the ugliest thing I'd ever seen—uglier than the choppy-haired brunette who'd been pulling the rope earlier.

Scars ran horizontally across her cheeks and over the bridge of her nose. She didn't have any eyebrows left, because the area was covered in lumpy scars, too. Even her lips had been slit several times horizontally, giving them a zebra-like pattern.

She must have noticed my reaction, because she smirked, revealing a short canine tooth, and said, "This is why they call me Z—"

"Zsasz!" the choppy-haired Norther hissed.

Zsasz swung around, her hairless eyebrows lowering on her face.

"Didn't you hear that?" the brunette whispered. Her big eyes danced all around behind that mask of hers, and she held on to her bow with a tight fist.

I stared at it, wishing I wasn't tied up. If only I could get my hands on that thing...

"I didn't hear anything," Zsasz said, but I could tell she was on high alert.

"Footsteps," the brunette said.

Zsasz raised her arm up and licked the blood from her wound, her pasty tongue dragging across her skin like a dry cloth. "Keep your eyes open and let's keep moving."

CHAPTER 2

Where's Penguin? I should have said. Or maybe, *How's Gotham?* Zsasz... What kind of a person chooses that name? But a few measly insults weren't worth losing my life.

I could hear Zsasz's goons walking stealthily at the back of the line. I call them goons because the other three women carrying bows were nothing more than obedient dogs. There was nothing remotely memorable about them—no unusual feature, no colored marking that made them stand out. They followed Zsasz, and sometimes even Rebel when she gave an order, without ever questioning their decision.

Zsasz could have asked them to walk the entire path backward, and they would have done it. What had she done to get them like this? Was this Rainer's doing? Had she brainwashed them into becoming so complacent? And what about Zsasz? Had she always been this psychotic? Or had Rainer trained her to be exactly as she'd wanted?

I swallowed hard, realizing that if Rainer was to

blame, it meant she was worse. I couldn't imagine anyone worse than Zsasz.

"I'm telling you," Rebel went on, "something's following us."

Zsasz swung around, tugging on our rope at the same time. "I said keep moving."

Rebel grumbled something but kept walking, pointing her arrow at every little sound she heard.

"Anyone who follows us onto Northern territory is suicidal," Zsasz said, but her voice barely carried, because she was facing straight ahead, her shoulders drawn back.

I noticed loose animal skin hanging from her shoulder blades and down her back. Its fur was light brown with a hint of red. What was it, anyway? Why did the Northers feel the need to carry body parts on them? Most of them were wearing sharp-tooth necklaces, and the leader wore dark gray fur around her neck.

An image flashed through my mind: a woman with long dark hair, a long cape made of either cotton or suede that dragged behind her, and a thick layer of fur atop her shoulders. She'd been walking through the Village smoke, her dark silhouette highlighted by the orange glow emitted from the fire's devastating flames. She'd also held on to two battle axes as she moved forward, her tall boots stepping over carcasses in search of something specific.

I knew exactly who Rainer had been looking for—Murk.

Had she found her? Was Murk still alive? If Zsasz had killed Trim for believing she was the leader of our little crew, there was no doubt in my mind that if Murk had been found, she was now dead.

Zsasz led us through a shallow stream of water that looked more like mud than anything else. I stepped in it, cringing at the thought of my crocodile leather boots getting wet. Hammer had worked hard on these, and I remembered her round face in front of mine when she'd warned me about their nonexistent water-resistant functionality. I'd thought it weird being that they were crocodile boots, but she'd explained to me that over time, moisture would damage the skin.

One of Zsasz's goons made a piglike snorting sound, and I turned my head around.

"Keep movin', pork chop," one of them said.

Hammer shook her fat face, which was now the shade of a ripe tomato. It was obvious she wanted to kill them, probably as much as I did. She didn't deserve to be treated like a piece of shit because of her weight. Even though I'd once wanted to kill her myself, I'd come to see the true Hammer—she was a decent human being who was maybe a little rough around the edges, but I'd come to think of her as a friend.

Poor Hammer.

She was breathing hard and the dark hair on her head stuck to her slimy forehead. It was curly, and although less than an inch long, it was the longest I'd ever seen on her. She'd always had it shaved short on her scalp.

She looked at me, but one of Zsasz's goons gave me the stink eye from behind her mask, and I turned away.

How long had we been walking, anyway? It seemed like an eternity. Ten, maybe eleven hours? That was my guess. I'd never been so exhausted in my life. My muscles burned, and my stomach felt like it was eating itself from the inside out.

But what shocked me the most was how far the Northers had traveled to attack us.

A heavy weight suddenly fell on my back, and my boots dug into the jungle floor, helping me maintain my balance.

"Coin!" Franklin said.

I swung around and caught Coin on my chest. Her eyes rolled in the back of her head, and her lips were cracked and pasty white.

"She needs water," I said, my tone a bit harsher than I'd intended. I nudged her with my shoulder, attempting to keep her on her feet. "Coin, come on."

If she went down, we were all going down. I needed her to stand.

"Rebel," Zsasz said with a flick of the wrist. "Give her a sip. We're too close to cut her loose."

Too close to cut her loose? Would Zsasz have killed her for being dehydrated? For slowing down the group?

Rebel grunted something and plucked a red and brown water bladder from her hip. She grabbed Coin by the face and forced the water bladder into her mouth, nearly knocking out her front teeth, including her golden one.

"There, you fuckin' little bitch."

"Back off!" I spat, lunging forward and yanking Johnson along with me.

Rebel flinched back, then glared at me when she realized I had my hands tied behind my back. The whole line went out of balance, and everyone danced back and forth to stay on their feet, creating a wavelike motion.

"Hey!" Zsasz shouted in a deep voice, her oversized figure marching toward us.

How big was she underneath all of that gear? She was much taller than me—probably reaching six feet tall—and her hands were the size of a man's. I could understand why her goons feared her.

"I said give her water," she said slowly, enunciating every syllable. "Did you give her water?"

"Yeah," Rebel said, shifting her weight from

side to side.

Zsasz stomped her way over. "I shouldn't need to fuckin' babysit you." She snatched the water bladder out of Rebel's hand and brought it to Coin's lips. Coin latched onto it like a baby on a nursing bottle.

"All right, that's enough," Zsasz said, pulling the bladder away from Coin's moist, light brown lips.

She slammed the bladder against Rebel's chest and droplets spat out into the air. "Everyone gets a sip. Rainer asked to have them alive, so make sure they stay alive."

Rebel nodded, her beady eyes lingering on me a little longer than necessary. She knew I hated her as much as she hated me, and I was happy about that. I wanted her to know, because one day soon, I'd be hovering over her with a knife dug into her chest and she'd look up at me, on the verge of death, realizing how stupid she'd been for having thought she had the upper hand.

That image was the one thing keeping me alive—that, and Ellie.

Hatred and love.

Revenge and desire.

I hoped to God Ellie was okay. Had she survived the waterfall? It destroyed me to picture her falling several hundred feet into a pool of water, her body gliding through the air like a rag doll. What if there were rocks at the bottom... What if...

I shook these thoughts away because all they did was make me sick to my stomach.

What about Fisher? Had she survived it? Were they on their way to the Cove? Was Rocket still alive? Because they needed her. She was the only one who knew how to find the Cove. And they also needed Proxy, because she was the one chance Fisher had at surviving her wounds.

"Open up," Rebel said, pointing the bladder toward my face.

I nearly turned away, but I couldn't let my ego get in the way of my survival. I swallowed hard as the warm water slipped into my crisp, dry mouth, moistening my gums and unsticking the back of my throat.

I realized I'd bitten down on the bladder when Rebel gave it a hard yank and my teeth made a clicking sound. "You heard Zsasz," she said. "A sip."

She moved on to Johnson who was lunging forward like a dog on a chain.

"Relax," Rebel said. "It's comin'."

Johnson gripped on so hard to the bladder that water splashed all over her face, and after a few seconds of heavy gulping, Rebel had to push her away with her hand. She went on to the back of the line to hydrate Franklin and Hammer when I heard it.

At first, it had brought me back several years when I'd gone to my first rock concert with Melody after a work shift. It was the sound of people yelling—cheering, really. Hundreds of people, if not thousands.

Had we finally reached Northern territory?

As Hammer finished what was left in the water bladder, Zsasz yanked on the rope and led us to the edge of the forest.

I knew it was the edge because a burst of sunlight unexpectedly lit up the jungle floor around our feet, warming the cool, moist air around us.

With her hand, she pulled aside as many banana leaves as she could, revealing a sight that led me to believe I was dreaming.

She slid her mask up again, allowing it to float over her forehead, and her deformed zebra lips curved into a malicious smile.

"Welcome home."

CHAPTER 3

There was too much to take in.

First, I saw the elephants. There were four, from what I could tell, walking through the massive crowd of women. On their backs sat their keepers—women sitting in basketlike saddles—swaying from side to side as they moved forward.

One of the elephants threw its head back and let out a trumpetlike sound through its massive wrinkled trunk before its keeper raised a stick over her shoulder and jabbed it in the back. It shook its head—a huge heart-shaped mass of clay gray—and its ears waved from side to side.

What was she doing? Hurting it? Is that how they'd tamed these wild animals? Had they stolen them from their mothers? I'd read the articles—I knew that for elephants to allow people on their backs, they had to go through a "training crush" process which basically involved inhumane beatings at a very young age. The purpose was to "break their spirit" so that they could begin interaction with human beings.

I'd learned this after visiting one of the biggest zoos near my hometown. Melody had been the one to refuse to get onto an elephant's back. She'd said it was disgusting that they even offered rides to children. I didn't understand why until I did my research afterward. I also remembered reading that in countries where elephant rides were a big thing for tourists, the captors often killed the mother elephant because she was too protective of her baby, making her dangerous.

I stood stiffly beside Zsasz, my eyes scanning the crowd. A large mass of multicolored specks moved about chaotically in what appeared to be a market you'd find in a third world country.

Everyone spoke over one another, either trying to sell or buy something.

Outside of the market-like space were huts lined up along the edge of this village, or city, or whatever it was they called it. Their home, or land, was a massive clearing against the side of a mountain and around it were palmlike trees forming a barrier, the same as there'd been in the Village. Maybe Rainer had learned a few tricks from Murk, after all.

The base of the mountain—a rocky surface with patches of greenery every few feet—caught my eye because of what lay around it: a tall wooden barrier, at least ten feet tall, that formed an enclosure. I couldn't see anything inside, though, because the brown pickets stood side by side almost as if glued together, their carved tips pointing up. It reminded me of something from a medieval movie.

Why was this entire section blocked off to the general population?

The only explanation I could think of was Rainer.

An elephant's foot stomped down, the sound resonating across the merchant huts. The woman on top of it was shouting something, but I couldn't understand what she was saying. She looked like a toy from this distance—a black silhouette with waving hands and a long spear pointed at the sky. With her spear, she reached over the wooden gate and must have unclipped a latch on the other side.

What was Rainer trying to protect? Why did she need a ten-foot fence to block out her people? A fence that couldn't be opened by anyone from the outside unless they were elevated in the air.

The gate creaked open and the woman atop the elephant disappeared inside, before slamming the door shut again and locking the latch.

I wanted to take it all in—to see where it was these mysterious Northers lived—but Zsasz let go of the wall of leaves with a swoosh and everything disappeared.

"Well, let's go," she said, turning to her side and leading us through a path of broken branches that had likely been stepped over thousands of times.

We moved on an angle down a small slope, careful not to catch a patch of mud or slimy rock. The last thing we needed was for one of us to fall—if that happened, we'd all look like a set of dominos.

"Did you see that?" Coin muttered in my ear, her voice sounding like dry leaves crumpling.

I was glad to know she was a bit more lucid than earlier. I didn't turn around or answer her because I didn't want to draw any attention our way. I had seen it, or at least, some of it, and I couldn't believe my eyes. I was afraid to enter the actual city because I had no idea what I was in for. Was the crowd going to tear us to shreds? Cook our body parts and eat them?

When we reached the bottom of the slope, the sound of the city amplified, becoming a cacophonic mess. There were women lamenting, some yelling, and others grunting amid the sound of swords, or sticks, clashing together.

But the moment we stepped out of the jungle and into the open, everything went quiet as if a volume knob had been turned all the way down.

But it wasn't the sound—or lack of it—that took me aback. It was what I was looking at.

Women were everywhere: filthy, sweat-stained women who stared at us like vultures around a fresh carcass. Their eyes looked translucent in comparison to their dark, dirty faces, and I couldn't tell if they were intrigued by us or thirsty for blood.

One of them, a frail old woman with elbows bigger than her arms, waved a crooked finger and opened her toothless mouth. "Heeeeeeere," she said. "*Aye bala mayun!*"

I turned sideways and cocked an eyebrow at Coin. For God's sake, did they speak a different language?

"Move aside, you crazy old hag!" someone shouted, nudging the old lady in her bony ribs.

She fell to her knees and threw her head back, revealing a big black hole for a mouth, and started moaning at the sky.

Everyone moved closer to us, and she disappeared behind dozens of limbs.

"Don't mind her," someone from the crowd whispered. "She's fuckin' crazy."

"Are these the Southerners?"

"Who the fuck calls them Southerners?"

"The traitors!"

"You don't even know them!"

"You heard the stories... Don't act like you have all the answers."

"Shut up!" Zsasz snapped, slicing her knife through the air.

The women all lunged backward at the same time, avoiding Zsasz's blade by mere inches.

"Make way," Zsasz ordered, and the crowd split

apart, their heads bowed and their eyes aimed at the ground.

One old woman stepped out of the crowd, a water bladder in her trembling hands. She rushed to the back of the line, where Hammer swayed from side to side and pressed the bottle against Hammer's lips.

But I didn't have the time to appreciate her kind gesture because all of a sudden, an arrow pierced right through her tiny thigh. She let out a scream so loud that I flinched.

Rebel, who was holding her bow in one hand, grabbed the woman's water bladder and threw it into the crowd, water speckling onto a few faces. She grabbed the old woman by her throat with her free hand, and as hard as she could, threw her into the crowd. The woman fell back into the arms of the crowd, her eyes sealed shut in agony and her veiny hands clasped around the arrow in her thigh.

"When Zsasz says make way, you fuckin' move!" Rebel growled. Her menacing eyes shot at everyone around us, who were now all bent forward even more than before, their heads nearly at the height of our waists. "Next person to step out of line gets an arrow in the eye!"

No one spoke—they stood like statues, avoiding eye contact with us at all costs.

There was a tug on our rope, and we were led through the narrow path of women and alongside the market. I crunched my way through dead branches, pieces of bone, and decaying vegetation. How did these women live here? The conditions were abysmal. It looked like they'd torn down a bunch of trees several years ago and had never bothered to clean up after themselves.

I hopped and nearly tripped when I saw my foot coming down on a dead bird's carcass. Unfortunately, Coin hadn't been so lucky. I heard the crunch before she let out a disgusted grunt.

My eyes darted over the crowd and toward the market-like living space to get a closer look. There were mesh nettings hanging from tree to tree; huts positioned so close together it was a wonder how anyone got around them; cotton blankets and leafy vines hanging in between the huts; cages filled with turkeys flapping their wings against one another; women carrying jugs of water at each end of long sticks over their shoulders; baskets filled with fly-infested fruit; and women yelling over one another to market their products.

The clothing these women wore wasn't what I'd have expected a Norther to wear. They weren't dressed in battle gear as our attackers had been, nor did they carry any weapons. They wore scraps for clothing—pieces of rags and leather held together by string and slim sheets of cotton wrapped around their breasts and groins.

They looked like slaves.

I stared at their grimy foreheads and filthy faces as their eyes remained locked on the soil at our feet.

Is that what they were? Slaves?

"Back off!" Zsasz yelled again as we moved to the outer edge of the city, and the women scattered like vermin, revealing a cage-like contraption big enough to fit dozens of women—a prison cell.

It was difficult to see through it because the walls were built of a braided bamboo, giving off a fence-like texture with tiny diamond-shaped holes. Shapes and colors moved inside, but I had no idea who was trapped behind there. Zsaszs reached for the latch at the front—something made of solid wood that was inaccessible from the inside—and opened it up.

Not even bothering to untie the ropes behind our backs, she grabbed Johnson by the base of her neck and threw her inside, propelling the rest of us forward.

I landed on my knees in what felt like dirt, my face against Johnson's back, then fell to my side when Coin tripped over me. Zsasz stood at the entrance, her rough shape outlined by the gloomy gray sky behind her, before slamming the door shut and darkening the prison cell almost entirely.

I slowly crept back up to my knees, my eyes rolling up to meet our prison mates.

CHAPTER 4

Was I hallucinating?

She was sitting in the dirt, her rag-like chestnut hair masking one eye and her thin stick arm cleaning a young woman's leg wound.

"Is that...?" Coin mumbled.

"Tegan," I said, matter-of-factly, even though on the inside, I wanted to scream.

She wasn't dead. The one person left who held enough knowledge to help Fisher wasn't dead. She'd know exactly what herb or plant was needed to save Fisher.

"Tegan?" I asked.

She didn't respond. She kept rubbing a leaf over the woman's leg, her hair swaying back and forth over half of her face.

"Don't bother," the wounded woman said, her face contorted in pain. "She's broken."

"Broken?" I asked.

As my eyes began to adjust, I noticed the markings on her arms, her shoulders, and her neck. She had cuts that had recently scabbed over and bruises so dark it looked like she'd been in a paintball fight.

"What happened?" I asked, awkwardly trying to get back on my feet.

Someone grabbed my wrists, and the sound of sharp material against rope scraped behind me. My hands came loose, and I brought my wrists up in front of me, rubbing the hot inflammation. The woman behind us—a short, tiny thing who could have easily been mistaken for a teenage Mexican boy—went on to remove everyone else's ropes.

"They beat her," the short woman said from behind. I knew her face, but I couldn't pinpoint who she was. I must have seen her in the Working Grounds or in the Village at one point.

"And tortured her," said the wounded woman.

Tegan didn't budge. It was like she was deaf.

"Why?" I breathed.

The short woman came around us after having untied the entire crew. She placed two hands on her shapeless hips. "They call her the Witch. Said somethin' about her knowing magic. They forced her to help a few Northers with their wounds after the attack, but she said no. So, they beat her over and over and over until she turned into this... Poor chica."

"But she's not a Medic," I said. "She's not Navi. How could they have expected her to heal them?"

"Doesn't matter," said the wounded woman,

her eyes sealed shut. "She's the best they have right now. Apparently, their Medic died a few weeks ago. Something about the flu."

Franklin scoffed. "How ironic."

It looked like she was back to her old self.

"And what about us?" I asked. "Why are we alive? Why'd they kill so many of our people, but not us?"

The short woman shrugged. "We don't know, man. We've been trying to figure that one out since we got here."

"How long have you been here?" I asked.

"*Tres noches*... Three nights," the short woman said, her Spanish accent forcing r's to roll off her tongue. "They've been feedin' us scraps and forcing us to sleep in our own piss and shit." She pointed at the far back corner of the cell—which wasn't all that far considering the small space—where a small brown pile had formed. It looked like plain old dirt, so I assumed they'd attempted to bury their feces.

And then, as if my nostrils had woken from a deep sleep, the smell hit me. It stank of fresh shit and dried-up urine—a pungent combination that smelled like an overall sickness. It didn't bother me much, though. I'd grown accustomed to rancid smells on Kormace Island.

"So, they haven't let you out since?" Franklin asked, crossing her sticklike arms over her chest.

The woman on the floor with the leg wound shook her head, her fingernails clawing at the skin beside her wound. "Locked us up in here and left us to rot."

Coin let out a sigh and brushed a rough hand through her short fuzzy hair, which had started growing in. "That don't make no sense. Why wouldn't they have killed you? Killed us? Man, this is fuckin' bullshit. They kill our people, burn down our home." She started pacing back and forth, making agitated hand gestures near her face. "And for what? To capture the survivors like damn animals? We ain't no animals. We're human beings! This is bullshit!"

"Coin," Johnson said, resting a hand on her shoulder.

It was all Coin had needed, because her rapid breathing slowed, and she gave Johnson a brief nod.

"I don't know what's going on," I said, "but they're obviously trying to hurt us somehow."

"You think?" Franklin said, rolling her eyes. She made her way to the side wall—something that looked like it was constructed of mud or clay.

There were little bits of grass and weeds sticking out of it. It reminded me of the bird's nest I built in fifth grade. The teacher had brought us all outside at the edge of the schoolyard and into the forest. She'd allowed us in a few meters to gather dirt, sticks, leaves, and clay from a hole she made.

I thought of my young self—the shy kid in class who'd cry every time someone got hurt—and wondered, who would have thought this is where I'd end up? On an island with a bunch of psychos, having to kill to survive?

I let out a long breath and slid down on the wall beside Franklin, my back gliding against the cool lumpy texture. I grabbed the hair on the sides of my head and pulled, causing my temples to stretch out, and it brought me immediate relief. A piece of dirt broke off from the wall behind me and rolled down my arm and onto the damp earth by my feet.

"Couldn't we break through this?" I asked, reaching a hand up to touch the surface.

It was hard and dry, but it wasn't cement. With enough force, or with enough fingernails, couldn't we find our way past it?

Hammer limped toward me, obviously hurting from the ten-hour trek we'd endured, and pressed a chubby hand flat on the wall behind me. She scratched it with the tip of her index finger, and I looked up, seeing her wide nostrils flare and her chin form two rolls.

"I don't know," she said. "I'm sure with the right tools, you could. But I don't see the point." She took a step back, turned around, and dropped down beside me, a loud sigh blasting out of her lungs as she hit the ground. "You guys realize this is probably a game to them, right? See how long we last?" She threw her head back in frustration, and a soft *clunk* bounced across the room. "Besides, even if we did manage to get out... Didn't any of you see the hundreds of filthy ladies out there? They might not be wearing masks or carrying weapons, but they're still Northers."

Tegan placed her leaf into the dirt beside the wounded woman, rose to her feet, and walked to the other end of the cell. She sat at the very corner against the gate, the outside light forming diamonds on her arm, and closed her eyes.

Everyone went quiet, hoping she might say something. But she didn't. She sat still and silent.

The wounded woman rubbed her shadowed face and said, "They might be Northers, but they're not *them*."

"Them?" I asked.

"The ones who attacked us. Those filthy Northers"—she made air quotes with her fingers—"are the one reason we're still alive.

"What's your point?" Franklin said. "Spit it out."

The wounded woman's eyes rolled up at Franklin as if contemplating whether getting up and strangling her would be worth the pain in her leg. "My *point*," she spewed, "is that they're not all the same. Some of these women have been pushing pieces of bread through the holes in the gate."

We turned our heads toward the gate, where there was movement on the other side.

"Only at night," the woman continued. "One of them got caught during the day, and, well..." She waved a finger at the gate and everyone's eyes followed. At the very center was a bloody patch of braided bamboo.

"They killed her?" Coin spat out.

The woman nodded. "I'm Alice, by the way, and this is Arenas." She stuck a thumb out at the tiny shapeless woman.

Arenas gave a brief wave of a hand and joined Alice against the back wall. Everyone else followed suit, sat down, and introduced themselves.

"So, what?" Franklin said, scooping a handful of dirt and throwing it into the air. "We're supposed to sit here and rot? Starve to death?"

Alice picked at something in her wound. "That's the thing... They're not letting us die. They're making us suffer."

Franklin let out a forced laugh and threw her thumb in Hammer's direction. "I realize some of us might not be affected by starvation, but there are some"—she pointed at her chest—"who don't handle no food very well."

"What're you, hypoglycemic?" Coin asked, curling her upper lip over her front teeth.

Franklin barely had any meat on her as it was, so I could understand her anxiety about inadequate caloric intake. She glared at Coin, then shifted her gaze out through the gate. "None of your business," she mumbled.

What was she hiding from us?

"We have to be smart about this," Alice said, grinding her teeth. "We can't let them tear us apart."

I stared at Alice as she spoke. Her bottom lip was swollen, most likely due to a blow, and her scraggly auburn hair had been cut messily into uneven lengths. It looked like straw more than anything—dry and crispy strings that wiggled atop her head as she spoke. She was so worked up, her eyes round and hands moving about sporadically as she spoke.

"We need to plan," she went on.

She looked like a mother on the verge of a mental breakdown—a fragile woman containing a dangerous amount of bottled-up anger.

That was it.

That was what the Northers were doing.

They were trying to break us.

CHAPTER 5

Warm, muddy water splashed my face before I heard her voice.

"Wake up!" Zsasz shouted, her dark figure towering over us.

Behind her were two of her goons and Rebel, whose beady eyes remained glued to me the way they had in the jungle. What the hell was her problem?

I wiped my face and sat upright.

"Now!" Zsasz growled.

Franklin was the first to stand up, and the moment she did, Zsasz grabbed her by the arm and pulled her out of the prison cell.

"Franklin!" I shouted, bouncing to my feet.

But the door was slammed shut in my face, and all I could hear were Franklin's feet kicking the ground as they dragged her away.

"Get off me, you f—" she went on, her voice slowly fading into the distance.

The sound of something hard hitting flesh exploded and Franklin instantly went quiet. I swung around, my hateful glare fixated on all the cowards in the cell, not understanding why no one had bothered to try to help.

"She'll be back," Arenas said calmly as if human emotion were too volatile to express.

"Be back?" My shoulders bounced up and down, and I tried to catch my breath. "They dragged her away! For what? To torture her?"

Alice, who was waking up at last, stretched her lips into an upside-down smile while clasping both hands around her leg again. Her skin was as white as chalk, and there were beads of sweat sliding down her face and leaving trace marks on her dirt-stained skin.

She grunted in pain. "There's nothing you can do."

"Man," Coin said, her gumball eyes popping out at Alice, "you don't look so good."

"No, she doesn't," Johnson added.

"It's this—this damn spear wound..." Alice said and threw her head back against the wall.

I could tell she was in excruciating pain. Her leg was entirely swollen, and the wound, a crusty, pus-infested hole that was oozing out a clear liquid, looked worse than it did the day before.

"Sepsis," Tegan mumbled from her dark corner.

Everyone's eyes turned toward her. She poked a finger against her temple, then poked again, and again. What the hell had the Northers done to her?

"Sepsis," she repeated.

"I'm assuming she's talking about Alice," Johnson said. She got up, crouched beside Tegan, and looked her square in the face. "What can we do?"

Tegan shook her head, her rag hair dropping forward and masking her face entirely.

"Don't bother," Arenas said.

I kicked dirt from the ground, flinging bits and pieces into the air by Tegan, who flinched and cowered even farther against the wall.

"Will someone tell me what the fuck is going on?" I snapped. I hadn't meant to, but I couldn't help myself. Everyone was acting like we were sitting on a rollercoaster from hell, waiting for our next stop. Why wasn't anyone doing anything? Why were we sitting there like caged animals?

"Where are they taking Franklin?" I asked again, widening my eyes on Alice and Arenas.

I realized they didn't have all the answers, but they had a few days on us—they knew more than we did.

"They're beatin' her," Arenas said, her eyes fixated on my crocodile boots.

"That's it?" I asked. "Just beating her?" I laughed. "Well, I'm glad to know it isn't anything serious. I'm glad to know she's having a good fuckin' time!"

"Jesus, Brone," Johnson said.

"Shut up, Johnson!" I shouted.

I was exhausted, I was hurting, I was starving, and I was dehydrated to the point where I was barely able to swallow. I wasn't in the mood to be told to calm down.

I threw my head back, pulled at my hair, and screamed until my lungs ached and my voice cracked. The silence that followed was almost too much to handle. I stood there, breathing heavily, absorbing the energy around me: a combination of fear, anxiety, and angst. What was wrong with me? I looked around, and no one made eye contact. It was like they were afraid of me.

Is that who I wanted to be? Someone they feared? Trim wouldn't have wanted...

"Pssst."

I swung around, prepared to swing a fist at the next person who told me to calm down, but when I realized the noise hadn't come from inside, my eyes darted to the gate. There was a dark finger wiggling through one of the holes.

"Pssst, over 'ere."

I looked closer and saw a big brown eye pressed up against another hole a bit higher.

"Is what dey want, you know," the woman said. "Don't let 'em. Don't let 'em 'ave it. Be strong."

"Barbara!"

Her eye went even bigger and she pulled away.

"Don't be stupid," the other voice hissed. "If

they see you..." Her voice trailed off, along with rapid footsteps.

"You okay, Brone?" Hammer asked, her puppylike eyes rolling up at me.

I waved a hand and shook my head. I didn't want to talk about what had happened. I wanted to be left the hell alone.

"Sepsis," Tegan muttered again, her body now rocking back and forth.

"What are they doing to us?" Johnson asked, from the corner of the cell, her arms wrapped around her knees. I'd never seen her so afraid before.

No one answered.

"Did they take any of you yet?" Coin asked, breaking the silence.

Arenas shook her head. "No... They've only been taking Tegan. She comes back more messed up every time."

Coin ran both hands over her face and through her fuzzy hair over and over again, then let out a long sigh.

"Sepsis," Tegan said again and this time, slapped herself across the face.

I observed her as she pulled her bottom lip, her wild eyes rolling around in every direction, and it seemed like I was sitting in a mental asylum. What on Earth had they done?

What were they going to do to us? To me?

Maybe this was it.
Maybe this time, we weren't going to survive.

CHAPTER 6

Where was I?

I wiped the muck from the corner of my lips and inhaled a slow, painful breath. My muscles felt like they'd completely melted, leaving behind bones, tendons, and ligaments.

What was that smell?

"Snap out of it, Brone," someone said.

Snap out of what?

How much time had passed since Franklin was dragged away?

Why wasn't I hungry? When had I last eaten?

"Give her some water."

"She doesn't need any," someone growled.

"Johnson, back off. If we don't share, we won't make it."

"She's already had a lot!"

I rubbed my eyes with the back of my hands. Everyone was so blurry—a bunch of colorful pixelated figures sitting around the dark cell.

"What's that smell?" I moaned.

What—what was going on? I couldn't...

Something cool slipped over my cracked lips and into my mouth. I lunged forward, wanting to inhale it all at once, but all I felt was water splash on my face and down my neck.

"Goddamn it, Brone!"

"Our water!"

"She spilled our water!"

A round figure stomped its way over to me, and something hit me hard across the face. I raised a hand against my cheek, feeling the warmth of my skin underneath my fingertips. "What... what was that for?" I asked, gazing up at Hammer.

She stood stiffly with two hands on her waist, her nostrils flared and her shoulders drawn back. "A, to snap you the hell out of it. And B, because you wasted the bit of water we had."

I sat upright and reality set back in. I was sitting in the middle of the cell, my legs straight out in front of me. My boots were missing. Where were my boots?

And what was that smell? It was like sour rot combined with a teaspoon of honey—a sickening smell I'd encountered before.

I looked around the room, trying to understand what was going on when I saw her lying there looking like a porcelain doll with both hands resting on her chest. Dirt had been pushed up around her, forming a small contour that enveloped part of her body up to the height of her elbows.

I jumped back, my palms sinking into the dirt underneath me.

"Wh-what happened?" I asked, staring at Alice's ghostly face and blue lips.

"She died two days ago, Brone," Coin said, staring at me like I'd lost my mind.

She looked like everyone else in the room—a lightened complexion, crisped lips, and dark bags underneath her eyes—yet paler.

Johnson was curled up beside Arenas, whose eyes were red and swollen—most likely a result of her friend's death. Tegan was still in the same corner she'd been for as long as I could remember, and Hammer, having gained satisfaction from hitting me across the face, moved to the side of the cell and plopped herself down in the far corner. She looked smaller than usual, her pants sagging and her shirt looking too big for her.

I threw a hand over my nose. "W-why haven't they taken her out?"

Coin shook her head and shrugged.

"Out of the way!" someone shouted from outside.

Heavy footsteps approached the bamboo cage. There was a soft click, and the door swung open. It was Rebel, looking like a Cabbage Patch Kid with her horrible haircut. She stood arrogantly with her fingers wrapped around Franklin's tattooed arm, then smiled venomously and said, "Special delivery."

She threw Franklin into the cell, but Franklin didn't have the strength. She collapsed flat onto the dirt floor, crushing her bony arms underneath her. There were red gashes all over her shoulders—most likely a result of either being whipped or cut. But they weren't infected. They were scabbing over, which meant whoever had done this to her hadn't intended to kill her, only to make her suffer.

"Franklin!" Johnson said in a panic. She rushed to her side as though they'd been friends for years, even though several weeks ago, Johnson would have been more than happy to beat the living daylights out of her.

She pulled on her shoulders and rolled her onto her back. Rebel grinned a set of rotten teeth when Franklin rolled over, revealing a disfigured face. There were gashes across her cheeks—two on each side, to be precise—and they'd been cut deep enough to form permanent, unsightly scars.

"What did you do?" I shouted. I jumped to my feet but my knees gave out, and I landed in Coin's arms. I couldn't remember the last time I'd eaten.

"Ah, ah," Rebel said, pointing an ivory shiv straight out at me. She winked, making me want to tear her eyes out with my fingernails. "You'll get your turn, sweetheart."

She threw a piece of crisp carcass into the cell

and slammed the door shut. I didn't have time to see what it was because everyone lunged on it like a pack of starving wolves.

"Back off!" I shouted, my voice hoarse, and everyone froze as if they'd made eye contact with Medusa.

I stood hunched forward, my arms dangling on either side of my body. I wanted to hurt someone—anyone. Never in my life had I experienced so much rage. Why was this happening? Why couldn't they have killed us instead? They were torturing us. Making us lose all sense of reality.

But that was it, wasn't it? I was feeling exactly how they wanted me to feel. I wouldn't let them.

I stepped forward, and everyone stepped back.

Hammer stared at me the way a child does when they don't get their way—full of hatred and resentment from behind big eyes. "Just 'cause you're the leader, Brone, doesn't mean you get to eat first."

"Yeah!" someone else chimed in.

"It isn't for me," I said through clenched teeth. "And we're not goddamn animals. Stop acting like it! All it's going to do is get us killed. Is that what you want? To kill one of your own over a piece of"—I glanced down at the dirt floor, noting the bottom half of a burned rabbit—"rabbit? They're trying to turn us against each other. Can't you see it? They're trying to break us, and it's working. They won't have to kill us because we're going to do it to ourselves!"

Everyone stared at me, their eyes wild and nostrils flaring.

"I, for one, think Franklin needs this more than we do," I said. "We can share what's left."

No one answered, but their eyes shifted from side to side, at the rabbit and at each other.

"Brone's right," Coin said, her lips sticking together as she spoke. "We... we need to stick together." She coughed into her elbow, and her eyes rolled back up at everyone. "We need to be a pack if we want to survive this."

Tegan suddenly hovered over Franklin, brushing her fingertips over the wounds on her face.

"Clean," she said, then stood up and returned to her corner. She looked like a bag of bones or a dinosaur. Her spine formed bumps along the back of her shirt, and her elbows looked bigger than her actual arms.

"You need to eat something, too, Tegan," I said, but she didn't respond.

Johnson dug her nose into her elbow. "How's anyone supposed to eat with that smell?"

I followed her line of sight at Alice's dead body. Flies hovered around her face now, and her skin looked like Play-Doh.

"I don't know," I said impatiently. "Plug your

nose."

I could hear my own irritated tone as I spoke, but I couldn't stop myself. I was exhausted in every sense of the word. I reached down and tore the leg off the rabbit, a loud snap resonating off the walls, and handed it to Franklin.

She lay there, her swollen lips parted and eyes fixated on the ceiling above.

"What did they do to you?" I asked.

She didn't speak.

"Franklin," I said.

Nothing.

I rested a hand on her shoulder. "I can't even imagine the things they did to you, but we need you. Please don't disappear on us."

Her red eyes slowly rolled toward me, and I couldn't tell if she was about to laugh, cry, or scream. She stared at me like she'd never done before—a mindless gaze covering a deep, indescribable pain. It was as if the Franklin I'd known no longer existed.

All at once, her already disfigured face contorted so drastically she seemed unrecognizable. Her mouth hung upside down, her eyes disappeared behind two slits, and she let out a wail so intense it sounded like she was dying.

I reacted in a way I'd never thought myself capable of—empathetically. I wrapped my arms around her neck and pulled her head onto my chest. Where was this nurturing instinct coming from? I'd never had it before. All I knew was that one of our own was in pain and needed comfort.

"It's okay," I whispered, resting a firm hand on her head.

I could feel scabs all over her scalp, underneath my fingertips.

She cried and cried and cried, and everyone stared in absolute silence at the wreckage before them. No one attempted to take the rabbit meat, either. They bowed their heads as a way of showing respect for her suffering until finally, she stopped.

"You don't have to talk about it," I said, staring her in the face.

She nodded briefly, then cleared her throat. "Don't want to."

I let her go when I sensed her pull away. She sat up, reached her stick arm beside me, and picked up the rabbit leg.

"At least you're not *dead*," Arenas said grudgingly.

Franklin's eyes rolled up at her, and I thought for sure she'd slit Arenas's throat with a piece of broken rabbit bone.

"Might as well be," Franklin said, slowly taking a bite of meat. "I have lung cancer."

CHAPTER 7

I played at the skin of my thigh by pinching it and letting go.

It barely moved.

I laughed, and everyone looked up at me.

"What's so funny?" Coin asked.

I wondered if I looked like her—a skeleton figure they use in grade school with two dark holes for eyes in my face. She looked like a zombie, or even better, a vampire.

I laughed again and plopped my head back against the dirt wall.

"A few years ago, I'd have done about anything to be this skinny," I said. It wasn't all that funny, but all I could do was laugh. It was the closest thing to any emotion I'd felt in a long time.

Hammer scoffed. "You were one of those."

"I think everyone was one of those," Coin said, a subtle laugh under her labored breathing. "'Cept for me." She gave us a crooked smirk. "Alls I wanted was muscle."

She raised her arm and attempted to flex her

bicep, but nothing happened. Her body had already started eating away at her muscle.

Maybe they were trying to kill us—slowly and painfully.

The sun had gone down, and the only light within our cell came from two torches fastened on sconces outside the gate. It supplied a tiny bit of heat, which Franklin seemed to appreciate. She was pressed up against the bamboo gate, her fingers dangling through the holes and her scarred face pressed flat against her hand.

The sun had come and gone a dozen times, and she hadn't spoken a word about what had happened. And as the days went on and we decayed from the inside out, I wondered when they would come for me. I thought about my death and wondered if the afterlife existed. If I died, would my soul float up into the air? Would I be able to levitate myself to the Cove to check up on Ellie? Or would I find myself colliding with her soul somewhere atop Kormace Island? Maybe she'd died a long time ago.

* * *

I remembered thinking he didn't look real. He looked like a doll made of rubber or silicone.

I hadn't wanted to go to my grandfather's funeral, but my mom insisted. She said if I didn't go to say goodbye, I'd regret it. But the one thing I regretted was *going* to the funeral.

Before that day, the last memory I had of my grandfather was of him sitting in a nursing home with a toothless grin on his face and an oxygen tube inserted into his nostrils. I'd gone to visit him with my mom on his birthday and offered to play a game of chess with him.

The nurses had been wonderful. They'd baked him a batch of his favorite cupcakes—rainbow cake with vanilla frosting—and even sang a little birthday song for him.

That was the memory I wanted to hold on to.

Not this one.

Not his lifeless body lying in a wooden box for everyone to stare at.

That night, after we went home, I snuck into my bedroom and cried the night away. I hadn't cried when I found out about his death—only after.

It must have been the middle of the night when my mom came in to check on me. My bedroom door creaked open, and she slipped in past the sliver of yellow light. Her footsteps approached my bed, and I kept my eyes sealed shut. I didn't want her to know I'd been crying for hours.

I hated crying around anyone, and I cried a lot, which meant I spent a great deal of my time in bathroom stalls at school or under my blankets at home.

But she didn't say anything. Instead, she raised the corner of my blanket and slipped in beside me, the warmth of her body giving me all the comfort I needed.

She wrapped an arm around me, snuggled closer, and said, "It's not over for him, sweetheart. His soul is still with us, and one day, we'll all be together again."

I didn't answer.

I squeezed her arm tighter and started crying again until I fell asleep.

* * *

Now I was stuck with Ellie's last moment in my head—her panicked face when she realized I'd thrown her into the river. She'd looked so confused and betrayed all at the same time.

I wanted to cry, but I couldn't.

I couldn't feel anything.

Maybe this is what it was like to die of starvation and dehydration. Maybe my body was eating away at my emotions, too.

A soft plop sound caught my attention, but it was Franklin's jagged movement that told me someone had just dropped food into our cell. She scrambled onto her hands and knees until she found it and shoved it into her mouth.

"Hey!" Hammer growled, but another piece was pushed through the same hole in the bamboo gate.

This time, Hammer lunged forward with her elbows out. She stomped on it before Franklin had the chance to grab it, then reached down, picked it up, and shoved it into her mouth without even wiping it off.

I dashed into the growing crowd of prisoners, squeezing my way past Coin and Johnson, and pressed myself flat against the gate.

"Who's there?" I asked. "Can you let us out?"

"Sorry," the voice whispered. "If I do, they'll kill me."

The voice was soft and timid—almost familiar. I pictured a petite middle-aged woman with thin hair, sun spots, and a hunched back. I wasn't sure why; that was the face I'd associated with the voice.

"Who will?" I asked.

She shoved another piece of bread into the prison, and this time, Coin pushed Johnson out of the way and picked it up.

"Back off!" Johnson shouted.

"You back off!"

"Get out of the way!"

"Shut up!" I yelled, and the argument stopped.

I returned my attention to this mysterious woman by sticking my eye against the hole. She was wearing a hood over her head, masking her face from the torches' orange glow. She held a small basket filled with what appeared to be pieces of bread and mushy fruit.

"What's your name?" I asked, but she didn't answer. "Please," I continued, wrapping my fingers through the bamboo links. "Who's going to kill you? Who are they?"

She slowly raised her head, revealing a partially burned face that resembled melted plastic. The skin was pink and drooping underneath her dark eye, and her lips were missing entirely. I couldn't see her full head, but the part that I could see was bald, with a patch of black hair hanging over her missing eyebrow. What had happened to her?

"Northers," she growled.

I tightened my fingers on the gate and pulled myself closer. Was she one of ours? One of Murk's people? Why else refer to these monsters as Northers? It was our terminology for them—not theirs.

Coin pushed her way to the front of the crowd, throwing her elbows out to make space. She must have overheard the woman talking to me because her eyes were bulging out and she pressed her dark face against the gate.

"Who's there?" she asked. "Who are you? You one of us?"

But the woman didn't answer Coin, either. Instead, she shoved another small piece of bread through one of the holes followed by several pieces of fruit.

"Hang in there," she whispered. "You'll be out soon enough."

And with that, she swung away and

disappeared into the darkness of the night.

CHAPTER 8

The sun pierced the morning sky, forming a bumpy orange line at the bottom of the bamboo gate. I didn't know how many sunrises had passed since we'd been captured. I rubbed my eyes with the back of my hand—something I knew was a big no-no on the island.

As Rocket had once explained to me, eyes were very sensitive and were usually the first organs to absorb an infection or an illness. But I didn't care. Maybe I'd finally catch something. I still couldn't understand why I hadn't caught anything when I first landed on Kormace Island. Many women did, and many of them died. Yet, here I was, alive and well for the most part.

It was my turn, now, to catch some incurable disease, because I couldn't handle this anymore.

Yet I thought of Franklin and the news she'd let spill. Why hadn't she told us? Why keep something as serious as cancer to herself? It all made sense now. I understood why she was so angry all the time. She was dying, and she knew it.

I watched her as she sat with her legs crossed in the middle of the cell. Her knees were bigger than her legs because she'd already lost so much weight. She looked like a doll or a character built of sticks you'd find in one of Tim Burton's movies—an obsession my mom had. These movies were apparently over fifty years old, and my mom held a collection of something called DVDs.

I thought of my mom and smiled.

God, I missed her so much.

How was I supposed to continue living while knowing I'd never see her again?

Did she think of me? Was she thinking of me right now? Would she look for me after three years, or would the government come up with some fabricated tale about how I didn't survive the island? Even if they did, they'd probably be right—I'd die here sooner or later.

"Piss off!"

"Get off me!"

Footsteps shuffled.

"Guys!"

"Let—let go!"

Coin grabbed Hammer by the throat and pinned her against the back wall. She raised a tight fist and smashed it into Hammer's face.

Hammer tried to swing back but missed when Coin swung another fist into her stomach.

Johnson jumped in, grabbing Coin by the arms,

but she was thrown off before she could get a strong grip.

"Guys!" Arenas shouted, her short figure bouncing up and down beside the fight.

I rushed toward them and wrapped two solid arms around Coin's upper body.

"Get off me!" she growled.

I wasn't sure how I was managing to hold on to her, but I was.

"Stop it!" I said.

"Let go!" Coin shouted, trying to squirm out of my grip.

But I didn't. I did exactly as Eagle had done to Elektra when she'd had one of her tantrums. I held on, hoping for her anger to pass.

Hammer stepped aside, rubbing her fingers against her rosy cheek. It was obvious she hadn't wanted to fight.

Coin drew in a long breath and let it out, her chest deflating under my hold.

"You good?" I asked.

She didn't answer. Instead, I felt her chest bounce up and down in rapid movements. What was she doing? Laughing?

But the sound that came out of her mouth wasn't laughter at all. It was a long, choppy lament that filled the room with dreariness. She collapsed to her knees, bringing me down with her, and I held on to her as I'd done for Franklin.

She threw her head back, releasing another loud howl, her mouth wide open. She clawed at her cheeks, her fingernails digging into and pulling at the skin under her eyes.

"It's okay," I said, and she dropped her head onto my neck, sobbing the way I'd never seen a grown woman do before.

I caught Hammer's eyes and then Franklin's, and it was clear we all felt the same thing—a dark hopelessness capable of shattering one's will to live.

"It's o—" I tried, but the gate blasted open, and there stood Zsasz with that same horrid smirk on her face.

She stepped inside, rolled up her sleeve, and revealed a fresh cut on the inside of her wrist. She stared at us from behind her bright eyes that looked white in contrast with the dark paint around her eyes. Her skull mask was hanging at her chin, which meant she'd been wearing it.

Had she left the city? Gone out and killed more of our own?

She grinned this time, revealing a set of yellow canine teeth. "Wore the same clothes as you," she said, almost tauntingly.

I glared at her, imagining what it would feel like to rip out her heart with my bare hands. I'd make her pay when the time was right. I'd kill her. I'd fucking kill her.

"Little redhead," she went on. "Looked pretty young, too."

Little redhead? Who was she talking about? None of the Hunters were redheads.

"What do you want?" Johnson shouted.

"Sweet little brown eyes," Zsasz continued. "Got all big when I stuck a knife in her stomach, though."

I couldn't. I just couldn't.

I lunged straight at her face, swinging my arms to grab anything I could. Hair, skin, her eyes—I didn't care. I needed to hurt her, make her suffer. Even if it meant she'd kill me afterward.

But something hard suddenly knocked me against the side of my face. My ear rang, and everything went fuzzy. I took a few steps back and collapsed flat on my side.

Someone rushed over; I couldn't tell who—only that they were checking to make sure I hadn't died.

Then, there was screaming, followed by what sounded like punches or slaps.

What was going on?

"Let her go!"

Another scream.

I tilted my head up, but all I saw were blurry silhouettes that appeared to be dancing with each other.

Someone was fighting, but I couldn't see who it was.

I was able to make out Zsasz, though, because of her heavy equipment and that jiggly bun on her head. She swung a backhand fist, and whoever was trying to attack her was propelled into the air and back into the prison cell.

Two other people from the outside of the cell came in and scooped someone up.

I blinked.

"Fr-Franklin," I tried.

They were dragging her away again.

CHAPTER 9

"She's back."

I blinked hard and opened my eyes, immediately regretting it.

Coin's swollen face hovered inches away from mine, and her rancid breath crept into my nostrils. It looked like her left eye had been injected with Botox—the same look I'd given Hammer awhile back. She must have noticed the grimace on my face, because she gave me a sly smirk and said, "Shiner, or what?"

"What happened?" I moaned.

I stretched my jaw, and a shooting pain radiated into my neck and down my back.

"We tried to defend you," she said. "Crazy bitch ain't human."

I sat up. "We?"

Johnson was sitting against the wall with one arm over her knee, and one hand over what appeared to be an injured arm.

"Dislocated her shoulder," Coin said, following my gaze.

I cringed.

"You feelin' okay?" she asked.

Dizzy, I rubbed my jaw and shook my head. "What happened?"

"She clocked you with a stick or somethin'."

"Nice," was all I could say.

And then, it all came back to me. "Franklin!"

But Coin pressed a hand on my shoulder, forcing me back down. She looked at the ground solemnly and shook her head.

"Nothing we can do," Johnson said. "Story of our lives, though, isn't it?" she scoffed. "Always suffering at the hands of someone else."

I wasn't sure where this was coming from.

Unexpectedly, she let out a laugh—a deep, unpleasant laugh that sounded more like a grunt than anything else. "Three years," she said. "Three fucking years! That's what they gave me. I've sat on this nightmare of an island for over fifteen years now. I think. I don't even know. Maybe it's been twenty. Not like we keep a calendar handy! Why do we even try? I mean, what's the point? I'd rather be dead. I'm done. I'm fucking done."

The cell went quiet until Hammer cleared her throat. "Been about the same for me, Johnson. I hear you. I do. I hate it here. This isn't a life anyone should ever have to live. But so help me God, I'm not givin' up until those demons"—she pointed a stiff finger at the bamboo gate—"pay for everything they've done."

Hammer was right. As much as I hated the prospect of being alive right now, I was living for one thing and one thing only—revenge.

I stood up, using the wall behind me for support, and drew my aching shoulders back. I was so weak it seemed like venom was seeping through my muscles, as though my bones might snap like autumn twigs if I were to shift my weight the wrong way.

"Hammer's right," I said. "They need to pay for this." I pointed a finger at the ground but closed my fist when I realized I was shaking. "They're doing everything they can to break us, but we can't let them. We have to stay strong." I swallowed hard, and my throat made a sticking sound. "We need to support each other when one of us wants to give up. And we can't be turning against each other." I eyed Hammer and Coin, and they nodded awkwardly.

No one objected. They stood like a herd of sheep, awaiting a command.

My mind was made up. We would devise a plan—something well thought out and calculated. There had to be a way out of this. These women were primitive savages. Surely, we could outsmart them.

Somehow...

I stared at the prison gate, the dirt floor, and

the filthy women around me, including Alice's dead body, which had already started decomposing. Everyone was covered in so much dirt, their eyes looked like brand-new golf balls.

But something caught me off guard: the sound of footsteps approaching. What was going on? Why were they coming back? It wasn't like Zsasz to come back on the same day. She usually waited days, or weeks, before returning.

Heavy boots ticked against the bottom of the gate, and the latch unlocked.

Several figures darkened the space behind the gate, and it opened, revealing Zsasz and Rebel. They stared at us for a moment as if contemplating who they were going to choose next.

Dear God...

This was it. They were going to pluck me out and torture me. Torture me for having lunged at Zsasz. They were going to make an example of me.

And if not me, someone else. We needed all the women we had. I glanced at Tegan. Why couldn't they take her? She was already a mess. Guilt crept into the pit of my stomach for even thinking it, but I was in survival mode—I couldn't control my thoughts.

Zsasz opened the door even farther and a humid gust of wind came sweeping in. Yet she didn't come in or try to grab anyone.

What was she doing?

Her hideous stripe-scarred lips curled up and she extended an open palm out and away from the prison cell.

"Welcome to General Population."

CHAPTER 10

"This way," the old woman said, tugging at Coin's arm.

But another woman who looked a little less beaten stepped forward and grabbed my hand. "No, this way."

The old woman—the one who'd grabbed Coin's hand—bared her partial set of teeth and let out a hiss.

"Barbara!" the young woman snapped. I knew that name. It was the name of the woman who'd come to see us that one evening—the one who'd told us to be strong. She looked familiar, too— maybe she was the crazy lady I'd seen when I'd first stepped foot on this territory. "Do you remember the agreement?"

Barbara nodded her matted head. She reminded me of an unkempt submissive dog—the kind who liked to push their boundaries, but when scolded, quickly retreated in fear of being punished. I could tell she was more of a follower than a doer.

"New girls go with... with food people," Barbara said slowly.

"That's right," the young woman said. "So, these women are coming with me."

Barbara scowled at her from behind narrow hazel eyes, turned her hunched back away from us, and left with a noticeable limp.

"Don't mind her," the woman said, eyeing each of us. Half of her head was shaved on one side, and the other half hung down to her jawline in orange waves. Freckles covered her face, her neck, and her shoulders. She didn't look very old—maybe early twenties—which meant she couldn't have been here that long.

"I'm Alice," the woman said, pressing a flat hand on her chest.

Arenas scoffed, and Alice's wild eyes turned on her.

"That's great," Arenas said, shaking her head over and over. "Just fuckin' great... Goddamn *cabrona*."

Alice looked at me and cocked her brow. I shook my head. "The dead woman in the cell was named Alice."

Alice's face went flat as if she were trying to process an empathetic response. But nothing happened. She stared at Arenas for a few seconds, the freckles on her face looking yellow underneath the afternoon sun, then swung around on her heels. "Well, she's dead. Now, follow me."

Arenas stiffened and formed balls with her fists, but I pressed a hand over her chest.

"Alice Number Two," she grumbled under her breath.

I squeezed her forearm and nodded. "Alice Number Two."

Alice Number Two led us through a crowd of women who circled us like vultures. Someone clasped their cold hand around my wrist, but when I swung around to see who it was, they'd already let go.

"Come on, Alice, you can share! We need help at the Materials Station!"

Alice Number Two didn't respond. She kept walking, her head raised high as if she'd won a bid at an auction.

We walked passed a wooden shelter that looked like a tiki bar you'd see in the Caribbean by the ocean. It had a hay or yellow grass roof, and four thick wooden poles supported the entire structure. Underneath it was a woman with a bald, scarred head that looked deformed, almost like she'd been slapped with a bible over the head as a baby.

There was something off about her—she looked disabled. Her bottom lip was drooping on one side, and she twitched every time she swung her metal rod against what appeared to be another piece of metal. It made a sharp intermittent clunking noise as we walked by, but what bothered me most was the material she was using.

How the hell had they gotten ahold of metal?

"That's Smith," said Alice Number Two, and Johnson let out a chortle. Alice Number Two's eyes shifted to her. "That's the name she was given."

"Given?" I asked.

I glanced over at Smith, realizing something I'd missed before. Her ankle was tied and fastened to the stool underneath her.

"She's the only one who makes the weapons," said Alice Number Two. "The Originals don't want anyone else having access to them. So that means"—she pointed a crooked finger at our faces—"don't go near Smith because she's been trained to gut anyone who gets too close."

"Originals?" Hammer said, watching Smith with an alien admiration.

Alice Number Two cocked an eyebrow. "Did Murk not tell you anything about us?"

I gritted my teeth at the mention of Murk's name. She had no right using it. Not after what her people had done to ours. I swallowed hard, fighting the urge to tackle her to the ground and bash her face in until it turned to soup.

But I couldn't do it. There were too many of them.

"The Originals," she repeated. She cocked her

head to the side when we didn't react. "The Orphans? Does that mean anything to you?"

She was staring at us as if this was supposed to trigger a memory. But it didn't. The only thing Murk had ever told us was that Rainer decided to leave, along with dozens of women, to build her own colony. What on Earth did orphans have to do with Kormace Island?

"We don't know what you're talkin' about," Coin said. "And honestly, we don't give a shit about you or your shitty little civilization you have here. Y'all a bunch of crazy bitches anyway. And where the hell is Franklin?"

It was obvious that Coin was sleep, food, and water deprived. She wasn't usually this bold.

Alice Number Two stared at her for a while, not once blinking. But Coin didn't back down. She crossed her frail arms over her chest and pulled her shoulders back. It didn't do much, though. She'd lost so much muscle mass in the last few weeks or months, that her bulldog look had become more of a Boston terrier look.

"Who's Franklin?" Alice Number Two finally asked, not a shred of emotion on her face.

I couldn't tell whether she was mentally delayed or downright psychotic—it was hard to differentiate between the two.

"Our friend!" Coin snapped, lunging forward.

Hammer and I both grabbed her at the same

time, stopping her midair.

"Oh," said Alice Number Two. "You mean that lanky woman with the tattoos?"

Her voice was so monotone, it was irritating.

"That's the one," Coin said through clenched teeth. We were still holding her by the arms, her head sticking out ahead of her body, and caramel-colored veins popped out of her neck.

Alice Number Two smirked. "First of all, your *friend* is no longer your friend." She wiggled a finger at Tegan, who was at the very back of the line, her head bowed low and her fingers interlocked in front of her. "Like this one. There's no one left in there."

I realized I was digging my fingernails into Coin's arm when she grimaced at me and yanked herself out of my grip.

"And secondly," she continued, "you might want to reconsider your next move."

This time, she'd directed her words at Coin. What was that supposed to mean? Coin breathed hard through wide nostrils, her eyes fixated on the Norther in front of her. Hammer was still holding on, and I feared that if she let go, Coin would snap this woman in half.

"We have a few rules here," said Alice Number Two, waving around that same freckled finger. She twirled in a circle as she spoke, pointing her finger out in every direction. "Nothing major... You'll get to learn them as you go. But when it comes to violence..." She let out a laugh, and it sounded like a car stalling—loud and choppy. "If you value your life at all, I'd suggest you fight your violent tendencies."

Everyone was watching her intently, trying to understand what she was getting at. Would a swing of a fist cost us our lives? I wouldn't have expected that on Northern territory—not by how violent and merciless they'd already proven themselves to be.

"The rule goes as follows," she continued as if reading notes off a piece of paper. "If a fight breaks out, all participants must enter a death match until one survivor remains. Should these participants refuse to battle to the death, it is the duty of surrounding women to terminate all parties involved."

"A death match?" Hammer blurted out. "With who? And terminate? What the hell are you talking about?"

Alice Number Two brushed the tips of her fingers against Hammer's cheek, and a cryptic smile formed on her galaxy face.

"It's simple, really," she said, using her own words this time around. "If your friend here"—she poked Coin in the chest—"takes a swing at me, we fight to the death. And if we refuse to fight, which I most definitely wouldn't..." Her smile turned into a grin and she patted Hammer on her cheek. "We both die."

CHAPTER 11

I didn't know what to think of them. They looked like slaves, but on the other hand, some of them stared at us with savage eyes as if prepared to rip the skin off our faces with their bare hands.

"Try not to make eye contact," Coin said, dipping a long pepper into a bucket of warm water.

I scoffed. "Kind of hard when they're all staring at us like zoo animals."

Johnson, Hammer, Tegan, and Arenas were sitting in the dirt with piles of long-rooted vegetables at their feet. They'd been told to tear off the roots and clean the vegetables while Coin and I cleaned off any remaining dirt.

There was another group of women working in the food section, but it was apparent they wanted nothing to do with us. They sat at the opposite end of the cultivation station, grunting and growling as they tore food out of the ground, cut through raw bloody meat, and skinned animals I couldn't even identify.

As we'd had in the Village, there was a cage with

turkeys and wild birds inside of a wooden shelter with bamboo fencing. It wasn't very big—maybe the size of a small bedroom closet—but only big enough for the birds to breathe and hop over each other's heads.

"So, this is what we survived for?" Coin tore a leaf off an ugly ginger-looking plant. "Slavery?"

Hammer splashed a long pepper into water, then pulled it out and shook it off. "Better than death."

"Is it?" Arenas asked. "This is worse than the life I grew up in. Worse than gangs. Worse than havin' your mom come home with a new guy every night. Worse than your own *hermano* tryin' to sell you heroin. Worse than—"

"We get it," Johnson cut her off. She glanced up toward the group of women who were chopping up slices of bloody meat. "None of us are happy about it. So, shut up and keep your head down unless you wanna end up like Franklin."

"Or like Trim," Coin mumbled.

"You shut your face!" Hammer shouted, pointing a wet finger at Coin.

"Guys!" I hissed as dozens of eyes rolled toward us. "You heard Alice—"

"Number Two," Arenas slipped in.

"Unless you want to be forced to fight to the death," I continued, "keep your mouths shut."

"You ain't got no say in this," Coin said, her dark

eyes narrowing on me. "You're the reason Trim's dead."

I clenched my fists and stared at her, my eyes widening to the point of discomfort. Why was she suddenly defending Trim? Taking her side? She barely knew her. She didn't need to remind me of what had happened. I already felt responsible. I already believed Trim had given her life for mine. What was she trying to prove?

"Whose side are you even on?" I asked, narrowing my eyes into a hateful glare.

"Trim would have a plan," Coin went on. "She'd find a way outta here. Yeah, maybe I didn't know her all that well, but Trim was the leader of the Hunters. Everyone knew that. And now, what? We're supposed to be relyin' on you? For what? Girl, you ain't cut out for this. You're unpredictable and emotional is what you is. And if you'd had half the balls Trim did, you'da stepped up when the Northers asked us who our leader was."

I couldn't believe it. Why was Coin turning on me? She'd been by my side for weeks. Where was this coming from? I bit down, my jaw clicking, and breathed in slowly through flared nostrils. I was enraged and hurt by her betrayal, but I had to think with my head, not my emotions, before reacting.

I contemplated keeping my mouth shut to avoid escalating the issue, but I couldn't. I couldn't sit there and let her bash me in front of everyone—

not after what Trim had done. Not after she'd sacrificed herself to save me.

As I stared at her, biting down on my tongue, I considered stripping her of her ego—pointing out all of her flaws until she felt like nothing more than a molecule invisible to the human eye—but that wouldn't resolve the situation.

So instead, I swallowed my pride and did what I thought any reputable leader would have done; I reassured her.

"I get that you're not yourself right now," I said, "but turning on me isn't going to bring Trim back. I didn't know she was going to step forward. If I'd known, I'd have stepped up first. I froze. I'm human, like you. I get scared, same as you. I got scared, okay?" Her eyes softened, and she sat quietly, taking in every word. "I'm not perfect. I didn't ask to be looked at as a leader. Because I'm not a leader, and I never have been. But all I can do is try my best. We're all trying our best in this hellhole. You think I want this? You don't think I've thought about dying every single day?" I pause, eyeing everyone in our circle. "I can't possibly be the only one who's thought about suicide."

A few nodded but they broke eye contact.

"So please," I continue, returning my attention to Coin, "give me a break. I'm going to figure this out. We're going to figure this out. But we have to be on the same team. It's us against them. Don't forget that."

Everyone stared at me, a heavy silence weighing down amid the cacophony of the Northern city—metal clanging against metal; muscles and ligaments being torn off carcasses; women bickering back and forth; elephants stomping through the crowds, and monkeys screaming at the tops of their lungs.

I looked back and noticed a small brown-and-white monkey sitting atop an old woman's shoulder. He pointed straight ahead, his mouth wide open with sharp canine teeth revealed, then hopped on her head, climbed back down onto her shoulder, and dropped to the ground.

Was that thing a pet? What a bizarre place.

"I'm sorry," Coin said, breaking the silence.

I turned back to her and caught her guilty gaze but didn't say anything.

"Ain't myself," she said.

Hammer patted Coin on the back. "No one is. That's what they wanted."

"Let's stick together," I said. My eyes slowly found their way back toward Smith's cabin, where she stuck a blade over a hot flame, pulled it out, and beat down on it with another piece of metal. "And find out where the hell this metal is coming from."

CHAPTER 12

"Get in the back of da line if ya know what's good for ya," the woman growled, her exaggerated overbite making her look like a witch you'd read about in fairy tales.

She limped forward, keeping pace with the lineup. There were at least a hundred of them—women wearing dirty, bloodstained rags—forming a crooked line, waiting to be fed. Every time we tried to step inside the line, we encountered ferocious eyes and bared teeth.

"Get to the back!"

"Worthless scum!"

"Let's go," I said, walking down the line.

Something unexpectedly caught my foot, and I was thrown forward and flat in the dirt. I jumped back to my feet, wiped the dirt from my lips, and swung around with clenched fists.

A woman wearing a bonnet hat and a necklace made of rocks opened her big, toothless mouth and let out a laugh that sounded like an explosion. She stuck a finger straight out at me, placed a hand on her stomach, and kept on laughing. Everyone around her joined in like a bunch of dumb hyenas.

As much as I'd have loved to tackle her to the ground and bash her face in, I knew it wasn't worth it. I'd seen enough death over the last twenty-four hours, and I didn't want more blood on my hands. And honestly, I didn't have the energy to fight.

I turned away and continued down the crowd of hungry women. When we finally reached the end, Hammer punched a fist into her palm. "Should've decked her."

You're unpredictable and emotional, I recalled.

Even though Coin's words had manifested out of anger, exhaustion, and starvation, there had been truth in them. Every time someone upset me, my first thought was to attack. Who was I becoming? What was I becoming? An animal like everyone else on this godforsaken island.

I shook my head. "We don't know how these women are. Just because Alice Number Two said fighting leads to a one-on-one death match, doesn't mean it's true. They might've all jumped us. We should hang low for a while and keep our eyes open. Get to learn the ropes first."

"What happened to her?" someone asked.

I turned around.

A woman with a scabby hairless head and an unhealthily round, almost swollen face stared past us and at Tegan, who was scratching her head and squishing herself up against Hammer.

"Orphans got her?" the woman asked.

What was she talking about? Who were these *Orphans*?

"What are you talking about?" I asked.

The woman shook her head and smiled, revealing two front teeth. "I'm assuming you 'aven't heard of the story, then?"

"What story?" Coin cut in, crossing her bony arms over her flattened chest.

The woman shook her head again, and this time, her eyes darted in every direction. "The dangerous ones. They're orphans... All of them. They came here a long time ago."

"Get to the point," Coin said.

"Murk never told us the full story," someone said.

I recognized that voice.

From behind the scabby-headed woman came a figure—a hooded woman bowing her head to mask her face from the sunlight.

"You," I said.

She'd been the one to bring us bread. She didn't look up. Why had she spoken of Murk? She was obviously one of us. Why was she hiding?

She stepped forward, her face dark and hidden beneath her hood.

"What're you talking about?" I asked. "Who are you?"

The woman slowly raised a hand—a pink, bubbly-skinned claw that looked like raw flesh—and pulled the hood off her head.

I couldn't believe it.

Half of her head was completely unrecognizable—a mess of red, brown, and translucent bubbles for a face and melted skin with patches of black hair for a scalp—but the other half—porcelain skin, eyes as dark as coal, and thin flat lips that made her look like she was always in a bad mood—I recognized perfectly well.

It was Sumi—our old Village cook.

CHAPTER 13

"Who else was with you?"

"How did you get out?"

"Sumi, say something!"

"Guys, back off!" I shouted, and Hammer and Coin took a step back with their hands up by their faces.

Sumi pulled the hood back over her head and averted her gaze, obviously embarrassed by her scars.

"It's only me," she said, her voice barely audible amid the chaotic sound of women yapping away in the lineup.

We all took a small step closer, and the woman with scabbed skin waved a hand in the air as if to say, *Carry on*, and walked away, keeping her place in line. The last thing I was thinking about was food. I needed to hear what Sumi had to say. I needed answers. I'd miss mealtime if I had to.

"They caught me and Sara"—she looked at Coin as if this name meant something—"a few hours after we made it out. It was Trim... She brought us out. Is she okay? Have you seen her? What about the Hunters? A few of them were helping us get out of the burning Village, but I don't know... I just..." She shook her head, and her hood danced from side to side. "It was too chaotic. There was so much screaming. So much smoke. I couldn't tell who was who, so I ran."

I swallowed hard, my throat swelling.

Why was I even here? If anyone deserved to be living and breathing right now, it was Trim.

"Some of the Hunters are okay," I said. "But Trim didn't make it."

She raised her head, her dark eye staring at me from underneath red bubbly skin, and I looked away. I couldn't own up to what had happened.

"They grabbed me, and they found Sara on the ground before the fire spread." She turned away and pulled the hood down even farther to shield her face. "She had an arrow in her back... The infection spread before she even made it here."

"I'm sorry," Coin said.

I didn't know who Sara was, but it was apparent that Coin knew her and Sumi cared deeply for her.

"It's okay," Sumi said. "I'm glad she isn't here."

"Why didn't they kill us?" Arenas asked, brushing a delicate hand through her black hair. "Doesn't make sense to me. Why us? What do they want?"

Sumi shook her head. "I haven't figured that out

yet. It's a big game. I think they're keeping us, the healthy ones, for work."

Johnson scoffed. "By torturing us?"

"By breaking you," Sumi said.

"Look," I cut in, "what can you tell us about them? About the Northers? The more we know, the easier it'll be to get the hell out of here."

Sumi let out a forced laugh. "Still as stubborn as when I first met you."

"I wasn't stubborn," I said sharply. "You were a bully."

She let out a long sigh and raised her head, one eye catching mine. "You're right... I'm sorry. I resented you for being new... for being a Hunter."

"I know," I said. "Fisher told me. She explained everything."

"Fisher?" Sumi asked. "Is she—"

"Guys," Johnson cut in. "I hate to break this family reunion, but we have more important things to talk about right now."

"Girl's right." Hammer crossed her arms over her chest, the skin of her triceps flattening against her sides. I couldn't believe how much weight she'd lost. "Where's the metal coming from? And what're they doing with Franklin?"

"Franklin?" Sumi asked. "That tall girl with tattoos?"

Hammer nodded.

"I remember her," Sumi went on. "She used to

ask for—"

"The Northers have her," Coin cut in. "Or whoever the hell they are. Man, I don't know what's goin' on anymore. Ain't they all Northers? Who are these women?" she swung around on her heels, her eyes darting from side to side.

Sumi slouched. "I don't know what they're doing with Franklin. She isn't the first to be taken away. A few of our people have disappeared, and they haven't come back."

"That's great," Arenas said, waving her arms from side to side. "Just great."

Sumi ignored her. "And these women are all Northers, technically. I think I've figured it out, though."

Dozens of women gathered in the empty space in front of us, moving us farther back in the line, but I didn't care.

"I think they're divided by class," Sumi said. "Peasants, I guess... And royalty, or military. I don't know how else to describe it. We don't have any rights here. We do what we're told and when we're told by the Originals or the Orphans. It's a long story. We cook for them... make clothes for them. Forge weapons for them. And the Peasants, meaning us, come from everywhere. Some of them are fresh drops and the Orphans catch them. They're not all bad. The Northers, I mean. It's the Originals and the Orphans who are the most dangerous, aside from a few Peasants who try to control the city. Most of these Northers are slaves."

"Who are these Originals? Or Orphans?" I asked. This wasn't the first time I'd heard the term. "And where's the metal coming from?"

"Whoa," Hammer said, sticking out a flat hand in front of her face. "You're confusing me. Too many terms being thrown around. We've always known the Northers as being bad... Evil, even. So, let's keep it that way. When we say Norther, from now on, we're talkin' about the crazy ones." She twirled a finger in the air. "These women aren't Northers. They were captured."

Coin shrugged. "Yeah. That makes sense to me."

"Originals, Orphans," Hammer went on... "They're Northers. Plain and simple."

Sumi barely moved. "Okay, fine."

"Keep going," I said. I wanted to hear more.

"We could talk about this for hours," Sumi said and paused, her hooded head swiftly turning from side to side. "But it's better if I show you."

CHAPTER 14

You sure it's safe for us to be leavin' the city?" Coin asked, slipping through a wall of banana leaves.

Sumi didn't turn around. "We have to be quick about it, that's all. There are Northers positioned around the territory, sealing us inside. It's not like we can run away. As long as you're not on duty, it's fine."

After supper, which had been nothing more than a piece of bread, two nuts, and a handful of fruit, Alice Number Two had relieved us of our posts. She'd said something along the lines of, "Go make friends," which was a patronizing way of telling us to get lost. She hadn't even bothered to tell us where we were to sleep, and when Johnson brought it up, Alice scoffed and turned away as if the idea of a bed was a luxury we'd never experience again in this lifetime.

There were hammocks lined up along the edges of the city—some hanging from trees, others from wooden posts—but it was evident by their uniqueness that these were all individually crafted, which meant they belonged to specific individuals or crews. I had the feeling that if we were going to create a living space for ourselves, we'd have to be willing to fight to keep it. Until we understood the social class system in this city, we weren't building anything.

"We need to be back before sundown," Sumi added.

The sky above us had turned a bright marmalade orange, although it was difficult to see with all the leaves and branches overhead. In a few hours, it would darken to a light indigo filled with bright stars resembling snowflakes in a winter storm.

The last thing we wanted was to traverse the jungle at night. We'd always avoided doing that, and it wasn't about to change anytime soon, especially if Northers were positioned around the city's perimeter. One little rustle in the darkness would attract arrows to our backs.

"Don't make much sense to me," Coin said, stepping over a diseased branch. "Why would the Northers keep a bunch o' women as slaves, but let them walk outta the city? Ain't much control there if you ask me."

"If you think about it," Hammer said, "it's pretty"—she tripped over something and stumbled forward. Johnson let out a laugh, but Arenas helped straighten her back up. We were lucky that

Tegan had stayed behind. She'd returned to the bamboo prison, sat by the gate, and refused to get up. "It's pretty genius," she continued. "It's an illusion. A false sense of freedom."

"What you talkin' about, you?" Coin asked.

But it all made sense to me. Had they decided to chain us, or build walls around us, they'd have increased the risk of a rebellion. This way, they were able to make demands, while also brainwashing the women into believing they had a comfortable life so long as they stayed within the city's perimeter.

"It's perfect," Hammer went on. "These women are abused and forced to live in certain conditions, but it's all they know. Then they're taught that they can explore a bit, but only a bit. Kinda like Stockholm Syndrome."

"Stalk—what?" Coin asked.

"This is nothing like Stockholm Syndrome," Johnson said.

"Kinda makes sense," Arenas said. "They're being abused."

"You don't know anythin' about these women!" Coin said, her voice reaching a little farther than necessary. "You can't say they're happy here! No one said they even wanna be here!"

"No one said anything about being happy," I cut in. "The Northers know how to maintain control of their people—plain and simple. They have a leash on these women, but they let it loose enough for them to feel a false sense of independence."

"D'you see them cower away when Zsasz walked through the crowd?" Coin asked. "Ain't no independence in that."

"Either way," I said, "the Northers aren't stupid. Let's try to remember that. They may be barbaric and uncivilized, but they know what they're doing, which means we have to be careful."

Something glistening in the distance caught my eye, and the cool scent of salt water filled my nostrils. The ocean?

Sumi stopped walking and turned toward us, her hood resting on her shoulders. "Murk told us that Rainer turned against her in the Village—that she convinced other women to join her in starting a new civilization."

Everyone nodded. We all knew the story—it had been told countless times around the Village fire. It was the kind of story you'd find in the Bible, similar to Satan, once having been God's right hand, turning against him and convincing others to follow.

"That's not exactly how it happened," Sumi said, and everyone stared at her with big eyes.

"A few months after being dropped on Kormace Island, Rainer got into a fight with Murk's right hand, Baretta, and accidentally killed her. So, Murk banished her. Told her to get out.

Apparently, Rainer begged her to stay and told her she was pregnant, but Murk didn't believe her. A few dozen women, disgusted by Murk's decision to banish a self-proclaimed pregnant woman, left with Rainer and together, they made their way up north in search of a place to call home. They're the Originals—the few women who turned against Murk. They're hateful and think Murk and anyone who stayed behind deserves to burn in hell."

"So, is Zsasz an Original?" I asked.

"No," Sumi said. "When the Originals made their way north, that's when they found them... The Orphans."

Johnson flung two hands in the air, her unkempt hair wiggling atop her head. "Spit it out already! Who are the Orphans?"

But Sumi didn't answer. Instead, she took a step back, the melted half of her face looking silver beside the ocean's reflection, and pulled aside a curtain of leaves.

What I saw next was the last thing I'd expect to ever see on this island.

It lay there in the sand, looking like an ancient artifact. Its wings had been taken off, and all that remained was the cockpit, half of its body, and leather seats that looked like they'd either been eaten away by the ocean's salt or stripped down by the Northers for resources.

On the side of the plane, along what remained

of the passenger windows, was red writing. It wasn't in English, either, and although I couldn't make out what it said, I knew it was Russian.

"There were twenty-seven of them," Sumi said somberly. "At least, that's what I've heard around the city. Twenty-seven Orphans. Now there're twelve remaining. Russia decided to ignore the airspace restriction and dropped off a bunch of little girls."

No one spoke. It was like staring at a crime scene. I couldn't believe my eyes or my ears. But it all made sense now.

"Did it crash?" Hammer asked, the loose skin of her face jiggling.

Sumi shrugged. "After being shot down, yeah."

I cringed. I didn't want to imagine a bunch of little girls screaming for their lives as their plane came crashing down. They hadn't asked for any of this.

"What're you saying?" Johnson asked. "Those crazy bitches are Russian orphans? Zsasz and others like her were raised on this island?"

Sumi nodded. "Rainer's the one who found them. I'm only telling you what I've heard from a few of the Peasants. And all I know is that those Orphans have been raised in combat and taught to think that Murk and all of her people deserve to burn in hell for what they did to Rainer."

PART FOUR

PROLOGUE

I looked up at her and wondered if she was real.

Maybe this was all a dream—a horrific nightmare that would eventually lead to me waking up in a pool of cold sweat. I'd get up confused, wondering if maybe I'd pissed myself, before realizing I was fine, that I was home safe in the comfort of my apartment and I'd left my bedroom window open on a cold autumn night. I'd probably bundled myself up too tight in my duvet, which always led to a night of tossing and turning.

I'd then sit up, frustrated for not only having soiled my clothing but also for having dampened my bedsheets.

But I didn't wake up.

Crack.

I blinked hard, a tingling sensation spreading across my cheeks and along my jawline. It looked like she was enjoying it. She smiled down at me, her zebra-striped scars on her lips widening.

What a fucking monster.

This time, it was her boot that came down at

me, and my entire head shook.

Although I didn't know what was going on, I knew I was in pain but couldn't feel it. I could taste it though—a warm, rusty fluid in my mouth—and I licked the blood over my teeth and spat out a glob.

"Don't know your place yet?"

Smack.

I fell flat on my side, my eyes rolling back momentarily.

I reached out a hand, clawing at dried-up dirt and debris at the center of the city, but her boot suddenly came down hard, and I heard the crack before I felt the excruciating pain radiate from my fingers and into my hand.

I let out a scream, but it was cut short when she stomped down on my head, nearly dislocating my jaw. Everything went blurry, and all I could see around me were women who looked like nothing more than empty shells, their heads bowed and shoulders slouched. They stood around the spectacle, their filthy faces barely visible beneath their cowardice.

How could they stand there watching?

"You all know how it works around here," Zsasz shouted, and all I could see was the silhouette of her now shapeless boots walking away from me. "But it seems you need a reminder!"

"A reminder!" someone repeated in the background.

I knew that voice—it was Rebel, Zsasz's dumbass sidekick.

She was probably reveling in this.

"Stick to the rules," Zsasz continued, "and you'll have a nice life here. It's not complicated."

"Got it?" I heard nearby, and the next thing I knew, Zsasz was crushing her weight down on my now broken fingers.

I let out another scream, but she didn't budge. I clawed at her shin, begging for her to stop, but she stood there, pushing down even harder.

"This helping you remember?" she asked.

"P-please!" I shouted, tears streaming down my face and saliva splashing on my cheeks. "Stop! Just stop!"

"What's the rule?" she asked.

"Please stop!"

I pulled on her pant leg, but it did nothing. She twisted her foot, the weight of her body shifting and my finger crunching, and I yelled louder than I'd ever yelled before.

"What's the rule?" she repeated, her voice carrying out over the spectating women.

"N-n-n," I tried. "Eye... Eye contact. N-n-no eye contact!"

She raised her boot off my hand, and I immediately clutched my wrist against my chest. I couldn't see anything through my quickly swelling eye, but two of my fingers were out of place.

Zsasz's blurry, fur-outlined figure circled me a few times as she spoke, but it was impossible to make out what she was saying. I was too out of it and in too much pain.

No eye contact.

No eye contact.

No eye contact.

A heavy blow suddenly knocked me square in the face and everything went black.

CHAPTER 1

"You shouldn't have tried to stare her down," said Alice Number Two, handing me a wet cloth.

What does she care? Why is she even talking to me? I pulled away. I didn't want her sympathy. I didn't need her help, either.

"You should at least clean the open wounds," she said. "You don't want that getting inf—"

"Would you fuck off?" I said, my eyes slowly rolling up toward her.

I was prepared to throw the ginger root I held straight at her face if she didn't shut the hell up. I'd use my damn teeth to fight her if I had to.

She must have sensed my rage because she raised two open palms. "Just tryin' to help."

"Well, don't."

Everyone looked away and I was glad they did—I could barely look at any of them either. Not one person had tried to defend me. Not one.

"Can I see?" Arenas asked.

She sat beside me with both legs crossed in front of her. I glared at her. What did she want?

"Your hand," she said, her long-lashed eyes shifting down to my hand, which I held close to my chest.

"Look, I've broken every one o' mah fingers, muchacha," she said.

What kind of life had she lived? I'd never taken the time to look at her because all I'd cared about was trying to get out of the Northern city.

She looked like she was in her early thirties. Despite the puffy bags underneath her eyes, she had no wrinkles or age spots. She was small—smaller than Franklin, but also much shorter—the kind of woman who was lucky enough to buy sneakers in the kids' section for half the price of adult shoes. Her skin was a creamy warm brown color, which might have once been beautiful, but now it was damaged, covered with dozens of scars of lighter shades and tribal markings that looked like they'd been tattooed here on Kormace Island and maybe even infected.

Her coarse hair—a choppy mess that looked like she'd stuck her head in a blender—didn't suit her small pointed nose and square jawline. She'd probably once had hair pulled back into a high ponytail running all the way down her back, the kind of slick-looking Latina you'd see in movies with hoop earrings, obsidian eyeliner, high-rise pants, and a leather jacket. The kind who wouldn't back down from any fight, even if her opponent was three times her size, which was most likely always the case for her, given her small frame.

But all that remained now was a broken woman.

She wiggled her fingers as if to say *Come on*, and I reluctantly gave her my damaged hand. Two of my fingers now shifted to the side, and the skin around my joints was turning midnight blue—almost black.

Her fingers were cold to the touch despite the hot, humid air around us, and she wrapped them delicately around my wrist. I stared at her narrowing eyes, not quite certain why I was trusting her given my vulnerable state.

With her other hand, she brushed a soft finger along each one of mine.

"Feel that?"

I grimaced. Even the lightest touch felt like a nail scraping along my skin.

"At least you feel it, muchacha," she said, squinting and smiling faintly with her pale lips. "You know, girl, sometimes—" she started, but she didn't bother to finish her sentence. In one rapid movement, she clasped my wrist as hard as possible and with her other hand, snapped my fingers back into place.

I yelled out and stomped my feet into the dirt. I hadn't even had the time to contemplate punching her in the face for what she'd done because I was in too much pain.

She let go of my wrist and patted my knee. "Sorry, girl. You wouldn't have let me do it if I told you what I was about to do."

Although I hated her at that moment, I knew she was right.

"Try not to use that hand for the next month or so," she said. "Gotta let the bone heal in the right position, and it ain't like we got any splints around here."

"I-I could make one," Hammer said, sounding like an abused teenager, her voice muffled and her head bowed low.

This place had already changed her. It had changed all of us. The Northers got exactly what they wanted—they broke us. And every time we accumulated even the slightest bit of courage or desire to rebel, they came crashing down on us to remind us of our places, as Zsasz had done to me this morning for having stared at her cold in the face.

She'd been doing her morning rounds, throwing water in people's faces and kicking women down if they weren't on their knees as she passed, and I stood there, watching her with such hatred, I envisioned laser beams shooting out of my eyes like Superman. If I'd had that power, I wouldn't have hesitated to melt that ugly face right off.

The worst part is, right before she came strolling into the city with Rebel and her goons, I overheard a woman say that Carlson, whoever that was, had attempted to run that night. They called them Death Sprinters. Basically, anyone who tried to run away was suicidal and a masochist because once caught—and they were caught every time—they were beaten beyond recognition, stripped of their clothing, and hung upside down a few miles away from here for Ogres to find.

They didn't need a gate or a prison wall to keep us inside. They had our fear and that was all they needed.

"Keep up the pace," came Alice Number Two's voice.

She stepped over Coin's legs, which were stretched out in front of her, and everyone moved a little bit faster. If we weren't washing vegetables, we were cleaning roots, curing meat, or pulling seeds out of fruit, and it was never-ending.

I understood now why Sumi had been so resentful about being the Village Cook. It was a shitty job, and if you didn't do your job, you were letting down the entire society—everyone needed to eat. A few other nearby Peasants nodded their dirt-stained heads and started peeling corn.

"You got guts," I heard.

I turned sideways toward where the voice had emerged. A woman who sat several feet away from

Hammer was holding an ear of corn in one hand and its peel in the other. She looked about my age with soft skin and pink lips. She stared at me, a strange look on her face—it wasn't malicious or territorial in any way, but rather, intrigued.

"What you did," she went on, her eyes darting from side to side. She leaned forward, her voice lowering even further. "No one's ever had the balls to stare down one of 'em Orphans like that."

Everyone around her nodded, and the air filled with whispered bickering.

For the first time since this morning, I didn't care that my fingers were broken.

CHAPTER 2

I flinched when the elephant trumpeted and stomped its feet into the dirt. The woman atop it jabbed her spear into its side then slapped the back of its head.

Farther ahead, near the wooden gate that remained closed off to the general population, women scattered, and shouts fired back and forth.

Coin was the first to stand up, her meatless shoulders drawn back and her lip curled up over her golden tooth.

"What's going on?" Johnson asked. She tossed aside a handful of things that looked like nuts, the names of which I probably wouldn't even know how to pronounce.

"Don't," said Alice Number Two, her freckled face aimed toward what now appeared to be a fight unfolding.

I realized then that the women weren't scattering at all—they were forming a circle: a fighting ring.

Hammer jumped to her feet, ignoring Alice

Number Two's command. I barely recognized her as she ran toward the scene. She'd lost all her extra weight, and what remained was loose skin and baggy clothing. Her hair, which had always been shaved down close to the skin, had grown out in curls.

"Sorry," Johnson said, side-glancing Alice Number Two as she ran away from her post.

Alice Number Two sighed, no doubt well aware that she couldn't hold us all back. I caught Coin's glance, and together, we got up with Arenas close behind. I didn't bother dragging Tegan along—in fact, I didn't bother talking to Tegan at all anymore. I didn't know what the Northers had done to destroy her from the inside, but whatever it was, it had worked.

I had more important things to worry about than trying to rehabilitate someone's mental state.

We pushed our way through the crowd until we reached the edge of the group. Hundreds of women formed a massive circle by the wooden gates, and at the very center were two women hunched forward, staring at each other with bared teeth and fingers forming claws in front of their faces.

A Norther with padded shoulder plates and a wooden club in her hand stepped inside the circle, swinging her weapon in circular motions. She paced around the two women with a frown as if prepared to kill them both if they didn't start fighting soon.

The woman on the right—a young blonde with a deformed nose and torn clothing—let out a wild scream and ran straight for her opponent. The other woman, a black-haired Asian woman with a thick unibrow and blood on her chest, screamed right back at her and stiffened her stance.

The impact sounded like someone taking a hammer to a piece of drywall—something cracked, and what followed next was animalistic grunting and screaming. The Norther with the wooden club kept circling the fighters, her lips curving up at one end.

What a sick piece of shit.

I wondered if she was one of the Russian Orphans raised on this island or one of the Originals who'd followed Rainer out of the Village. She looked young, and with her smooth-skinned face and charcoal-outlined eyes, I could only assume she was one of the Orphans.

Another loud crack was followed by the sound of the entire city cheering. I wasn't sure what was more disturbing—the two women fighting to the death, or their audience forming a circle around them with hungry eyes as if prepared to harvest organs the moment one of them died.

The blond woman was now on top of the Asian woman, her hands wrapped so tightly around her opponent's throat that the other woman's face swelled until it looked like her unibrow might fall off. She then swung a fist straight at her face over and over again, the sound of impact making me want to turn away.

Blood splattered upward and under the blond woman's chin, but she didn't stop.

"No!" someone cried out, breaking formation and stepping inside the circle.

But the Norther didn't hesitate—with one quick swing of her club, she broke the pleading Peasant's nose, propelling her into the air and back into the crowd.

Rules were rules.

Like no eye contact, I remembered.

If we stuck by these rules, we'd survive.

We'd survived.

My heart began beating faster and faster until I felt like I couldn't breathe. Suddenly, all I could see was Trim floating in front of me, the cut in her neck split open and oozing thick blood out onto the forest floor. Then, I saw Sunny hanging upside down, her face swollen and her dandelion eyes looking like nothing more than two glass marbles.

My hands became clammy and my old Village shirt—my suede unevenly cut top—stuck to my back. Maybe I was dying. Finally dying.

"It's normal," I heard Proxy's voice. "Post-traumatic stress disorder."

Another image flashed through my mind—Northers slicing their blades in downward motions, cutting off limbs and slicing through torsos amid our Village engulfed in flames.

Make it stop. Make it stop. Make it stop.

"Whoa, whoa, honey, you okay?"

I looked beyond these vivid flashes to find who was speaking: a middle-aged woman with messy hair, a big round nose, and a belly that stuck out from underneath a shirt that was too small for her. If I'd seen her in the real world—the *old* world—she'd probably have been wearing a lot of makeup, fancy clothes, a big sun hat, and an unnecessary amount of gold necklaces around her neck. Her hair was dyed bleach blond, right down to the roots, which meant she was new.

I wiped a layer of cold sweat from my forehead. "Think so."

"You don't look so good, sweetheart," she said, a strong southern accent slipping off her tongue.

Honey? Sweetheart?

She was definitely new.

"Just memories," I said.

"I take it you been here awhile?" she asked, little rolls forming on her forehead as she glared at me from underneath the sun's hot rays.

What did she have to be so chipper about? She looked completely out of place. Her goofy grin and shiny attitude were sure to get her beaten.

"Name's Georgia." She offered me a perfectly manicured hand. With a wink, she added, "Just like the state, honey."

I stared at it for a second, then back up at her, and when she realized I wasn't in a touchy mood, she pulled away, the smile on her face not fading one bit. Her eyes went big, almost playful. "Can you believe this place? I knew things would be... archaic, but oh Lord, I never imagined somethin' like this."

Was I supposed to say something?

She reached a gentle hand on my forearm. "Soon as I get outta here... outta this strange city... I think I'll find myself somewhere quiet... Lay low until my three years are all up." She shook her head and let out a laugh. "Three years. I got lucky, let me tell you! Think they mighta made some sorta mistake. I was lookin' at twenty-five years in federal prison. But this..." She tilted her head back, closed her eyes, and took in the sun as if the sounds of women crying and screaming couldn't be heard behind me. "This is paradise."

Poor woman. Did she truly think they were coming back for her in three years? Was it up to me to break the news to her? She looked so happy believing the fantasy.

"What's your name, sweetheart?"

"Brone," I said. I stared at her hazel eyes and the little wrinkles at the edges of her eyebrows.

"You do know you can change your name, right? Or go by your last name?"

She stared at me as if I'd told her she'd landed in Wonderland, then tilted her head back, her face aimed at the cloudless sky. "Is that so?"

But then, out of nowhere, she smacked her perfectly smooth hand against my shoulder. "Thanks for lookin' out for me, doll, but I've been Georgia since I came outta my momma's womb. Ain't nobody gonna call me anythin' else."

Her puffy lips flapped up and down as she spoke, but all I could think about was the searing pain over my right eye, in my head, in my ribs, and in my hand...

"What're you here for, honey? Look at you. You're so young."

What was I here for? What was *she* here for? The idea of a cheerful, rosy-cheeked southern woman killing someone was inconceivable. I supposed that was what she thought about me.

"Killed my mom's boyfriend," I said, growing tired of having to repeat myself.

She pulled back, her chin blending into the folds of her neck. "A sweet thing like you?" She leaned forward and squinted. "I bet it was an accident. Am I right?"

What was that supposed to mean? Did I not look like the kind of person who had the potential to kill someone? Did I look *that* innocent? Or was she being condescending because she was older than me? And why was I so offended by the comment? It's not like I'd grown up wanting to one day look like a murderer.

"What're you trying to say?" I asked, my tone coming out a lot harsher than expected.

But she didn't frown or retreat. Instead, she smirked and winked at me. "A feelin' I get from you. You remind me of my sister when she was young. A sweet, harmless little—"

"Listen, lady," I said, pointing my crooked, swollen finger at her face.

"What's goin' on here?" Coin broke in.

I turned my head toward her, my broken finger still pointed in the approximate direction of the woman's face.

"Oh," Georgia said, her smile melting into a frown the moment she saw Coin. "And what do we have here? What'd you do, honey? Was it gang related?" She flicked her wrist. "I bet it was gang related."

"'Scuse me?" Coin puffed her chest out and bared her teeth.

"Oh Lord," the woman said, grimacing at Coin. "Look at that gold tooth. How on Earth did someone like *you* afford that?"

Coin's eyes went huge and her nostrils flared wider than her lips. "You fuckin' racist piece of—" she started, but I pressed my good hand over her chest and pulled her back.

"Not worth it." I turned away from Georgia. "She's an idiot... a close-minded bigot."

"You two are actually *friends*?" Georgia said. "Oh, Brone, darlin'—"

"Georgia." I slowly turned around. "Word of advice. Shut your mouth and go make yourself a comfortable bed."

Her eyes popped out and her jaw went loose. "I beg your pardon?"

"You heard me," I said. "Better get comfortable around here because the truth is, no one's coming back for you. Not now, not in three years, not ever."

With that, I grabbed Coin's arm and walked away.

CHAPTER 3

"Man, you shoulda seen the look on her face!" Coin said, clicking her fingers in the air.

"Well, I didn't," Arenas said. "I was too busy watchin' someone die."

The smile on Coin's face disappeared and she looked away.

"What's going on here?"

I turned around to find Alice Number Two staring at us, her arms crossed over her stomach. She stood with the weight of her body on one leg, her hips bulging out on one side. She made her eyes go big as if to say, *What are you, deaf?*

"Get back to work," she said. "You can watch a fight, but when it's done, you don't stand around like a bunch of headless chickens."

"We weren't—" Johnson tried, but Alice Number Two raised her chin and stuck a flat hand out in front of her face.

I wasn't in the mood to put up a fight, so I started walking toward the Food Station, and everyone followed.

"She's such a bitch," Johnson muttered.

I turned my head around to see Alice Number Two still standing there, watching us make our way to our post.

I forced a laugh. "She's something, all right."

"Where's Ham?" Coin asked, craning her neck to see over the dozens of heads around us.

"You shouldn't call her that," I said. "It's degrading."

Coin stopped walking, rested her hands on her hips, and gave me a playful up-and-down. "Girl, look at you. Carin' about people's feelings and shit."

"Yo," Arenas said, "Brone's right. It's insulting. How would you like it if we called you chocolate? Or cocoa?"

Coin pointed a stiff finger in Arenas's face. "First off, that don't even compare. I was shortening her name, not callin' her piggy. And second"—the corner of her lip curved upward—"I love chocolate. Ain't got no issues with that. But I'd kill any of you bitches for a piece o' chocolate right now, so you prolly shouldn't be usin' that word around me."

I raised both eyebrows at her, and she let out a laugh. "I wouldn't actually *kill* you... Jesus, Brone. Lighten up."

How was she cracking jokes when we were barely surviving on Northern territory?

Coin wiped her nose with the back of her

hand—something she did to look tough when she was feeling undermined—and threw her chin out at the crowd. "Seriously, though. Where's Hammer?"

"Aren't any of you affected by what just happened?" Arenas burst out. "*Están locas!*"

"Who you callin' crazy?" Coin said, the brown skin around her nose wrinkling.

"All of you!" Arenas continued. "You're all acting like this is normal. Like it's no big deal that some woman bashed another woman's face in. She's dead. She died right there! Right in front of me. And you're all talking like it's something that happens all the time. What's wrong with you?"

I filled a wooden, seaweed-coated bucket with warm water from the Food Station and glanced over at Arenas. I knew where she was coming from. She had every right to feel this way. Personally, I hadn't been sick enough to stay and watch the whole fight, so I didn't have to live with another image of someone dying.

"Here," came a woman's low voice.

She dumped a wooden box full of fruits, vegetables, and nuts on the ground by our feet. "Cut and clean them."

She must have been one of the cultivators. A few women came and went from the Food Station throughout the day. They disappeared into the jungle and returned with all kinds of unrecognizable foods. Others stayed behind, planting seeds in a massive garden. It was surrounded by a fence-like barrier covered in crisscrossing vines and leafy branches.

There must have been at least a dozen of us working at the Food Station. I'd have much rather gathered food from the jungle than sit here on cleaning and prepping duty.

I grabbed a round, hard-shelled thing and rubbed my good thumb along its ridges. Arenas reached for a pile of multicolored berries with an exaggerated scowl on her face.

"How long have you been here?" I asked, watching her.

She plucked a berry from its twig and looked up at me, hesitant. She must have sensed that I was trying to help because she shrugged. "Few months."

"It takes awhile," I said. I paused and inhaled a deep breath. Even talking hurt.

Fucking bitch... I'd kill Zsasz for this...

I breathed in again and looked at Arenas. "I've been here about a year, and I'm only now starting to accept it. This place isn't like anything I would have imagined. It's barbaric and completely disgusting. I know how you're feeling—"

Her dark eyes rolled up at me.

"You feel like you're caught in some horrible nightmare. Like any minute, you'll wake up in the comfort of your bed."

She nodded, and her lower lip trembled. "I've never seen nobody die like that before… I mean, I know I wasn't a good person. I did some shit, too. But that… that was something else. I can't even—"

"You don't have to understand it," I said. "I don't think anyone can understand it. I, for one, don't understand how any of this is happening. We're all human beings. We're all women. We should be working together, not against each other."

"Amen," Coin chimed in.

"You religious?"

Hammer appeared behind me carrying another bucket of water.

"It's just a sayin'—" Coin tried.

"Yeah, yeah," Hammer continued. "Keep believing in your Santa Claus."

"'Scuse me?" Coin jumped to her feet.

"All I'm saying"—Hammer raised her pointer finger—"is that if there *is* a God, he or she doesn't care about us. In fact, he or she is pretty damn twisted to let a place like this exist. Wish God would do us all a favor and send a hurricane our way."

"You seriously shouldn't be talking about religion," Johnson said. "Some people are sensitive to that."

Hammer scoffed and sat down. "Maybe people need to let go of their little baby feelings."

"Yo, man," Coin said. "Just because you—"

"Guys," I said, and Coin stopped talking. "Stop, okay?" I couldn't handle this. Not with this amount of pain. I couldn't think straight. "And Hammer, Johnson's right... Why are you trying to start a fight? I'd be willing to bet that some people on this island are only alive because of religion—because of faith."

Hammer let out a chortle. "Pathetic."

Maybe it was. I wasn't in a position to argue with her, especially since I wasn't religious. But so long as religion wasn't causing fights, I didn't see a problem with it. Surprisingly, I hadn't seen anyone fight over religion on Kormace Island, unlike in the real world, where people killed each other over it.

Now *that* was pathetic.

Arenas dropped a handful of berries into my bucket of water, her sad gaze meeting mine. "Thanks."

"I didn't do much," I said. "But if you ever need to talk about it, you can talk to me."

She smirked and nodded quickly. I felt sorry for her. She looked like such a badass—a big mouth— yet here she was, completely devastated after having witnessed someone get killed so violently.

I wanted the violence to end. But how could it? We were trapped in a massive prison surrounded by violence every day. The same principle still applied—kill or be killed. There was no leveling with these women—no talking things through in a civil manner. Especially the Orphans; they'd been raised to hate us. How could anyone rationalize that?

But, as I stared at Arenas's slouched posture, I wondered if maybe there was another way to bring peace to this city. Maybe we didn't have to resort to violence. I sat quietly, staring at the dirt by my feet and my fingers dipped in warm water. Maybe the answer started with me. Maybe I had to let go of my anger first.

"Get out of my way!"

A woman's voice shook me from my daze. In a matter of seconds, the idea of a peaceful society shattered. All of my hatred suddenly resurfaced like a plastic ball tossed into a swimming pool.

My vision blurred and the berry I held exploded inside my fist.

It was Holland—the woman with bleached-blond hair and long dark roots Trim and the Hunters had found in the jungle. It all came back to me. She'd been shivering and looking starved when we'd found her, and Trim had brought her into the Village despite Fisher's hesitation. This woman... Holland... was the same woman who'd walked away unharmed the morning of the massacre.

She was one of them.

How was this possible?

Had she been sent by the Originals? Sent to

poison our entire Village? Because that was what she'd done. She'd infiltrated our society and somehow managed to poison our breakfast. Hundreds of lives had been lost because of her.

All because of her.

My heart skipped a beat, and my ears rang. I couldn't think clearly... couldn't see clearly. All I knew was that this woman was responsible for countless lives lost that morning.

Without thinking, I yanked the sharp cutting tool out of Arenas's hand, jumped to my feet, and ran straight toward Holland, my heart pounding out of my chest and my legs like jelly.

CHAPTER 4

The first hit was satisfying—her head jerked to one side and her jaw hung loosely before she came crashing down underneath me. I grabbed whatever I could to hold her still, but she kept swinging her arms around, as if she couldn't tell where the attack was coming from.

I swung another hard fist at her face, feeling alive.

"Fight!"

"Fight!"

"Fight!"

Pulling Arenas's cutting tool from my injured hand, I pressed it into the base of Holland's neck. She immediately stopped trying to fight me off. I sat, my muscles as hard as stone, my lips curled over my teeth, and my eyes popping out. I'd never experienced so much rage in my life. I'd have torn her throat out with my hands if one of them wasn't so injured.

I regripped its thin handle in my sweaty palm and pressed it into her skin even harder, a line of maroon blood appearing underneath the blade.

"You," was all I could say.

"Brone," she said. Her chest heaved up and down so fast it probably looked like I was riding a horse.

"Don't," I said through clenched teeth.

"You don't understand." She clasped her fingers around my wrists, trying to relieve the blade's pressure. "I didn't have a choice. Brone, I didn't—"

Wrinkles formed on her forehead and around her nose, and she let out a weird, choppy sound before bursting out into a full-blown sob. "I didn't want to... I didn't think it..."

"No, you didn't think!" I shouted, and my voice carried into the crowd that had formed around us: wild women with hunched postures and closed fists.

"Get up, Holland!" someone shouted.

"Fight!"

"Kill herrrrrr!"

"It was only supposed to be Murk," Holland said, her nails now digging into my skin. "They said—they said they were only taking Murk. I didn't know. I didn't know." And she burst out crying again. "I'm sorry... I'm so sorry."

I stiffened.

Was she lying? I stared at her face, a contorted mess that looked like it had gone through a blender, and my anger slowly dissipated. I'd never forgive her for what she did, but how could I possibly kill someone who was crying her heart out? I hated her, but at the same time, all I saw was a girl. A frightened girl who held onto an immeasurable amount of guilt.

How was I supposed to hurt someone who was hurting so much herself?

I got up by pushing myself off her, and she winced at my sharp movement. "You should be sorry," I said, and I straightened up, so everyone could hear me. "You killed dozens, if not hundreds, of innocent women."

She slapped two hands over her face and kept crying. "I-I-I know. I'm sorry. I'm sorry. I'm sorry."

Sorry wouldn't fix what she'd done, but it did do something because the idea of killing her was no longer appealing to me. Although I wasn't ready to admit it yet, Holland was a victim in this, too.

Whispers suddenly erupted around me, and I felt like a bearded lady in a circus act. What were they all looking at?

"Who is that?"

"Who's that girl?"

"Did she just give her mercy?"

"Isn't Holland the reason her people are dead?"

I dropped the cutting tool by Holland's face and stared at her for a moment. Her bloodshot blue eyes squinted beneath the sun's afternoon rays, staring back at me.

I could see her pain. She was already suffering for what she'd done. Death would only bring her relief.

I turned around and started crossing the open space around us when I heard someone's voice.

"Whoa, whoa, whoa," the woman said. She stepped into the circle, her massive leather boots stomping through the sand. I hadn't seen her before, but it was obvious she was a Norther (either an Original or an Orphan, going by Coin's simplification of terms).

"Fight's not over," she said.

I glanced back at Holland, who sat up slightly, her torso held up by her elbows behind her back.

Fight to the death, I remembered, and she had my weapon. She reached for the cutting tool and stood tall, her dark roots falling over half her face.

How was any of this fair? I'd shown her mercy, and now, what? She was going to kill me? With my own weapon? The crowd around us burst into a cacophonic cheer, and the Norther tried to smile, though it looked more like a hideous grimace. She held a wooden club in her hand, and she smacked it repeatedly into her open palm.

Holland walked forward like this whole battle-to-the-death thing was nothing more than a walk in the park. Had she played me? Manipulated me into feeling sorry for her? I clenched my good fist.

But when she got closer, she didn't lunge or swing a fist. Instead, she knelt on one knee, her scraggly half-tone hair still dangling in her face, and raised the cutting tool over her bowed head.

What was she doing? Why was she giving it to me?

The air around us filled with a heavy silence and all I could hear was my rapid breathing.

"Take it," she muttered. "Honestly, after what I did, I don't deserve—"

But she let out another whimper. I slowly reached for the blade, realizing this may also be a trick. But it wasn't. She didn't pull away or try to attack. She remained still on one knee, her gaze fixated on the ground at my feet.

The crowd started up again, and this time, solid fists pumped into the air.

"Fight!"

"Fight!"

"Fight"

How could I? How was I supposed to take her life? She wasn't a threat anymore. Yes, I was still angry about what had happened, but the blame couldn't be placed on one person. I reluctantly looked up at the Norther, who stood as stiff as a piece of plywood, her fingers white around her club as if waiting for an excuse to bash me in the face.

I couldn't do it.

I let the blade hang loosely at my waist, and the entire crowd went still—so still, in fact, that I could hear the Norther's fingers tighten around her club. Her bushy, untrimmed eyebrows came close together and she let out a grunt.

"You fight, or you die!" she shouted, and her voice carried across the entire city.

Only then did I notice that even the nearby elephants stood still, their ears flapping from side to side as their handlers pulled at ropes.

I wasn't sure what led me to stand up to a Norther, especially one willing to kill me, but the idea of dying at that moment was less disturbing than the idea of taking Holland's life—a woman filled with grief and self-hatred.

I stared at the Norther—the uncivilized animal now glaring at me—then dropped the blade into the soil at my feet and drew my shoulders back.

CHAPTER 5

The Norther with the wooden club took a step forward, her cracked lips now forming an ugly smile.

"Two deaths," she said, whacking the club in her palm.

Holland stood up and side-glanced me. "You don't have to do this. Get it over with, and you'll live."

I didn't answer her. Instead, I tilted my head back and closed my eyes, feeling the sun's warmth on my face, and imagined what was waiting for me on the other side. I didn't have the energy to fight, and I couldn't imagine a place harsher than this one, so the idea of death became comforting.

All I wanted was for all of this to end.

But then, another image crept into my mind—Ellie's face. She stood smiling with her head tilted to one side and her wavy brown hair brushed over one shoulder. What if she was still alive? What if she was waiting for me at the Cove? Then, I thought of my mom, who was probably sitting in her apartment, lonely and depressed and binge-watching old movies to keep her mind occupied. If I gave up, would it be selfish?

An orchestra of gasps filled the air around me and I cracked open my eyes in time to see the Norther raise her club into the air. It all happened so fast, but at the same time, everything moved so slowly. With her rotted mouth wide open, she swung the club straight for the side of my head. I had no time to think—only act. I dropped into a crouched position, feeling the club brush through the hairs on top of my head and suddenly, a familiar rage-fueled instinct set in. With my good hand, I grabbed the cutting tool by my feet and threw myself at the monster in front of me, digging the blade into her neck, right below her jawline.

It slipped in like a knife through butter, and warm blood came pouring out over my hand.

The skin on her face tightened, pulling her hairline back, and she dropped her club. My ears rang, and my heart pounded so hard I couldn't tell if the crowd was making any noise. I pulled the blade out of her neck and blood spritzed into the air and onto my lips. When I stepped back, she slapped two hands over the stab wound. She looked at me, her pasty lips parted, and I stared back, watching her bright eyes glaze over as her life slowly slipped away.

"Brone!"

I followed the voice, but everything was so bright, all I saw was a silhouette moving toward me. I hated this feeling. Hated the disorientation that came along with a surge of adrenaline. I clenched my fist around my bloody weapon, prepared to take another swing at the next Norther—because they were coming, I was sure of it. I'd killed one of theirs. There was no way I was getting out of this one.

"Brone!" the voice said again. This time, I recognized it.

"Coin?"

"Come on, let's go," she urged. She pulled at my arm and I dropped the blade into the dirt. Then, as if my hearing had suddenly come back, whispers erupted all around me.

"Oh my God."

"Did you see that?"

"I can't believe it."

Coin yanked on my arm even harder to lead me out of the circle—away from the vultures surrounding the Norther's dead body. I shoved my way through warm bodies, avoiding eye contact at all costs until I turned around briefly and caught Holland's gaze. She didn't move as the circle tightened around her. It was almost like she wanted to be accused of killing the Norther. Why wasn't she leaving?

"Brone!" came Hammer's voice.

My legs shook, and I didn't know what to say.

"Give her some space," Coin said, but that accomplished nothing.

Women started circling me, eyeing me with fascination. Coin swung her arms out again, but in scissorlike motions this time. "Back off!"

And then, to my surprise, the women did precisely that. They spread out, forming a long, empty stretch through the sand. But they didn't do it for us. They backed off for someone else. I raised a hand to my forehead, the afternoon sun now like fire against my skin, and gazed down the opening they made.

It led to the wooden gates—the ones with pointy pikes fastened tightly together. One woman atop an elephant stood beside its front gate, which was now open, and pointed her spear in my direction. She shouted something, but I couldn't make it out.

What I saw next made my stomach sink.

Zsasz came blasting out with six other Northers scurrying behind her. She walked toward me with a heavy step, her soulless eyes never leaving mine. Her chin was raised, and her zebra-scarred lips formed a flat line. I'd never seen her like this before. She usually had a sly smirk on her face—a look that told me she was always one step ahead of us.

But not this time.

And she was coming straight for me.

I swallowed hard.

CHAPTER 6

Her wide, crystal-blue eyes underneath hairless eyebrows were enough to make me want to drop to my knees. She stood inches away, staring down at me, her head bowed forward.

"I see you haven't learned your lesson," she said, eyeing my broken fingers.

I couldn't speak.

"Do you know what we do to bad girls?" She tilted her head to the side.

I shook my head. She made me feel weak and vulnerable. How did she manage it? Was it the abuse? Had she programmed me to fear her? Because I'd never been so afraid of anyone in my life.

"On your knees," she ordered, and I dropped like a dog, my knees digging into the dirt.

I hated her. I hated myself. Why was I even listening to her?

"Brone," Coin tried, but Zsasz swung the back of her hand at Coin's face, and she was thrown into the group of women who formed an enclosure around us.

"I asked you a question," she said, her chin elevated so high all I saw was the bulge in her throat.

What question? What was she talking about?

"Do you know what we do to bad girls?" she repeated.

"Bad girls?" was all I could say.

Why couldn't I think clearly?

She swung an open hand across my face and I fell to my side, not wanting to carry the weight of my body on my injured hand.

"Get up," she ordered.

The skin on my face was hot, and my cheek throbbed painfully. She'd already beaten me this morning, and now she was hitting the same bruises. It felt like nails were puncturing my face.

Smack.

Another hand smashed me across the face, this time, on the opposite side, and my vision went blurry.

She knelt on one knee, her bumpy, white-scarred face inches away from mine.

"Have you been a bad girl?"

I stared at her, and she slowly moved closer, her eyes never leaving my face. She pressed her dry, zebra lips against mine and through her nose, let out a hot breath that smelled like decay.

I cringed and she pulled away revealing that

familiar smirk. Then, without a single warning, her face transformed into a monstrous scowl and she grabbed my broken fingers. I yelled out in pain, and she squeezed harder until I heard a crack.

She pulled my hand upward, and I bounced into a standing position, trying to alleviate some of the pressure. Then, like a vicious master tugging on their dog's leash, she swung around, forcing me to follow.

I cried out and clawed at her solid grip, but it didn't loosen. She marched down the path the Peasants had formed, and I followed close behind, my bare feet nearly kicking the back of her boots with every painful step.

"P-p-please!" I begged.

She dragged me through the front gates of the barrier. The six other Northers following close behind, and one of them made a hand gesture at the closest elephant handlers, who I could only assume, closed the gate behind us. I was in too much pain to understand what was going on.

The moment we were inside, she let go of my hand, and I grabbed it, tears dripping onto the tips of my broken fingers. What was she going to do to me? Torture me? I blinked away tears, and my surroundings came into focus.

At the back of this strange space was the base of a mountain—a rocky, gray, pebbled surface that rose up on a steep angle. The farther up I looked, the more greenery was to be seen. In front of this were wooden steps fastened together by rope and wooden poles that formed a crooked path toward the side of the mountain. I hadn't seen this hidden path when I'd first laid eyes on the city. It looked like a secret passage into a cave and reminded me of Murk's headquarters.

Was this where Rainer resided?

Beside the bottom of the steps were two women—armed Northers—standing stiff like statues with metal-tipped spears pointed at the sky. It was obvious, the stairs led to something, or someone, important.

On both sides of the two Northern guards were dozens of small log cabins without windows and with roofs constructed of vegetation. Composed of dry wood and crisped leaves, they looked old and appeared large enough to fit a single bed inside. Was this where the Northers slept? Compared to our sleeping arrangements in the city, this was luxury.

Why had Zsasz taken me in here?

Several women with heavy gear—weapon belts, bows, blades, and even battle-axes—walked around, their chests puffed out and their hateful eyes raking me up and down. A handful were seated by a campfire, carving weapons, their backs hunched as they chewed on pieces of crisp meat. It was like I'd traveled back in time to the Stone

Age.

And then I heard it—the sound of women battling. I followed the clanging of metals, the hitting of sticks, and the puncturing of arrows. At the far back of this enclosed space, this territory that I assumed was designated for Orphans and Originals, and overtop vividly green grass, were women dressed in plain clothing—women who looked like Peasants—training for battle.

Had they chosen to fight for the Northers? They weren't as beastly-looking as the Orphans or the Originals—again, though I couldn't yet differentiate the two, I could tell them apart from regular women. Yet they were battling with such ferocity, I had a hard time believing they'd chosen this life.

Franklin, I thought.

What if they'd taken her to create a soldier? A Battlewoman? I searched the large group of fighting women, hoping to catch a glimpse of her, but all I saw were fast-moving bodies and weapons swinging through the air.

"Keep moving," someone grumbled behind me, and something hard nudged me in the back.

My head rocked back before straightening out, and I quick-stepped my way to Zsasz, who was headed toward the wooden stairs at the back—the ones that led up the side of the mountain. But when she reached the guards—two women staring straight ahead as if their personalities had been entirely stripped away—she stepped sideways and continued down a stone path behind the log cabins. I hadn't even noticed it.

Tall green grass and ginger-orange flowers decorated the edges of the path, and I flinched when a huge, shiny admiral-blue-shelled bug buzzed by my face. Her heavy footsteps crunched the stones beneath us, while I shifted every few steps, careful not to press the weight of my bare feet on something sharp. The air around us became cool and damp, and the sun was no longer visible.

I turned around to find that most Northers had stayed behind. Only one woman—a short, stalky thing with a pimply shaved head—threatened me to keep moving by pointing a sharp blade at my face.

Massive, drooping trees hung overhead, outside the wooden gate. How far did this barrier of theirs reach? It stretched all the way to the side of the mountain, forming a narrow path, almost like an alleyway.

When we finally reached the end of this tunnellike path, everything opened up again, the wooden pikes stretching out and forming a circular enclosure around a space I hoped was something I was imagining. It wasn't all that big, maybe several hundred feet in diameter, but the sight before me was enough to make me wish I'd let the Norther holding her club bash my face in.

Individual cages constructed of bamboo formed a crescent moon at the back of this garden-like space—small cells large enough to let one sit or stand. The prisoners inside them paced from side to side, dropped into seated positions, or stuck their fingers through the holes of the cages. I couldn't count them all because my heart was racing and my head swung back and forth as I tried to comprehend what was going on.

Everything was a rich green, almost wet looking, and flowered vines climbed over and through the prison cells, but all I saw was torment. At last, like a camera lens coming into focus, I saw her.

She was at the very center of this outdoor prison—this torture chamber if you will—crouched on her knees with her arms above her head. Her wrists were tied with vines that stretched all the way up into a drooping tree. Its slanted trunk originated from behind the wooden pike enclosure, but its branches, leaves, and vines extended so far that they formed a ceiling overhead.

At first, I didn't recognize her because both of her eyes were swollen shut. Her lip was split open, and the blood had crusted over it and down her chin. Her tied hands were purple and swollen, and

I wondered how long she'd been forced to sit in this position. Her beige suede shirt was torn in half, revealing long jagged cuts along her ribcage that seemed infected.

But that hair... It had grown out a bit, but it was still as silvery white as it had always been.

"Murk," I breathed.

Her sky-blue eyes stared at the ground by her knees like she was stuck in some never-ending daydream. I blinked once, then twice, to make sure I wasn't hallucinating. How was Murk still alive? Why hadn't they killed her?

An indescribable relief washed over me. Our leader, my leader, was still alive.

"Mur—" I tried, but Zsasz grabbed me by the collar of my shirt and my head rocked back and forth.

"No one talks to her," she hissed, her putrid breath mixing in with the taste of dehydration and stomach acid in my mouth.

She stared at me as if watching a mouse trying to escape a trap. A sadistic smile crept onto her demonic face. A feeling of pure hatred built inside me. My loyalty to Murk overpowered my fear of Zsasz. "What're you doing with her?"

She threw out a hand with snakelike speed and wrapped her short-nailed fingers around my throat, squeezing my jugular until I found myself unable to breathe properly.

"You will speak only when spoken to," she said.

I couldn't move, and my face was swelling up. I did my best to nod, and when she realized I wasn't trying to open my mouth again, she let go. I inhaled a sharp breath and rubbed my neck.

"Take a good look at your leader," Zsasz said, watching me more than Murk. "She did this to you. All of you. A true leader wouldn't have banished a pregnant woman to the jungle."

I almost said, "Maybe a pregnant woman should have thought about her child before murdering someone," but I bit my tongue. Besides, I didn't know what, or who, to believe anymore. But if I'd been allowed to talk to Murk... Have her explain everything to me.

"Please," someone groaned, and a few fingers slid through one of the bamboo cages. She wiggled them, then tightened her grip and shook the cage. "Please!" she shouted. "We haven't eaten in four days..." and her voice faded, almost as if she were too weak to finish her sentence.

Zsasz shook her head and laughed. "Ungrateful. I give them a home, food, and water, and all they do is complain."

Was she being facetious? She raised her hands over her head to tighten her blond bun, and that's when I noticed it. On her wrist, below her palm, was a black ink tattoo. It resembled a binary code, or maybe, an ID number. There were at least eight digits, but she'd moved so fast I hadn't been able to count. Underneath the digits was a word written in Russian. What did it mean? Was it her name? I remembered Sumi mentioning that Zsasz was one of the Orphans, so did this mean all Orphans had an identifying tattoo?

Had they been marked as children?

Over the tattoo were two long scars running vertically down her wrist. They were thick, crooked, and embossed most likely due to the severity of the cut. I'd seen this kind of cut before and it had nothing to do with one of her many kills.

Although I hated her, I couldn't help but wonder what kind of life she'd had—what kind of childhood she might have had if she hadn't been abandoned on this island. Maybe she'd be sitting in a coffee shop in Russia, sipping on a hot caffe latte in the dead of winter.

Instead, this woman—this trained killer who'd once been a scared little girl—was tormenting and murdering women every chance she got.

"What're you looking at?" she growled, and I turned away, realizing I'd been analyzing her this whole time.

Murk suddenly let out an incomprehensible mumble, and Zsasz swung her head in her direction.

"What was that?" she said. "Does the almighty

leader have something to say?" She moved in on Murk, her back rounded and her fists clenched. "Speak up."

I peered behind me and at the entrance we'd come through. The other Norther hadn't followed us in. Had Zsasz truly brought me here alone? Would it have been stupid of me to try to take her on? Probably. I was half her size and she knew it, and my fingers were broken.

If only I'd had a weapon, I thought, watching her walk away from me.

She leaned on one knee, her face level with Murk's.

"I'm listening," she said, and Murk's bright eyes slowly rolled up.

I could sense the hatred where I stood—the rage she held inside. But there was nothing she could do. Her hands were tied over her head, and she was at Zsasz's mercy. I knew that feeling. In fact, that was precisely how Zsasz made me feel, even when my hands weren't tied.

Zsasz brushed a rough hand through Murk's silver hair, making its ends stick out in every direction. I couldn't believe how different she looked. Her hair was scraggly and hung over her brows, and her skin had lost its beautiful orange, almost brown, glow. She was nearly as white as Zsasz aside from the reds, blues, and purples all over her face. Her arms were bony and bruised, and for the first time, she resembled an old woman.

Murk had always exuded confidence, certainty, and fearlessness. Who was I even looking at?

Zsasz turned her head toward me with a repulsive smile. "No wonder your Village burned to the ground. You had this"—she prodded Murk in the cheek with a stiff finger—"for a leader."

Without warning, Murk spat a glob of thick saliva on Zsasz, who, to my surprise, didn't budge. Instead, her head slowly turned sideways until she was face-to-face with Murk. She wiped her hand on her knee, where Murk had hit her, then swiped her hand along Murk's cheek, returning her the favor.

Murk pulled away, but Zsasz pushed harder and harder until Murk's face was covered in gooeyness. Then, in one swift movement, she swung a closed fist into Murk's stomach, forcing a loud groan out of her blood-encrusted mouth.

Zsasz stood up and patted her clothing as if Murk's saliva had contaminated her from head to toe. "Keep your germs to yourself, you old hag." And this time, she swung her heavy boot into Murk's chest.

Murk let out a yelp, with her eyes sealed shut, and her body swayed from side to side, her purple fingers clawing at the rope around her wrists. What was I doing? Why wasn't I attacking Zsasz? I couldn't move. My leader was being beaten, and I couldn't move.

I clenched my jaw, preparing myself to watch Murk take another blow, but instead, Zsasz turned around and marched toward me. My knees buckled, and I took a step back.

"See that?" she growled, leaning into me. Her nostrils widened, and a droplet of snot hung at the tip of her pink nose. She threw a stiff hand in Murk's direction. "Every time you pull something like that again... Every time you decide to stand up to any one of us, your leader will feel it."

I stared at her and then at Murk, whose eyes had shifted to the dirt in front of her.

"Get her, Brone!" someone shouted. "Kill that fucking bitch!"

I averted my gaze toward the voice, but Zsasz's cold fingers grabbed me by the face, forcing me to look her in the eyes. "I should've killed you when you first came at me," she said slowly, and then her zebra lips curved up on one side.

My jaw clicked underneath her hard fingers, but her grip didn't loosen.

"But after the stunt you pulled today... I'd rather make you suffer in ways you can't even imagine."

"Why?" I muttered through clenched teeth.

She pulled away, seemingly taken aback by my inability to stop talking.

"Why?" she sneered.

"Why do you h-hate us s-so much?" I asked, though I wasn't sure I'd made any sense with her fingers pressing my cheeks in.

Her hairless eyebrows quickly came together, forming a crease over the bridge of her nose. "Like I said earlier," she growled, "you speak only when spoken to."

"We're people, too," I continued. "I have a mom... I h-had a life. I d-don't want to f-fight anyone. I want—"

With her other hand, and without breaking eye contact, she grabbed one of my broken fingers and pulled up. I felt the excruciating, mind-numbing pain before I heard the snap, and I fell to my knees. She breathed heavily, her nostrils expanding with every breath, and the hatred in her eyes made it look like she wanted to skin me alive. She shoved me into the grass and onto my back. I pulled my arm to my chest and rolled from side to side, moaning in pain.

My eyes were too wet for me to see anything. I blinked repeatedly, but all I saw was Murk's figure sway from side to side as Zsasz delivered heavy blows.

She was doing this because of me. All because I'd talked back.

The cages around her started rattling, and women shouted things I couldn't understand—

some pleaded, while others yelled insults and threats at Zsasz.

Why was she doing this? Why was Rainer doing this?

Zsasz's fuzzy figure suddenly appeared by my face, casting a cool shadow over me. She crouched, her leather boots squeaking, and rested a gentle hand on my cheek. "You so much as repeat any of this to your friends on the outside and Murk dies."

CHAPTER 8

"Brone, talk to us."

"What happened?"

"Look at her hand… It's worse than it was."

"What did that evil bitch do to you?"

I closed my eyes and pushed the sound away. All I wanted was peace. Was that so much to ask for?

"I don't understand," came Hammer's voice. "I mean, why are they taking some of us and not all of us? Where's Franklin, and why'd they choose her?"

"You are all numbers," came a croaky voice.

I cracked my eyes open, my surroundings coming into focus. My back was pressed against a wooden box that stored all unwashed fruits and vegetables carried in by some of the Peasants. The sun was setting, creating long and wide shadows inside the market, and the sky had turned a papaya orange. I inhaled a deep breath of warm, humid air. Where would we sleep tonight? At our station again? We'd been sleeping in the dirt, too afraid to take over someone else's territory by approaching the hammocks at the west side of the city.

And then my gaze met hers. She sat across from us, at the other Food Station—the one filled with women who were constantly glaring at us like a bunch of wild dogs. But now, the looks we were receiving were those of intrigue and hesitation. This woman, the one who'd just spoken to us, had wrinkles deeper than any wrinkles I'd ever seen before and protruding brow bones that stuck out over somber gray eyes. Her chin, too, reminded me of a witch you'd find in a kid's fairy tale. She was old—much older than Murk—and her eyes were fixated on me.

"Numbers," she repeated.

"We heard you," Coin said. "What're you talkin' about?"

She raised a wavering hand, pointing at each one of us individually. "You're all alive 'cause yous can produce, plain and simple." She smacked her lips together, probably moistening what remained of her decaying teeth, then looked around to make sure the Northers weren't around. "Dey don't vant to kill you. Dey vant you to work. Dat's all. And if you cause trouble, dey'll teach you lessons over and over again till all you can do is work and not think."

"What about Franklin?" Hammer asked, her knuckles whitening around a coconut.

The woman sucked on her bottom lip, her chin moving back and forth, but didn't say anything.

"They took one of our friends," Coin said. "Why? What're they doing to her?"

I thought of the women I'd seen training for battle behind the pike gate and the ones who'd been caged in seclusion inside bamboo cells beside the mountain. What *were* they doing? I leaned forward, wanting to hear every word this old woman had to offer.

"Sometimes dey take women for torture... To teach 'em," she said, and her milky eyes rolled toward me. I looked away. "But if dey take someone for a long time, dey're not comin' back."

Everyone stiffened, but the old lady waved a crooked finger and continued. "Dey're not dead if dat's vat you're thinking. Dey train dem to become Fighters. Dey're the ones who helped attack dat old Village..."

"That was our Village," Coin growled, and the woman nodded slowly.

"Your friend," she said, her finger still wiggling, "she von't be da same if you see her again."

I bit down on the inside of my cheek. Why was she telling us this? Was she trying to scare us, or help us? I thought of Murk, and my heart started beating hard. I wanted to tell them. They all deserved to know that Murk was still alive, but every time I thought of speaking up, I remembered what Zsasz told me and how she'd threatened Murk's life. And I didn't know who was listening. For all I knew, Zsasz had spies throughout the entire city.

"Why her?" Arenas cut in. "I mean, why'd they take her instead of any of us?"

The old woman smiled and searched the sky.

"You deaf, you old fart?" Coin spat out, but Hammer swung an open hand at her shoulder.

"I've been here a long time," she continued. "Vatching. Observing. It isn't all calculated. Dere isn't always an answer. Dey act on instinct, the Orphans. If your friend seem strong, den dey took her to fight."

"Strong?" Arenas burst out. "That girl was a twig."

I cocked an eyebrow at Arenas. Who was she to call someone a twig? She resembled a preteen.

"Not physical strength," the old woman said.

"She was the first to stand up..." Hammer said.

"So unfortunate..." the woman continued. She averted her attention to the ground by her bare feet, which had thick yellow nails twice the length of her toes and curled into the dirt. "My sweet little girls."

Little girls? What the hell was she talking about?

"I thought if I came, too, I could protect dem," she said, though it came out sounding more like a whimper. She slapped two wrinkly hands over her eyes, her long brown fingernails poking out through her white bangs. "I tried so hard," she continued, her head bouncing through intermittent sobs. "Dey weren't like dis before... Is Rainer's fault." I recognized her accent. It reminded me of Everest, whose Ukrainian accent had always been so hard to understand. "She made dem into monsters. All of dem. Dey were such sweet little girls. So scared. All alone. I know vat is like to be all alone. Dat's vy I came with dem. I was like dem once. All alone. Vy did I even survive? I couldn't help dem. I should have died in dat crash."

"She high or somethin'?" Coin whispered, and Hammer smacked her again.

And then I saw it. She shifted her hands, and on the inside of her right wrist was an old tattoo with Russian writing and numerical digits. It resembled the one Zsasz had, but I could tell it was much older. The ink was a faded blue, and the digit was much shorter.

This old lady... It all made sense. She'd been with them on the plane. She'd probably been working at the orphanage, having once been an orphan herself. My mind raced as I watched her ramble on.

"What's going on here?" came Alice Number Two's voice.

She stood tall with two hands on her waistline,

the sky's rich purple overcast outlining her sticklike silhouette. The old woman quickly wiped her tears and let out a stupid laugh, revealing two chipped teeth at the front of her mouth. "Oh, you know," she said, rubbing her wrists. "Dis damn arthritis is killing me again."

CHAPTER 9

"Brone, wake up," someone said, and a soft nudge jabbed me in the ribs.

I sat up, my neck stiff and my back covered in dirt. The sun had already risen, and women were walking about the market, tending to their daily posts. How long had I been sleeping? What was going on?

The pain in my hand returned, and I grimaced. I wanted to tear off my entire hand. This was unbearable. It had swelled to twice its size, and the skin around most of my knuckles had turned eggplant purple with patches of yellow. The slightest movement caused a radiating pain to shoot up my wrist and into my arm.

"Rainer's coming," Hammer whispered.

"What?" I mumbled, my eyes widening at every face nearby. Women glanced at me as they walked with queer looks on their faces. There was no hatred, no hostility—only respect and empathy. I received a few brief nods, but I didn't nod back. I didn't know what to think. Was this because I'd killed a Norther? Were the Peasants happy about this?

"Did you hear me?" Hammer pressed. "Get up and look busy."

"What?" I said again. "What're you talking about?"

"Murk," Tegan suddenly spat out, and everyone's attention turned to her. She rocked back and forth like she did every day, her knees pressed to her chest and her matted hair barely moving as she swayed.

"What'd she say?" Coin asked.

"Don't bother," I said, "you know she doesn't make any sense."

Had Tegan seen Murk, too? Had she been locked in one of those cages, tormented day in, day out, forced to watch her leader suffer? Why hadn't Zsasz locked me up? My stomach sank because I knew that whatever she had in store for me would be worse than physical torture.

Maybe this was my torture—not knowing what was coming to me.

"Must be something big," Hammer continued. "I don't know what's going on. All I know is that someone said Rainer's coming out here today."

Was she coming out to make an example of me? Or, maybe she came out on special occasions, such as celebrations. And if that was the case, what were they celebrating? Their victory against our people? Burning our Village to the ground? I hadn't realized I was staring into nothingness until Hammer poked me in the shoulder.

"Brone, you okay?"

I was far from okay. How were they all acting so goddamn normal? I stared at Hammer's flabby-skinned face, the small curls on her head, and the long eyebrow hairs that were combed downward, giving off the appearance of multiple bald spots.

Stripes.

Striped eyebrows.

I thought of Zsasz, and my throat swelled. I didn't know whether to cry or scream. I wanted to hurt someone. Anyone. I glared at Hammer, feeling nothing but hatred. How had she let this happen? Why had she let me go after Holland like that? This was all her fault.

"Jesus, Brone," Hammer let out. "Why're you looking at me like that?"

I couldn't stop. I breathed in and out, imagining how long it would take for her throat to collapse if I jumped on her again.

"Yo!" Coin shouted, and my shoulders jerked forward. She held a balled fist in the air and stared at me with lips so tight they looked like a butthole. "Snap the fuck out of it!"

I was completely taken aback. Where was this coming from?

"I see that rage and shit," Coin went on. "Ain't

none of us responsible for what happened to you. You decided to go after that Holland bitch. Don't you be placin' blame where it don't belong!"

She'd never been so stern with me before. I blinked once, then twice, trying to understand what was going on. Hammer looked terrified, but Coin appeared ready to break my other hand if I so much as thought of raising it to any of them.

"I ain't stupid," Coin continued. "I'm sure they hurt you in lots of messed-up ways. And it's cool if you don't wanna talk about it. Maybe you can't talk about it. Maybe they threatened you. Man, I don't know. Alls I know is Trim's blood is on your hands, so you'd better grow a goddamn ballsack, get over what happened, and be the leader Trim would've wanted you to be."

Everything came into focus.

Coin was absolutely right. I was letting them win. I was allowing myself to become a victim.

"Ballsack? Really?" Arenas cut in. "*Chica*, why you gotta reference male genitals for strength? I mean, think about it. Balls are weak. You kick a man's balls, and he's down, you know? If you ask me—"

"Well I ain't askin' *you*, chica," Coin said.

Arenas rolled her eyes and pouted her thick lips.

"You know," Hammer said, "she has a point—"

"Yo, Ham, whose side are you on?" Coin said,

revealing her gold tooth.

"I'm not taking sides," Hammer said. "I'm agreeing with a statement. Besides, women need to stop using men as a symbol of strength and power. You don't see men giving birth to children. You don't see men lifting cars off—"

"What're you, a feminist?" Coin spat.

"What?" Hammer said. "No, it's not about—"

"Damn, girl." Coin's face stretched into a playful grin. "I get it, I get it. You play for *that* team. That's why you's a man hater."

Hammer pulled her face back, forming multiple rolls under her chin. "What does my being a lesbian have to do with this?"

Coin snapped her fingers in the air and let out a laugh. "Man, I knew it! I smelt your dykeness first time I laid eyes on you."

"Because I'm not feminine?" Hammer asked. "You're exactly what's wrong with this world."

"Oh, am I missing something here?" Arenas pointed a small finger back and forth between Hammer and Coin. "I thought you two were a *thing*."

"'Scuse me?" Coin said. "You sayin' I'm queer?"

Arenas shrugged and looked away.

"Bitch, just 'cause I got short hair and used to have muscles, don't mean—" But she cut herself short when she caught Hammer's glare. "All right, I get it."

"What's your problem with lesbians, anyway?" Arenas asked. "We're on an island full of women. What do you think that sound was last night? Man, love is love. You think those two women were only moaning in pain together?" She flicked her wrist in the air. "Chica, sounds to me like you're in the *armario*."

"Arma—what?" Coin asked.

"Think that means closet," Hammer said.

Coin raised a solid fist and her eyes nearly popped out of her head, but the second I parted my lips, everyone turned to me.

"Murk's alive," I said.

CHAPTER 10

It was like watching something out of a movie.

The elephant's handler waved a spear in the air, gesturing all the Peasants to make way. She wore a suede crop top that revealed a chiseled set of abs. She looked young—early twenties maybe—and that's when I realized she wasn't one of the Orphans or Originals. There were no identifiable tattoos on her wrists, and she was too young to be an Original. But one sign told me she wasn't one of them—the long gashes and scars across her chest, shoulders, and face. Was this Zsasz's doing? Because Franklin had had the same cuts. Was this a breaking technique? Did torturing and disfiguring them make them complacent? This woman, her face contorted in wild anger, had probably been brainwashed to become an elephant handler.

"How's she doing?" Hammer asked, leaning in.

What was she talking about? And why was she bothering me when I was trying to see Rainer, the abominable excuse for a human being responsible for the deaths of hundreds?

Hammer leaned in and placed a stiff hand over her lips the way one does when they're making it obvious that whatever's coming out of their mouth is a secret. "Murk."

I nudged her on the shoulder and gave her the stink eye. I'd already told her—told all of them—to keep their mouths shut about that. She must have sensed my irritation because she pulled back, straightened her posture, and focused her attention on the approaching platform.

Attached to the elephant was a harness built of wood, and attached to this, ropes made of vine that pulled the platform. Underneath the platform were four big wooden wheels that rolled slowly, pushing dirt out of the way as they moved.

At first, I couldn't see her because four Northers stood holding swords at each corner of the platform. Bows were fastened to their backs, but by the way the crowd cowered in fear at Rainer's very presence, it was evident they wouldn't need them.

The woman atop the elephant led the platform, or the carriage, out of the wooden gates and to the front of the market space, where two women had fought to the death a few days ago. There were still patches of bloody soil where the battle had occurred.

The wheels came to a stop, and the four

Northers at each corner of the platform knelt on one knee, their postures hunched and their heads bowed. They were geared up from head to toe, every inch of their skin covered. It was hard to see them with all the people in front of me blocking my view, so I stood on my tiptoes to get a better look. If only Biggie were here, I thought. She could have raised me up on her shoulders.

I didn't dwell on that too long. Every time I thought of the Hunters, of my friends, I fell into a deeper depression. Coin was right—I needed to stay strong.

Whispers erupted all around me. It was like standing in the middle of an atrium, or a hall, waiting for the president of the United States to give some big, fancy speech... with one difference: the energy around me was filled with both admiration and fear.

"Haven't seen Rainer in months," someone beside me whispered.

"Yeah," a tall blonde responded. "What does she do all day in there?"

"In there," I assumed, meant the mountain. As Murk had done, Rainer probably set herself up some sort of living quarters inside a cave.

After taking off, at the very least she could have been original, I thought, glaring toward the platform.

She stood up, and my heart nearly stopped. I

remembered her. She'd been walking through the fiery Village with two stone battle-axes in hand, stepping over dead bodies, her head swaying from side to side as if on a hunt. And that was precisely what she'd been doing—hunting. Hunting for Murk.

She'd obviously found her.

I'd seen her for a moment during the attack, but now, I saw her clearly. She had deep brown hair, almost black, pulled back into a high and tight ponytail that reached almost all the way down her back. It looked wet underneath the bright early afternoon sun, the top glistening. A thick streak of white hair originated from her left sideburn, all the way up to the back of her head. It was the strangest thing I'd ever seen. Her skin was a golden brown with an olive tint, and her eyes were jade green and outlined in black. She wore the same fur padding she'd sported during the attack—thick gray and onyx hair that stuck out in every direction imaginable, giving off the appearance of strong, broad shoulders. She was clad in a lot of leather— a padded chest piece, tight beige pants, and knee-high boots with suede lace and strange holes that I assumed were for ventilation. Behind her back hung a black cape-like material.

I remembered that cape and how it had dragged behind her in the Village.

God, I hated her.

I'd never hated anyone so much in my life.

"Good morning to all of you," she shouted, her voice carrying across the entire city.

It was a stern voice—not too deep, but not feminine, either. A uniquely neutral voice that could be distinguished from a distance with ease.

Everyone went completely quiet, staring at her as if she were a Greek goddess capable of magic beyond our understanding. But she wasn't a goddess—she was human. An awful, cruel human who didn't deserve to breathe the air around us.

"It has come to my attention that an attack took place yesterday within my city," she continued. She had an unusual accent, though I couldn't determine where it was from.

But there was one thing I did know—this was definitely about me.

I swallowed hard, my feet shifting in the dirt beneath me. Rainer's eyes scanned the crowd, and I turned my head to the side, my heart beating so hard I thought I might stop breathing. Then, several women stepped away from me, opening up the crowd and making me visible to Rainer.

What were they doing? Helping her? Or were they afraid to get caught in the crossfire? Was Rainer going to kill me herself?

"You," she shouted, her gaze fixated on me. "Step forward."

Holding my bruised and broken hand against

my chest, I moved forward as colors around me began to blend, as everyone's faces became distorted pixels and I felt myself trying to escape my own body.

Rainer walked past two of her kneeling Northers and hopped off the chariot, her feet making a soft thud in the dirt. With her chin raised high, she moved toward me, arms swinging back and forth with such confidence I feared she might kill me with her bare hands.

As she walked, everyone in the crowd knelt on one knee, but when she approached me, I remained standing. Was I supposed to kneel? Although terrified, I'd have been dishonoring Trim by kneeling. I was going to die anyway. I wouldn't give her the satisfaction.

She reached behind her back where a shiny, leather-wrapped handle stuck out. She clasped her fingers around it and pulled upward with a swoosh, revealing a medieval-style sword with a long blade constructed entirely of metal. It glistened underneath the beaming sun, and I swallowed hard.

"You killed one of my women," she said quietly, rubbing her thumb along the sword's handle. "One of my little girls."

"I defended myself," I said quickly.

Why was I talking? What was I doing? I was standing face-to-face with Rainer, the leader of the Northers, and I was running my mouth again. As if a mask were pulled off her face to reveal her true self, her brows came together, and she bared her yellow teeth in anger.

With her free hand, she swung a closed-handed fist at my face, and I nearly fell to the ground. Everyone inched farther and farther away from us, and Rainer stood tall, looking like the monster she was.

Without warning, she kicked me in the leg, right above my knee. I yelped out in pain before falling to the ground with one knee in the dirt.

She had me exactly where she wanted me—at her feet.

I slowly raised my chin, trying to salvage the bit of dignity I had left. My ears rang, and an electric pain shot up my jaw. I'd been hit so many times in the last twenty-four hours, I must have looked like a rotten apple.

Then, something cold pressed against the skin of my neck. I followed its source, realizing it was her sword. She held its handle with both hands and rested the blade on my left shoulder, against the skin of my neck.

There was a sick satisfaction in her eyes—a malevolent look that I thought only fairy-tale villains were capable of giving—and all I could think about was my mom.

I wanted to tell her I was sorry—sorry for

everything I'd done. In fact, I wanted to apologize to everyone for all of the trouble I'd created. The Hunters, Trim, Ellie... all of them. There were so many thoughts and vivid memories flashing through my mind, it was like watching a digital slideshow in my head.

I closed my eyes, watching the memories flicker, and inhaled a deep breath.

I was ready.

CHAPTER 11

There was no pain.

In fact, I felt nothing.

Was this what death felt like?

I flinched at the sound of her voice.

"Remember this day the next time you doubt my leadership," she shouted.

I looked up to find her standing in front of me with her sword jabbed into the dirt. Her chin was so high that her ponytail now hung all the way down her lower back.

"I am a merciful leader," she continued. "The rules I set in place are there to protect you, not harm you. Today, this woman receives my forgiveness."

She gazed down at me from behind her Egyptian eyes, and the last thing I felt was forgiveness.

"But if I hear of another attack on one of my women, you will all pay for the crime of one."

No one spoke, but instead, kept their faces aimed at the ground.

"Do I make myself clear?" she shouted, jabbing her sword into the air.

Everyone's shoulders jerked forward, but then and all at once, they closed their fists with their thumbs tucked in and pressed them hard against their chests, a loud thrum resonating in unison.

Was this their way of submitting to an authority figure? To leadership?

Rainer, instead of closing her fist, spread her fingers apart to form a star and raised her arm straight into the air. I assumed this was her way of acknowledging the wordless symbolism—her way of accepting everyone's loyalty.

Then, without any effort whatsoever, she threw her sword behind her back, its metallic blade slipping with ease into its leather sheath.

She didn't even bother looking at me again. Instead, she turned away, her heavy footsteps creating a flat path in the dirt as she returned to her wheeled platform. Two of the Northers kneeling on it each extended an arm, which she gripped to prop herself up as if they were handlebars.

"You okay?"

The voice took me aback because I hadn't heard it in a few days. I turned to my side where Sumi stood, her hood pulled far over her head and face.

I almost responded, "Do I look okay?" but

didn't.

"Mashi can help with that," she said.

I slowly got up, a loud pop coming out of my hip. Everything hurt, and everything made noise—as though I had the body of an eighty-year-old.

"What's Mashi?" I asked.

Although I couldn't see her very well, it almost looked like she smiled underneath her hood.

"Not what—who."

I grunted when someone bumped into my back and my broken hand jerked forward.

"She's a friend," Sumi continued. "She has a way of getting certain... things... to alleviate pain."

"You mean drugs?" I said.

"Don't make that face," Sumi hissed, and for a moment, it seemed like I was back in the Village—back to when she would dump half a spoonful of egg into my bowl and say, "That's all you get."

I hadn't realized I was making a face, but it was to be expected. Having dealt with Gary's drunk ass for over five years, I'd grown to hate substances with a passion. I'd seen how alcohol would change him—how it turned him into a shell, capable of atrocities without guilt or remorse.

When he was sober, it was easy to tell. I'd find him on his knees in front of my mom, pathetically wrapping his arms around her legs and pleading with her to give him one more chance. In the five years I knew him, that happened about five or six times.

"Sorry," I mumbled, though I wasn't sorry at all. I had every right to be reluctant to the idea of ingesting a mind-altering substance.

"Look," Sumi said, her shaded eye darting from side to side, "take it or leave it. It's not like I'm offering you heroin. It's all natural. It's coca leaves. Mashi plucks what she can when she goes out cultivating."

"She works at the Food Station?" I asked.

"Yeah," Sumi said. She raised a hand to her shoulder's height. "Little Asian lady, about this tall. Short hair that looks like a black ball on her head. Looks frail overall, but she's pretty fuckin' healthy for a sixty-year-old."

I knew who she was talking about. I'd seen the woman come in and out of the jungle carrying baskets of vegetation. Most of what she brought were foods I'd never seen before. I'd had to ask Alice Number Two, who had basically become a team leader figure, to help me out when it came time to cut the food open. Some had nuts inside, others, thousands of seeds.

What was Rainer's policy on drugs, anyway? Murk had fought long and hard to keep them out of the Village and the Working Grounds. Did Rainer even care? She must have if Sumi was whispering about it.

I stared at Sumi's partially bubbled face, then

down at my hand. It looked like a deformed balloon you'd find lying around after a kid's birthday party—swollen but not round, and full of mismatched colors, which, in a kid's birthday party, would likely be the result of cake, snot, and sticky hands. In my case, it all boiled down to plain old bruising.

The pain was nearly intolerable, making me frustrated and irritable. Every time someone so much as looked at me, I wanted to swing my good fist at their face.

But I couldn't get Gary out of my head.

I'd rather suffer in pain than alter my mind. Especially in this place. I needed to be clear-headed.

"No thanks," I said.

She cocked her crisped eyebrow and tightened her lips. "Suit yourself, but the offer stands if you need it."

"And if I change my mind," I said, knowing I probably wouldn't, "is this a gift, or is there a price?"

She scoffed. "Brone, nothing's changed. We're still living with a bunch of wild women. The one difference is *management*. There's a price for everything. You of all people should know that."

A price for everything, I thought.

My stomach sank. Rainer hadn't truly forgiven me. It was only a matter of time before someone came after me, whether in the middle of the night or through a brainwashed Peasant. I'd seen the way she looked down at me—the way those hateful, soulless eyes sat over her elevated cheekbones, gazing into me as if I were nothing but a piece of dirt on the tip of her leather boot.

I had to get out of here.

CHAPTER 12

"Are you insane?" Coin hissed, leaning over a pile of bright yellow pineapples.

"Do you have a better idea?" I asked.

"You think you're the first one to have this idea, chica?" Arenas asked. "You heard what they do to Death Sprinters. They hang you up for them Ogres to cut open. You really wanna take that risk?"

"What's more insane?" I asked. "Risking our lives to get out of here to live a somewhat decent life, or staying here?"

No one said anything.

"As slaves," I continued. "Is that what you want? We're already prisoners on this island, and now we're prisoners to these savages." I waved my one good hand in the general direction of the mountain.

"What about Franklin?" Johnson asked, tracing a line through the dirt with her cutting tool.

She was the last person I'd have expected to mention Franklin's name.

"Yeah," Hammer cut in. "We can't leave her

here."

I bit the inside of my cheek, carefully contemplating how to best approach this situation. I had two choices: I could either attempt to be a hero, which would most likely, if not ultimately, lead to some of us dying. Or, I could be realistic in my approach, even if it meant coming across as heartless. I thought of Murk, and although I didn't know whose story to believe anymore, I still respected her. Her having banished a pregnant woman—if it was even true—didn't take away from all of the good she'd done for her people. In this situation, the Murk I knew would have set her feelings aside and saved the majority, even if it meant sacrificing a life.

And although I didn't want to be the kind of leader who took that route—I would have preferred to find a solution to save everyone— there was one thing everyone seemed to have forgotten.

"Franklin's already dying," I said.

There was a heavy silence—the kind of silence that follows a heartfelt eulogy at a funeral. I prepared myself for retaliation, but none was received. Instead, everyone stared at the ground, and a few women shared brief nods.

"I don't mean to be morbid—"

Coin cut me short with a stiff hand in the air. "You're right, Brone. You don't have to apologize for sayin' the truth. Franklin could be dead in months, for all we know. No idea how bad the cancer is by now. Besides, tryin' to get inside those gates would be a suicide mission."

"You have no idea," I said, remembering all that I'd seen: women battling with all kinds of advanced weaponry, dozens of Northers gathered around a fire, and cabins lined up along the base of the mountain. These Northers, aside from their trained Fighters, were heavily equipped from head to toe. Going up against them with the limited resources we had would have been equivalent to citizens attacking a SWAT unit. "If we can get out of here... We can come back for others when the time is right."

"So..." Arenas said, fidgeting with her legs crossed in front of her. "You gonna tell us what you saw in there? What'd she look like? How's she doing?"

"Not now," I said sharply. I'd tell them all about Murk when the time was right. The one reason I'd told them was to give them hope. Seeing her had done the same for me. Zsasz wasn't going to kill Murk—she was full of shit. I wouldn't fall for her mind games. Murk was the only leverage the Northers had. And keeping it a secret wouldn't help me, or anyone for that matter. These women needed encouragement—motivation to *want* to do something instead of sitting around and waiting to die. The fact that our leader was still alive meant we had a chance to rebuild our society. I glanced around, noting all the eyes that kept darting my way. "Why does everyone keep staring at me?" I said, and it almost came out as a shout.

Johnson let out a snort. "Why do you think, genius? You killed a Norther and you're still alive."

"For now," I mumbled. "At some point, someone will come after me."

"Well, we have your back, Brone," Hammer said. "If anyone tries—"

"Never seen anything like that before," came a woman's voice. I craned my neck to catch her standing behind me. She wasn't chubby, but she wasn't thin, either. She looked solid enough to take someone out with one swing of her fist. She had short, messy pinkish blond hair that I imagined had once been hot pink or lilac purple, arms covered in colorful tattoos, and a septum piercing that made her look like a bull. I was surprised she still had it with how barbaric women were here—why hadn't anyone tried to tear it out to use the silver? It wouldn't have been the first time I'd heard about piercings being ripped out.

"Like what?" I asked.

"What you did... You fought back. No one's ever done that before."

I turned around in the dirt and looked up at her. She stared at me with big blue eyes, and for the first time, I didn't think of this place as *us* versus everyone else. Maybe there was only *us*.

"Listen," she said, "me and my girls camp out over there." She pointed toward the biggest tree at the edge of the city. Its trunk reminded me of Redwood, and around it were hammocks hanging from its massive branches. "You got a bed anytime."

A bed? As in, a hammock? This woman was offering me a comfortable sleeping arrangement? All for having killed one of the Northers?

"You and your girls," she clarified, eyeing my little crew.

Coin's face lit up like a Christmas tree and she smacked Hammer on the back. "Yo! You hear that, Ham? We finally get to sleep!"

Hammer gave her the stink eye and rolled her shoulders back. It was apparent that Coin was getting her strength back. That may have had something to do with the fact that we worked in the Food Station. I'd seen her sneak nuts into her mouth every chance she got.

"Name's Quinn," the young woman said, both hands on her waist.

Johnson's jaw hung loose and her eyelids went flat. "As in Harley?"

"Who?" Quinn asked.

"You know, Harley Quinn," Johnson continued.

"Seems to be a Batman thing going on here…"

Quinn cocked an eyebrow. "It's my last name," she said as if Johnson was too stupid to understand the concept of a last name.

"Oh," Johnson said. "I assumed you were into comics and stuff, 'cause, you know—" she pointed at her own nose, then at her arms, as if indicating invisible tattoos.

Quinn's eyes widened, and I stuck my good arm out toward Johnson. "What Johnson means to say is *thank you*." The last two words squeezed through my gritted teeth.

Johnson cleared her throat. "Thank you."

Quinn nodded slowly, her gaze leaving Johnson and landing on me. "What's your name, anyway?"

"Brone," I said. I extended my good hand, but I pulled it back when a dull pain set in my other one.

Quinn smirked and threw her chin out at me. "No worries, Brone. Listen, if anyone gives you a hard time around here, tell 'em you're friends with me. They'll back off."

"Oh," I said. "Um, thank you."

"You in charge around here?" Coin asked.

Quinn looked at her, but her head didn't move. "No one's really in charge here, n'case you haven't noticed." She looked around, and the loud cacophonous sound of the market suddenly filled the air as if for the first time. Women scrambled past us; others yelled while waving fabric—it was always the Clothes Makers who yelled the most.

I didn't mean to stereotype, but as I watched the women wave fabrics of all colors and textures and even some necklaces made of precious stones, pearls, or plain old plants, I thought, leave it to women to pursue something as trivial as fashion on a remote island full of murderous convicts.

"But some of us have more... say," she continued. "I run the Resources Station over there." She pointed toward the hammocks. I hadn't noticed, but behind them was a shelter made of wood. The structure resembled the cabins I'd seen inside the gates, in the Northers' domain, only it was entirely open and had no walls. Had she built their cabins for them?

"Wood, stone, metal, plant... A lot of bone, too, but your station usually brings it over to us," she said.

I shot a glance at the small group of women handling the meat. Blood covered them from head to toe, and they always looked tired, wiping their foreheads with the backs of their hands and panting in the hot sun. By doing so, they smeared more blood on their faces, but they didn't seem to care. In a wooden crate to the side of their station were clean bones forming a pile. The old Russian woman—the one with the orphanage tattoo— hovered over them, sticking her fingers inside. I never knew what she was doing. Most of the time, she sat around or circled her station. Maybe they were taking it easy on her because of her age.

"And these resources," Arenas asked, "you use them to create weapons?"

I didn't like where this was going. Her tone was cold, and the way the skin on her face tightened made me think she was ready to snap.

"We don't," Quinn says. "But yeah, Smith over there"—she wiggled a finger into the market, though with all the hanging sheets and clothes, I couldn't see her—"does all that."

"But you still provide the stuff," Arenas said, her mouth hanging loose. "So really, you contributed to Alice's death." Her head moved from side to side now with a fierce Latina attitude.

"Who's Alice?" Quinn asked. She didn't seem bothered by Arenas's reaction.

"My fuckin' friend!" Arenas shouted.

"Easy," Quinn said. "First of all, I don't know your friend, and unless you feel like dying today, I suggest you lose your attitude. Second of all, I do what I'm told. I'm still pushed around by the Beasts as much as you—"

"Beasts?" I cut in.

"You haven't heard that around here?" Quinn asked.

I looked around the group to make sure I wasn't the only one who felt like they were missing something.

"You know," she continued, "the Orphans... the Originals."

"You guys call 'em Beasts?" Coin asked.

Quinn shrugged, crossed her arms over her stomach, and made her eyes go wide. "Um, yeah. It isn't always easy to differentiate the two. They're all just *Beasts* to us."

Johnston snorted. "You know, with all that hair they wear over their shoulders, they kinda do look like—"

But she stopped talking when my eyelids went flat.

"Just saying," she mumbled.

Hammer slapped two hands together to clean them off. "Well, that made my life way easier."

Quinn stared at us, evidently not understanding what was going on.

"We've always known you as—well, not *you*, anymore... but them. We've always referred to them as Northers."

Quinn let out a short laugh that sounded more like a bark. "Northers..."

"If that's so funny, what'd you call us?" Coin asked.

"Who's *us*?" Quinn asked.

"Murk's people," Hammer clarified.

Quinn tilted her head back. "Ah, so the stories around here are true. You *are* from that southern Village. I heard you were the biggest colony on this island."

"Where else would we be from?" Arenas asked. She hadn't entirely lost her attitude, but she'd mellowed out quite a bit.

Quinn shrugged. "Number of places. I don't know all their clan names." She uncrossed her arms and pressed a flat hand against her chest. "Me and a few of my girls come from a small colony that used to live on the island's western shoreline. A lot of women here are Newbies, though."

"Clans?" I asked.

"Newbies?" Coin cut in, but Hammer leaned in and whispered, "Drops, I'm assuming," and Coin nodded with her mouth open.

Quinn scoffed, and I couldn't tell whether she was amused or shocked. "You didn't honestly think the only people on this island were you and the Beasts, did you?"

"What? No..." I stammered. "We knew there were others..."

"Didn't realize there were whole clans," Hammer cut in.

"So, what?" I said. "The Beasts"—I gestured an air quote with my one good hand—"are plucking people from other clans? I thought Rainer's hatred was for Murk and Murk only. Why's she going after everyone?"

Quinn smiled a set of crooked yellow teeth, but I could tell it wasn't a genuine smile. "She's a psychotic bitch. What do you think she wants?”

“To rule the entire island?” Coin asked.

Quinn formed a gun with her hand, pointed it at Coin, and made a clicking noise with her tongue. “Bingo.”

CHAPTER 13

"You're relieved—go eat something," said Alice Number Two.

"Go eat something," Arenas mocked when we reached a safe distance away from Alice Number Two.

"You do realize it's just a name, right? She didn't ask to be named Alice," Johnson said.

Arenas crossed her bony, dark arms over her chest. "I don't care. And it's Alice *Number Two*."

I ignored the back-and-forth bickering between Johnson and Arenas and focused on making my way to the Cooking Station as fast as possible and without landing myself in a fight. The last thing I wanted was to get stuck in line waiting for a hot slab of meat and to be told there was no more food left when our turn was up. Wouldn't have been the first time it happened.

"Back o' da line," came the Cook's voice.

She was as grumpy as Sumi had been in her old job but much older and less tolerant of back talk. Every day, this woman moved about her shack as slow as a tortoise, her back round and her eyelids heavy. She wore the same hat every day—a square cap made of pliable-looking suede that sat still in her short salt-and-pepper hair. She sliced through meat and tore apart tendons like she'd been trained to do it wearing a blindfold.

The moment we took our place in line, whispers broke out all around us.

"How long have they been here?"

"A few months, I think."

"And what about her? The Beast Killer? Where's she from?"

Beast Killer? Was this what they were calling me? A soft whistle suddenly caught my attention. It was Quinn. She was standing a few places up from us with a group of women who looked like they belonged to the Middle Ages—filthy faces, white-powdered hair that was undoubtedly being cleaned with nothing but salt, torn clothes, and fingernails as black as coal.

I gave her a brief nod, but she didn't let go of her stare. Instead, she jerked her chin sideways as if to say, *Get over here.* Was she trying to get me killed? The last thing I needed was to start a fight over cutting someone in line.

"Brone!" she shouted, and all I wanted to do was cower away in a corner. I didn't need more attention. But then, something extraordinary happened. The woman standing in front of me—a middle-aged Peasant with chicken legs and a round belly—stepped back with her head bowed. Then, the woman in front of her did the same thing, and this pattern continued until a clear path was created for us, leading all the way to Quinn.

She hung two open palms by her sides and grinned at us as if she'd orchestrated the whole thing.

"Beast Killer eats first," she said.

I couldn't believe it. Had killing that Norther—that Beast—really earned me respect among these Peasants? I hadn't done it for respect. I'd been trying to save my life. As I walked with my small crew of women, I realized something: these women, or at least most of them, hated the Beasts as much as I did.

Maybe this meant something.

Maybe we stood a chance, after all.

Maybe...

"Out of my way!" came Zsasz's voice.

She barged through the crowd of women leaving the market after a long day's work and my stomach sank. The bit of strength I'd felt seconds ago evaporated instantly. I was weak, pathetic, and vulnerable again.

God, why did she have that effect on me?

Behind her was Rebel, her usual sidekick, and two other Beasts I didn't recognize. These two were tall, wore padded shoulder plates, and stomped through the city like they owned the place—which, in a sense, they did.

But they weren't what bothered me. What shook me were the two women they dragged behind them. They were Murk's people as evidenced by their suede clothing, and although I didn't recognize them, one caught my gaze as if she knew who I was.

A gash ran across the bridge of her nose, and her shirt was doused with blood at the neckline. Rebel, who was the one dragging them by a rope, tugged hard when she caught her staring my way and the woman fell to her knees.

"Hey!" I shouted, but I regretted it instantly.

What was wrong with me? Why couldn't I keep my mouth shut?

Rebel's wild eyes flashed underneath the setting sun. She crinkled her nose and curled her upper lip over her front teeth, giving off the appearance of a rabid raccoon.

"Got somethin' to say?" she shouted, and she yanked even harder on the rope, forcing the two women into the dirt.

I didn't respond, but instead, stared at her, picturing myself beating my fist into her face. When she realized I wasn't breaking eye contact, she dropped the rope and marched over to me, arms swinging in an exaggerated motion.

I was doing it again—breaking rules.

To my surprise, Zsasz didn't get involved. She watched us, seemingly satisfied with whatever Rebel was about to do to me. I wanted to look away—back down and save myself the pain—but I couldn't. All I could think about was Trim, and how if she were here, she'd die before submitting to these pieces of shit.

And that was exactly what had happened.

"Brone," someone muttered, but it sounded like a distant dream.

Someone nudged me, and I yanked my body away from them.

"Just look away," someone else whispered.

But I couldn't.

Rebel came face-to-face with me, her putrid breath slipping into my mouth. Her head moved from side to side and the tip of her nose brushed against mine. My heart should have been racing, my palms clammy, but as I stood there, staring into her gunk-encrusted eyes, all I felt was an alien calmness.

"On your knees," she growled.

I didn't move.

Her nostrils flared, and I could tell she was on the verge of blowing. They'd already beaten me time and time again. They'd starved me, hurt my friends, threatened me, and threatened to hurt Murk, even. What more could they do? I'd live with the consequences, but I wouldn't submit to them.

Trim's death wouldn't be for nothing.

Rebel pulled a stone blade from her holster and pressed its tip into my neck, her nostrils spread wide.

What a disgusting piece of shit, I thought.

If only I'd had my arrows.

She dug the sharp tip into my throat, and I swallowed hard under the pressure, my stare never leaving hers. Her face was beet red now, and her forehead glistened with sweat.

"On your fucking knees before I—"

"Rebel," Zsasz said, calmer than I'd have expected from her.

Rebel pulled away, her hideous eyes staring at me with such hatred. She wasn't getting her way, and it was eating her alive. I didn't realize I was smiling until Rebel's brows came together. She let out a loud growl and with all her strength, swung a fist to the side of my head.

I fell to the ground, Rebel's boots a fuzzy haze in front of me. My ear rang and my vision doubled.

"Leave her be," Zsasz said. "She's mine. I'll take care of her later."

I heard footsteps and realized they were continuing their path toward the bamboo prison cells.

"Brone!"

"Brone, you okay?"

"Is she okay?"

"Give her some space!"

A solid hand grabbed me by the arms and pulled me up.

"You okay, kid?" Quinn asked.

I blinked once, twice, three times, until her face came into focus.

"You're nuts, you know that?" she said.

"They killed my friends."

"They killed a lot of our friends, too." Quinn grimaced. "But if you keep this up, you're gonna get yourself killed."

"I don't care."

Deep down, I knew that wasn't true. I did care, but, I was too numb to acknowledge it. I wanted revenge more than I wanted to breathe. If, by some miracle, I were to survive all this, I'd someday come to regret everything I'd done on this island. Eventually, reality would set in, and I'd realize that I became exactly what I fought so hard to prevent: feral, capable of taking a life without hesitation or remorse.

But right now, I didn't care.

"Come on," Quinn said. "Let's get you something to eat."

CHAPTER 14

I pulled my good arm out of Coin's grip.

"I need to know," I hissed.

Her eyes looked like glow-in-the-dark golf balls under the moonlight's glow. The city was quiet, for the most part. I could hear Beasts moving around in the jungle every few minutes. What did they do? Sit there all night guarding their territory? What kind of a life was that?

She mouthed something, but I couldn't make it out. Instead, I turned around and scurried my way over to the bamboo cages. Two torches resting in sconces illuminated the exterior gate, so I eased my way toward the sidewall, careful not to step into the light.

"Brone," Coin whispered, and I swung around, not realizing she'd followed me.

"Why you doin' this?" she asked.

"Doing what?" I asked. I was getting impatient. Everyone was sleeping—this wasn't the time to have a chat.

"Tryin' to be a hero? They're gonna kill you,

Brone. You're pushin' your luck."

"I'm not trying to be anything," I said. "Either follow and shut up or go back to your fancy hammock."

Her eyes narrowed into little white slits then darted from side to side. "Fine," she mouthed.

I continued my path, my body hunched forward and my footsteps calculated. The last thing I needed, especially after today, was to get caught trying to talk to the new prisoners. The heat of the fire warmed the tip of my nose as I drew nearer. Since being released from this cell, I'd never actually come back to it—I'd never wanted to.

But that woman—the one who'd looked at me as if she knew me—I needed to know who she was.

"Pssst," I said, but I immediately jumped back when dirty fingertips came popping out through the diamond-shaped holes.

"Who's there?" the panicked voice asked.

Then, an amber eye appeared from within the darkness. She clasped, and reclasped the gate with her fingertips, trying to pull her face closer to the bamboo gate.

"You," she breathed.

Although I couldn't see her face, I knew this was the woman who'd been looking at me earlier today.

"Do I know you?" I asked.

Her breath was short and labored as if she'd been running in circles for hours. Or, maybe the Beasts were doing precisely what they'd done to us—starving her. I remembered that awful feeling: being depleted and out of breath every few minutes, the way my muscles had burned after something as simple as standing up.

"Are you Brone?" she breathed. "The Archer?"

I nodded, but when I realized she probably couldn't see me well enough, I cleared my throat. "Yeah."

"I have a message for you." Her voice lowered even more, forcing me to move in closer to the gate. She spoke slowly as if reciting a poem off a piece of paper. "We're alive... Um. Fisher made it. And... W-We're coming for you."

I nearly fell back at the sound of those words. I wanted to scream—scream as loud as I could with joy. I couldn't believe it. Ellie... She was okay. And Fisher. Oh, God, Fisher. She'd actually survived. Proxy had pulled through. She'd saved her. She'd fucking saved her.

I slapped a hand over my mouth, my throat swelling. I hadn't felt anything other than fear and pain for so long that I thought I might implode. My eyes watered and I swallowed hard.

"Shit, Brone!" came Coin's voice.

A cold hand grabbed me by the shoulder and pulled me away from the cage.

"Wh...what're you doing?" I snapped.

I wanted to hear more, to ask this woman where she'd received this information. Ask her about the Cove. Ask her about everything. But then, dozens of footsteps filled the air around us, and shadowy figures came out from out from the edge of the jungle.

Shit.

I contemplated running the other way, but I didn't have time. These figures had already seen us. Oh, God... Fisher. Flander. Biggie. Rocket... Proxy. Elektra... All of them. I couldn't die before they came looking for us.

The first face to come out of the shadow and into the orange light took me by surprise.

Quinn.

What was going on? Had she faked wanting to be friends? Was she coming to finish me off on Zsasz's behalf? Maybe that was Zsasz's plan all along...

The next face I saw only confused me more—it was Tegan, and beside her, Hammer, Johnson, and Arenas. I looked from side to side. What the hell was going on? They weren't alone—there were dozens of women behind them, all slowly stepping into view beneath the black star-lit sky.

And then I saw Holland. She bowed her head, but it was obvious she wanted to be here.

Coin's fingernails dug into my arm, but I

couldn't feel the pain—I was too preoccupied trying to understand what all these women, including my friends, were doing sneaking out during sleep hours.

I wanted an answer, but no one spoke.

Instead, Quinn took a step closer and bowed her head. She made a fist around her thumb and slammed it into her chest. Everyone behind her followed suit, soft *thumps* filling the air.

I knew this gesture... They'd made this gesture for Rainer.

"We're stronger in numbers," Quinn said, and in a single moment, all the pain I felt—both physical and emotional—vanished.

My lips curved into a smile and my heart pounded against my chest. The dozens of women before me were willing and ready to stand by my side against the Northers—against the Beasts—and against Rainer.

I stepped forward, my gaze meeting everyone's faces, and drew my shoulders back. Although I hadn't done it on purpose, I'd given these women something to believe in; I'd given them something to fight for.

Hope.

I stared at them, noting the hunger in their fiery eyes. I wanted to laugh and cry all at the same time, but instead, I said nothing.

I raised my good hand into the air and

extended my fingers to form a star.
    Together, we'd fight back.

Visit **shadeowens.com** for more works by Shade Owens.